BLESSED
is the
ROT

Titles by Sheri Singerling:

ALFOM SHARED UNIVERSE

NOVELS
Nytho
Neuen
Blessed is the Rot

SHORT STORIES
The Badge
The Seed
Rogue
Wireworks
To Keep the Non-Euclidean at Bay
Paper Airplane Poet

All titles can be standalone reads and can be read in any order. Find the author-suggested reading order on her website at sherisingerling.com.

BLESSED
is the
ROT

SHERI SINGERLING

Cover design by Geoffrey Bunting
Cover illustration by Jack Hillside
Map illustration by Chaim Holtjer

ISBN: 979-8-9914752-7-3 (paperback)
First Edition
HypIn Publishing

Visit the author's website at sherisingerling.com

For Alan

Simetria
Church of Impermanence
Upper city
Bell tower
Lower city
Old World

THE TOLLER

The distortion greeted Fenrir. He sensed the foul thing lurking as soon as he stepped off the ladder and onto the tower's wheezing floorboards. No one else would have known it to be there, not without a detector to aid them. But Fenrir wasn't like them. He had a knack for seeking the corruption out. It was part of why he'd been such a lauded surveyor.

How times had changed for him. Now, he was as helpless as the masses. He had no glyph-inscribed garb to shield him or blessed chalk for scribbling wards, and even if he had, he was forbidden to touch such things. Under pain of death. Instead, Fenrir peered into the faint dawn light towards the corner of the tower where the distortion pulsed. The space was bathed in a diffuse shadow; the light hadn't yet crept over the wooden rail to expose the horror. But he couldn't stand to wait, and he didn't need sight to tell him what was there.

Fenrir inched forward, stopping with every step, turning his head to be sure the unease and discomfort that accosted him came from the spot he suspected. Once he was only five paces distant, Fenrir lowered himself to his knees and craned his neck forward. He could smell a trace of ozone. Then he saw it—just the smallest hint of wrongness, a pin-prick of destruction, the seed of their undoing. About a foot from the floor, a neat, little mote of non-Euclidean space.

It roiled the air around it so that a haze hovered. Looking through it towards the wooden rail behind, it seemed to melt and expand and collapse at the same time. The closest analogy that Fenrir had seen was the liquid in his hot tea or soup. Convection cells rising and falling and rising and falling in a never-ending dance. Much like the distortions. Some of those were nearly never-ending but worse because, unlike hot tea or soup, they didn't satisfy themselves with the contents of their vessel. No, many distortions grew. If it weren't for the surveyors, they would eventually consume the world.

Fenrir knew what he had to do. He backed away on hands and knees from the foul mote until he was halfway across the tower platform. Then he rose, moved to a horn-speak affixed to the side of the tower, and spoke through it.

"I need to send a message," he said. Silence on the other end. He waited one, two, three seconds then grabbed the mouthpiece and shouted. "A message, immediately. Potential distortion observed."

The word did the trick. The attendant called through the other end. "Messenger en route."

Within minutes, a boy came flying up the series of ladders that zig-zagged through the narrow tower. He panted as he stuck his head through the opening on the floor. He was unkempt with stray bits of straw sticking from his ashen hair. His eyes were red-lined and swollen. Fenrir cursed under his breath. Was this the best the Church could do for its own?

And what picture did he present to the boy? Equally dirt-encrusted with grime settled into the crevasses of his too-tanned skin. His own hair the color of straw when freshly bathed but now likely a dun. His tired and sagging eyes made more tragic by the contrast with their vivid emerald irises. Too-thin cheeks alongside a too-prominent jaw and cheekbones.

Fenrir had been good-looking before his fall from grace, but five years in a cold, dark, rat-infested cell had done its worst and spat out the broken shell of a man.

Of course, the boy couldn't know any of that. He looked at Fenrir with adoration through sleep-deprived eyes. For Fenrir was a blessed toller.

"You've a message, Sir Toller?" the boy asked.

"I need a surveyor, immediately," Fenrir said. "There are signs of distortion in the tower."

The boy's eyes widened, and he instinctively backed down a rung on the ladder. "You should get out of there."

Fenrir smirked. Here, at least, his past life served him well. He knew the true extent of the distortion's danger. He was safe, for the time being. The thing was barely there at all. If it was expanding, it would be many days yet until it grew enough to force him to vacate his post. In the meantime, he was obliged to fulfill his duty.

"Someone's got to toll the bell," Fenrir said.

He rose from his knee and gazed down at the boy. A pang shot through Fenrir's gut. Was that how his own son would have looked at him? Bad memories that served no purpose. He forced them away.

"Fast now," Fenrir said to the boy's retreating form.

The child traced the zig-zag of the ladders, down two hundred feet in minutes. Fenrir walked to the wooden railing furthest from the distortion and gazed out on the city. Simetria was waking. Little bodies filed out of brick and wooden buildings topped by clay shingles, tilted and haphazard in the slums near the tower. The edges of the city were occupied by single- and two-story structures jammed together or separated by narrow cobblestoned streets and alleys. Further afield, clustered on the hill, were stone palaces, the homes of the great families with their wrought-iron gates and stone walls.

But no matter where you looked in the city, from the haunts of the low bloods to the grand homes of the high bloods and everywhere in between, holy symmetry reigned supreme, reaching its pinnacle of perfection at the centerpiece of the city—the Church of Impermanence. That's where the boy ran to fetch a surveyor. They would come and do what Fenrir had done years ago. He'd be forced to stand by and watch them partake in the one joy he was forever denied. He gritted his teeth at the thought of it.

The dawn light shifted to daylight, but the perpetual cloud cover over Simetria made the change subtle. Fenrir pulled out his pocket watch and checked the time. The distortion had distracted him, and the morning was getting on. It was time to toll the bell. One of the other two tollers beat him to the task, the dongs sounding from the tower in the north of the city. Fenrir hurried to the center of his own tower, spread his legs wide, gripped the long, thick rope, and pulled down with all the force he could muster. Once, twice, thrice.

Even with the bell hanging thirty feet above, the sound was deafening. For Fenrir, the dongs continued to ring in his ears long after the bell had stilled. This was part of his role too. A toller was forbidden from stuffing their ears for it was their blessed duty to be bathed in the harmony of the Euclidean.

But Fenrir's task wasn't yet complete. Even the tollers had to perform the ritual demanded of all citizens of Simetria. When the bell tolled, everyone, everywhere stopped what they were doing and played their part in maintaining the Rot of the Link. For Fenrir, this involved making markings on a parchment. He took a seat in one of the chairs at a small wooden table, the only furniture on the tower's lonely platform. He opened a drawer set in the table and pulled out parchment and a graphite stick. He flipped an hourglass sitting nearby, ensured the sand was trickling down, and got to work.

For the next ten minutes, Fenrir drew triangle after triangle. Points A, B, and C. Connecting each with lines as straight as possible. Then below, he wrote out the Holy Theorem of Pythagoras: $a^2+b^2=c^2$. He was too distracted by the distortion to be more creative in his ritual and satisfied himself with this simple yet elegant fundamental truth. Once the sand in the hourglass was emptied, Fenrir rose and repeated the tolling of the bell. One of the other tollers was a bit earlier than him and the other a bit later, but the exact timing wasn't as crucial as the regularity of the ritual. Every day, they had to run through the routine three times. *Thrice per day to keep the non-Euclidean at bay,* as the Church liked to say.

That was the holy purpose of the tollers. They rang their bells to tell the people of Simetria to do their duty. First to signal the start then to indicate the stop. In between the three sets of tollings, Fenrir was free to do whatever he pleased. Normally, he would use the time to take a nap on blankets arranged in one of the corners of the tower. Fenrir wasn't an early riser by choice, but being a toller meant he didn't get a say. Today though, the distortion was disrupting more than space. Fenrir was forced to stay awake in anticipation of the surveyor.

And she was fast. Within a half-hour of the boy leaving, she arrived. She rose through the opening in the floor, first her tricorn hat, then the high collar and epaulets of her long coat, a glyph-gloved hand planting itself on the wooden planks followed by a shin-high, laced boot. She lugged up her pack of tools and let it thump against the floor. She was winded with a sour look on her face. But such a face. Fenrir's breath caught in his throat at the look of her. Freckles on pale cheeks. Eyes greener than his even. Orange-red curls sticking out from under her hat, chin-length near her face but held in the back by a braid that reached down past her backside. Tall and lean and regal.

Fenrir was dumb-struck. In his thirty-two years, he'd fallen in love a few times over, but that had been before. Since walking out of the iron-clad gates of the penitentiary, Fenrir had barely even felt the stirrings of lust. He certainly felt them now, but this flood of desires was different. It was more than the purely physical because he was also drawn to what she was—a surveyor.

They could take the title from him, strip him of his rank, remove his privileges, but he would always be a surveyor at heart. He had a soft spot for his kind. Only they understood the duality of their duties. How the distortions demanded fear and respect in equal measure, how there was only a half-truth to what the Church preached. And with this woman, there was yet another link between them. She was more than just a surveyor. As soon as she set foot on the tower platform, her eyes settled on the distortion. She was like Fenrir, gifted with another kind of sight, and like him, she hid it from a world that didn't understand. She looked away, pretending she couldn't sense it, then took note of Fenrir.

"Surveyor Sophie," she said.

"Toller Fenrir," he replied.

A dewy shine kissed Sophie's brow and upper lip. The morning was chill, but all the leather she wore did little to let her body breathe. Fenrir remembered that well and didn't miss the feeling, but he longed for the garb nonetheless. He tried not to see his torn sandals, threadbare pants, or stained tunic.

"You called in a potential distortion?" she asked.

"I did. It's over yonder."

Fenrir pointed, and Sophie squinted. She rummaged in her pack, fished out a detector and chalk, then headed towards the mote. She held the palm-sized brass circle in front and stared at the readout. Fenrir knew what she was seeing even without glimpsing the device. A little metal needle would be flipping from the low to the high end of the scale set behind the glass plating. As she approached the distortion, the needle would stay in the higher end of the range. Sophie stopped several feet from it, checked the readout, moved in an arc around it, rechecked the detector. She did this a few times before leaning down and setting the chalk on the wooden floorboards. Three white lines about two feet from the foul thing.

Sophie returned to her pack and hoisted it up. She glanced around, and her eyes settled on the table Fenrir used as his desk. She strode over to it and deposited her pack on one of the two chairs. Then, she pulled out her equipment piece by piece, arranging each on the tabletop. Fenrir moved in and peered over her shoulder. He knew the shape and feel and heft of every item she handled. The memories came flooding back with each of them.

Fenrir was in the Pullton Estate in the upper city, using the arc torches to contain a distortion wildly out of control.

Then he was on the dock, ripping up planks with a crowbar in search of an elusive distortion that was afflicting the rats.

Then he walked the cobblestoned streets of Simetria in the late evening fog, planting freshly calibrated attuners to rods arranged throughout the city.

His hands were coated in chalk.

His fingers buzzed with the fresh ink of glyphs scribed into them.

Then, he was back on the tower with Sophie, struggling to contain the wail that wanted to erupt from his throat. How he longed for those days past, for what he had been. If only there was a way back, some means of redemption, but there wasn't. Fenrir could never again be a surveyor. He'd committed the worst sin, sacrilege enough for any Simetrian but doubly so for a surveyor. His old life was gone. Yet he couldn't keep himself from longing for the impossible. The best he could do was bury the want deep. Pretend it wasn't there gnawing away at his soul, killing him by degrees.

Sophie finished arranging her tools, stuffed a notepad and graphite stick in her pockets, and grabbed a set of rulers and protractors. She spent the next hour making meticulous measurements, and it was all Fenrir could do to not step in and assist. Instead, he sat at the table and watched her work from afar, resisting the urge to touch the trinkets set out before him. He trained his eyes on the object of her labors, the distortion she was attempting to pen in. Such strange phenomena. He'd spent years of his life in close proximity to them, in studying them, and yet he knew so little about them. They all did, mired as they were by ignorance.

Sophie strode over to her pack. Fenrir sat up in his chair and watched her. He waited while she stowed her tools and stayed patient even after she took up the other seat and started to jot down notes, mumbling to herself. She had a habit of sticking the graphite pen in her mouth when she was thinking. It left a little stain of gray on her pale pink lips. She seemed lost in thought and almost unaware of his existence. He'd faded into the background of the tower, no doubt. His tanned skin and hair and clothes melding with the wood of the place. He was nobody and nothing to Sophie because, besides being a surveyor, the privilege trickled from her pores. She was a high blood. Most of her kind tended to play at work as clergyfolk or else bankers. But she was again like him, preferring the difficult and dangerous role of surveyor.

Fenrir leaned forward and scanned through the notes written in her spidery script. She was struggling with a calculation, stuck on converting her measurements as viewed from afar to the physical extent of the distortion. They used a projection equation, but she'd forgotten to include the lensing constant. Fenrir was forbidden from touching the tools of his former trade, but that didn't include the theory behind it. This was just text set to paper after all.

Fenrir rose from his chair and came up behind Sophie's. She was so focused on her work that she didn't even notice. He extended his arm, and she jumped when it came into view. She twirled around with haughty annoyance written on her face. He smiled and tapped his finger on her notepad.

"You left out the lensing constant," he said. "That's why the buffer zone is too large."

She glared at him then looked at the text below his finger. He moved it aside, and she craned forward and scanned it. Her eyes widened, then she set her graphite stick to the paper and furiously scribbled away. She struck through lines of numbers and symbols then made additions above and below. The page was a mess by the time she'd made her corrections, but she had the long-sought result. There it was, nestled at the bottom of the page, circled three times over. One radial yard. She tapped the graphite stick to the result and grinned.

"That looks much better," she said, glancing back up at Fenrir.

He nodded, hands in pant pockets, waiting for the realization to dawn on her. It happened within seconds. Her smile faded, and her brow wrinkled.

"How do you know about the lensing constant?" she asked.

"I'm learned," Fenrir replied.

Her lips protruded. "Fine, keep your secrets, toller, but how did you notice the distortion? It's barely even there."

It wasn't impossible for an ordinary person to observe the distortions or rather their effects, but it depended heavily on how potent a given foul mote was. Large ones could be spotted by the undulations they gave off, making the air ripple. They could be felt too by a subtle fluctuation in temperature or a kind of ethereal breeze. But one as faint as that in Fenrir's tower? It was just a pin-prick. Impossible to detect without aid unless one was gifted with another kind of sense.

"I'm observant," Fenrir said.

Sophie blew air through her nose at his claim.

"I didn't touch it," he said, "if that's what you're concerned about. You can check me for affliction, if you like."

"Oh, I most certainly will, but first, I need to erect a ward around the bothersome thing."

He pulled back at her choice of word. Distortions were the stuff of nightmares, an awful curse set on their world, meant to be feared. Bothersome was a grave understatement.

Sophie stood from her chair, grabbed her ruler and chalk, and headed over to the distortion. Fenrir watched again from afar as she inscribed the wooden floorboards of the tower with symbols meant to stunt the foul mote's growth. She was careful and methodical such that the process took her another half hour. She groaned and held her lower back when she finally rose, her ward complete.

Fenrir migrated over to inspect her work. The ward was elaborate—lines of equations repeated unnecessarily, arcs and curves where they weren't needed, extra lines in empty spaces that required none. But the ward's inefficiency, the excessive flourishes and wasted chalk, was eclipsed by its raw beauty. Sophie had made it a work of art precisely because of its imperfections. Fenrir gaped at it.

It was already working. He could feel the difference. The tugging was lessened, and the wrongness ever so slightly diminished. She'd done well. She was skilled. He pulled his eyes away from her creation and searched her epaulets for signs of her surveyor rank. Navy blue. Tier 2. Very good. Almost as good as he had been.

Sophie clapped the chalk off her gloves then moved back to her pack. She stowed some of her tools.

"Take off your clothes," she said, turning round with the detector in hand.

Fenrir's face flushed. The truth was, he was filthy. The shack he lived in was distant from the nearest water spout, so if he wanted to bathe, he had to pay a pretty penny at a local bathhouse. A toller's work was blessed but not well compensated. Besides, he didn't associate with anyone at the tower, lived alone, and kept to himself. Naturally, hygiene had gotten pushed to the wayside. He hadn't been trying to impress anyone, until now.

"Can't you do it without me having to go through all that?" he asked.

Sophie scrunched up her nose and shook her head. "Even a layer of cloth can interfere with the reading. Now, disrobe."

She was correct, according to theory, but in practice, the detector rarely encountered such issues. Still, there was no point in arguing. Fenrir sighed then removed his clothing more akin to rags than proper attire. When he got to his loincloth, he stopped.

"That too," Sophie said, angling her head at the area near his crotch.

Fenrir's face burned as he untied the knots holding his undergarment in place. The old and weathered fabric fell to his feet, and he cupped his genitals with his hands. It was the penitentiary all over again. He was less a person and more an object. Just a mass of flesh that the distortion could have embedded itself into. The skin or muscles or bones or organs mutated by the non-Euclidean into something horrible and strange. It slowly encroaching and transforming more and more of his body until it reached his brain and caused him to go insane. That was the fate of the afflicted. He shuddered at the thought of it and held back the torrent of horrid memories that rushed at him.

Fenrir stared at the tower floor, trying his utmost to

avoid making a scene. Sophie's hand appeared in his line of sight holding the detector, and he latched onto the view for dear life. He focused on the glyphs inscribed into her glove. Brown leather with a white stitching. Surveyors took pride in their gloves, the styling and contents of the glyphs unique to each of them.

Fenrir had paid a small fortune for his first pair. They had been black leather with red thread tracing his favorite axioms. He'd had a fetish for triangles in particular, and those had featured frequently in his attire and gear. Sophie's gloves tended towards the geometric. Polygon nested in polygon in polygon, smaller and smaller until the sides of the shape met at a point. She moved around him, tracing every curve, hovering so close sometimes his hair felt contact. This went on for what felt like ages.

When Sophie strayed towards his groin, she cleared her throat and looked up at him, her head tilted to the side to see him past her tricorn. Fenrir glanced down, met her gaze, and held it. Then he let his hands drop to his sides, and she inspected his delicate parts for signs of affliction. Of course, there was nothing to find. Fenrir hadn't gone anywhere near the foul thing, but she couldn't simply trust his word. When people became afflicted, the first thing they did was lie to themselves about the severity of their condition. No one wanted to believe it had happened to them, this curse that had no cure. The only way to free an afflicted was a mercy killing.

"You're clean," she said.

He grimaced at the word choice then grabbed his clothing and dressed. Sophie headed over to her pack.

"The good news," she said, over her shoulder, "is that the distortion is of mild potency. The bad news is, based on my preliminary measurements, it's long-lived rather than ephemeral and likely to expand so that the tower will have to be abandoned."

She glanced at Fenrir. He didn't give much of a reaction, as he'd suspected this would be the case. Even in the two hours since he'd arrived, the distortion had grown in volume. The question was, how fast would it grow? And what would the Church do without one of the three bell towers?

"Will the Church be able to build a new tower quickly enough?" he asked.

Sophie finished stowing her tools in her pack. She fastened the three metal and leather clasps then heaved it onto her shoulders. Her hat got nudged by the movement, and she readjusted it to have a slight angle down towards her face.

"The Church won't have a choice," she said. "But fret not, it seems to be expanding slowly. I'll know just how slowly once I've made more measurements. I'll be back tomorrow and every day thereafter to check its progress."

Fenrir tried not to smile. Despite the fact that the distortion was a foul thing, it had given him something to look forward to. Yes, it would expand until it consumed the entirety of the tower. Yes, he would have to relocate to another tower to toll the precious bell. But it had also given him Sophie. A link to his old life. A reminder of his glory days.

"I look forward to it," he said.

Sophie headed to the opening with the ladder, stepped down, then glanced up at Fenrir. "Since we'll be seeing a fair amount of one another, maybe I'll manage to unearth your secrets, Toller Fenrir."

PROCLAMATION

Construction of a Replacement for the Most-Holy Southeast Bell Tower

WHEREAS, a foul distortion was observed on the platform of the Most-Holy Southeast Bell Tower on the fifteenth day of the ninth month in the year of our Lady five hundred and twenty-nine, and

WHEREAS, the measurements of said distortion indicate the long-lived type of mild potency with expanding nature, and

WHEREAS, the current Most-Holy Southeast Bell Tower will be rendered unusable in the near future;

NOW, THEREFORE, be it resolved that I, Archbishop Torrington, do hereby proclaim the immediate construction of a new Most-Holy Southeast Bell Tower that meets the specifications for harmonious spaces as outlined in the Axioms of the Euclidean.

And I hereby beseech the devout of Simetria to volunteer their time and effort for this most worthy and noble cause.

IN WITNESS, WHEREOF I have hereunto set my hand and caused the Blessed Seal of Our Beloved Lady to be herein affixed.

Archbishop of the Church of Impermanence
Reginild Torrington

The Rot of the Link protect us. The Hand of the Lady guide us.

THE SURVEYOR

Sophie didn't like the toller at first. He seemed like all the other low bloods. Dirty, simple, vacant. But then he'd mentioned the lensing constant and caught her attention. She was skilled, yet for all her ability, a toller had pointed out her mistakes. It was humbling, and if she'd been the prideful type, perhaps she would have despised him. But Sophie wasn't like the other high bloods. She bore scars and deep-set wounds that had softened her. So instead of viewing Fenrir's interference as a jab at her competence, she was intrigued.

Sophie returned to the tower the morning after her first survey, and there Fenrir was, sitting at his table, waiting, freshly washed and shaven. His hair was the color of hay now and straight, reaching to his cheekbones in the front but shorter in the back. His clothes had been mended, poorly, but it was the effort that made her smile. He rose from his seat and nodded to her. With the dirt and grime gone, Sophie realized Fenrir carried himself too well for a low blood. Beyond that, there was something so achingly familiar about him.

"Good morning," he said.

"Good morning," she replied.

Sophie took off her pack, carried it to the table, and

rested it on the floor next to the seat she had used the day before. Two mugs steamed in the morning chill.

"Would you like to rest before taking your measurements?" Fenrir asked, waving at the mugs. "The ascent is difficult, even without all that equipment."

"What's this?" Sophie asked.

She sat in the chair meant for her, pulled the mug towards her, and sniffed.

"I'm sure you're accustomed to better brews," Fenrir said, taking the other seat, "but I thought you might appreciate the refreshment."

"Tea? How did you get that up here?"

Her eyes scanned the tower then spotted a small barrel with a strap nearby.

"The same as myself," he said. "Hands and feet, rung by rung."

Fenrir grabbed his mug and took a sip. The way he gripped the vessel—holding the handle with just the thumb and first two fingers, using the other hand to support the base—confirmed her suspicions. Fenrir was well-bred. That begged the question, why was he serving as a toller? It was a blessed duty, true, but one delegated to the low bloods.

"The gesture is thoughtful," she said. "Many thanks."

They sat in silence and drank their dark and bitter drinks. Sophie gazed over the railing at Simetria. Despite the clouds and grayness of everything, it was beautiful in a melancholic way. Her eyes ran from the southern gate up through the main thoroughfare of the city. The buildings shifted from horrid lean-tos into sturdier constructions of wood and stone. Simple and practical but not beautiful. As the slope of ground signaled the transition into the upper city, the architecture morphed into a lovely thing. Expertly crafted stonework meant to last the ages. Ornate but with a focus on sharp edges and clear angles.

This culminated in the grand palaces of the great families, which formed a kind of ring around the centerpiece of Simetria. Its pride and joy, the Church of Impermanence. It was topped by a massive dome, itself capped with a globe bearing a light that blazed unerringly. That light alone told them the Rot of the Link persisted over all these long years.

Sophie's eyes strayed to the two other bell towers further out, perfectly arranged to complete the symmetry in the city at large. How would the construction of a new tower affect the harmony of the alignment? One imperfection, one stone out of place, and the distortions might increase. Sophie didn't envy the architects assigned this task.

"If you'll excuse me," Fenrir said, rising from his chair, "I have to toll the bell."

"Of course."

"It's quite loud," he added.

Fenrir moved to the center of the tower platform, grabbed the rope affixed to the massive bell, and pulled down hard. The sheer force of sound almost knocked Sophie out of her seat. He hadn't been exaggerating. She clapped her hands over her ears and winced at the two dongs that followed. Then, Fenrir was back at the table already pulling out a parchment and graphite stick. Sophie rummaged in her pack for her notepad.

The two of them spent the next ten minutes scribbling equations and drawing diagrams. Anything from the axioms would do—Archimedes, Hypatia, Euler, Fibonacci. The specifics weren't as important as the act itself. The rituals were all about reducing the probability that the distortions would form. It was a means of reminding reality of its truest, purest state, that of the Euclidean.

Sophie glanced at Fenrir's work a few times, but his writing was too fine for her to make out the contents. After the ritual had been executed, Fenrir tolled the bell yet again, and Sophie took that as her sign to get to work. She finished her tea and pulled out her tools. Fenrir sat and watched, but something about how he looked at the devices told her they weren't strange and mysterious objects to him. Less wonder and awe in his eyes and more of something almost like longing.

"I won't bother you for very long today," she said, "I just need to ascertain if the distortion has grown or changed in any way."

She already felt it had, even before she'd reached the top rung of the ladder. A subtle but tangible growth. The bishops had told her the tower needed to be kept functional as long as possible. It would be weeks until a replacement was constructed.

"Then, there are the wards to reinforce," she added.

Fenrir nodded and stayed seated while Sophie moved to the distortion with her supplies. She measured and remeasured the extent of the thing then set her chalk to wood. Her ward was solid, but it could be improved upon. After reporting her findings to the Church, she'd spent the rest of the previous day researching methods and techniques she could employ. Four hours she'd pored through old texts written by surveyors of the past before settling on an elegant, although controversial, addition.

It would be difficult because it had to be exceptionally precise. She started by drawing dots on the outermost edge of the ward, one close to the rim then one a bit further then closer then further over and over again until she'd run the circumference of the ward. She repeated this, filling in another set of points between each of her previous ones. She made two more passes in this way until her dots traced a sinuous curve, a dashed approximation of a wave wrapped in the shape of a circle. The Exalted Sine Function.

Just when she was ready to connect the dots into a line and complete the addition to the ward, the tower floorboards creaked. She looked over her shoulder to find Fenrir staring down at her handy work, his eyes wide.

"I'm bolstering the ward," she said.

She knew what this must look like to the uninformed. With the exception of circles, it was unusual to incorporate any form not composed of hard lines into a ward. Triangles, squares, pentagons, hexagons, whatever other polygon suited one's fancy. Those were all commonplace, but what of this curving line that undulated? It looked borderline forbidden. Erring towards the non-Euclidean.

"I know this seems odd," she said, standing up, chalk still in hand, ready to scrawl, "but it's permitted. And given the need to keep this distortion contained for as long as possible, I'm required to take unorthodox measures."

"A Sine Function?" he asked.

Sophie's face mirrored Fenrir's now. Only learned members of the clergy studied the Exalted Functions. She didn't understand how the man could know about the Sine Function let alone identify one in a ward.

"How do you know it?"

Fenrir's eyes darted away, and he shrank. This was the version of him that she'd first met. The silent, sullen toller, but now, she saw that wasn't the only Fenrir. There was another one, tucked away. It was the one who had found that miniscule distortion, knew the lensing constant, and could spy a Sine Function set in a ward.

"I'm learned," he replied.

"As you said yesterday. But why would a learned man be living the very unlearned life of a toller?"

Sophie put her hands on her hips and stared Fenrir down. He looked at the ground with defocused eyes.

"It's my lot in life," he said.

She sighed in exasperation and turned back to the ward. Fenrir headed to the table. Sophie spent the next ten minutes connecting the points with a smooth curve. Crest and trough, crest and trough, caging the distortion in tightly. She dusted off her hands, stowed her gear, and sat down at the table opposite Fenrir. She waited for him to glance up. After a few seconds, he did.

"It's not my intent to be deceptive," Fenrir said. "You simply ask questions I cannot answer."

Sophie leaned forward. Fenrir moved to mimic her posture, chest to table, arms folded and flush with it.

"But you want to tell me something, don't you, Toller Fenrir? Otherwise, you wouldn't bother to give me little hints as you do."

Fenrir smiled. "Be that as it may, Surveyor Sophie, I'm not at liberty to divulge the information you seek."

Sophie leaned back and crossed her arms. "Fine, as I said yesterday, keep your secrets."

She rose, hoisted her pack, and headed to the ladder. Fenrir followed. She went down a few rungs until only her head showed from the opening in the floor then stopped and looked up.

"If you can't tell me how you're learned," she said, "perhaps you'd be willing to share some of that learning regardless?"

Fenrir's eyes lit up, and he grinned wider than she'd seen thus far. The movement exposed his teeth, and those too gave him away. Straight and whole and well-maintained. Not exactly shining or whitened, but too good to for him have been raised as a low blood. There were many mysteries to this toller, and Sophie liked nothing more than tackling enigmas. She spent so much of her time and energy keeping her own horrid nature hidden. It was freeing to unearth others' secrets for a change.

***

Every day, Sophie made the climb up the tower. Every day, Fenrir was waiting with two cups of tea and a smile that became more assured. As he grew comfortable with her, the toller-side retreated while the learned-side took center stage. They talked of distortions, of glyphs, of wards, of the tools of her trade. She showed him what each did. He listened attentively but refused to touch any. He said he was afraid to damage the blessed things. She knew he was lying. He wasn't devout. That became clear when their conversations strayed to the Church.

"A toller that doesn't attend mass?" she said in mock horror.

"The sermons are vague," he replied.

They leaned against the railing near the table, gazing out at the city and the Church. Sophie had finished her measurements on the distortion nearly an hour ago. This was becoming a common occurrence, her lingering.

"And the chapel closest to my home is too crowded," Fenrir added.

Sophie smiled and laughed. "A true servant would take the pilgrimage to the next nearest chapel or the next."

"I prefer to read the sacred texts on my own," Fenrir said, "rather than have a priest who doesn't understand them lecture me."

"That's not the same. You have to bathe in the wisdom of our Lady's servants even if they are lacking in said wisdom."

"To maintain the Rot of the Link."

They both laughed. It was refreshing to be able to speak openly about the faults of the Church. It was something Sophie couldn't do with anyone else. The politics of being a surveyor were fraught, and she had the added complication of also being the head of a great family ever since her father had passed the year before. She was watched at all times and had to be on her best behavior. It was exhausting.

Sophie told herself she stayed to converse with Fenrir long after her duties were complete because he was inconsequential enough to not be dangerous. In truth, there was more to it than that. She liked him for him. And she learned from him. She brought texts with her that they pored over together. At first, simple ones for her to gauge the extent of his knowledge, which was expansive, then ones she herself struggled to digest.

"This is where I found the suggestion to use the Exalted Sine Function for my ward," she said, pointing to an entry in a tome on ward construction.

Fenrir leaned in and scanned the contents. They sat side by side at the table, close enough that their arms occasionally brushed.

"Who made this entry?" Fenrir asked.

"Surveyor Grimwool," Sophie said. "He was tier 1 and lived a century past."

The theory behind the efficiency of utilizing a Sine Function as the outer layer of a ward is not well established at present. Normally, any curvilinear form is ill-advised in the construction of wards as such representations can cause the Euclidean and non-Euclidean to momentarily invert. Although these inversions tend to be short-lived, they cause the distortion to behave erratically henceforth. However, the Sine Function is an exception to this rule. This is perhaps related to the origin of said Function, which is fully Euclidean. Although the Function can appear curvilinear when plotted in x-y space, it is best understood in the context of a triangle of rights, such that the sine of an angle equals the side opposite over the hypotenuse.

"This is obscure," Fenrir said. "I'm surprised you found it."

Sophie scrunched her nose and shook her head. "And I'm surprised you understand a word of it, learned toller."

Fenrir blushed.

"I can bring something still more obscure tomorrow, if you'd like," she said.

"If it's not too much trouble."

Neutral words but eyes that begged her to do so.

The next day, Fenrir was waiting for her at the tower's base, in the street just outside the entrance. She stopped short on seeing him.

"Is something wrong with the distortion?" she asked.

Fenrir smiled and shook his head then looked at the ground. He wore a new tunic, simple, beige, adorned with nested squares stitched with red thread along the hem.

"You mentioned bringing a new tome," he said. "I wanted to offer to carry it or any of your supplies in return for the favor."

The attendant who sat at the tower's base leaned back on his stool and glanced at them. There was a typical low blood. The dead eyes. The slouch of the shoulders. Such a contrast with Fenrir. Sophie heaved her pack off her back and handed it to Fenrir.

"This climb is my least favorite part of my visits," she said. "So by all means."

Fenrir smiled wider, lifted the pack with a grunt, and slipped his arms through the too-small straps. Sophie moved in and loosened the clasps until the pack sat more comfortably on Fenrir. They stood close, and she lingered longer than she needed to, pretending to fiddle with the clasps. She loved this feeling—the tension, the hum, the buzz of want. But did she want him? Or was she just rerouting her unfulfilled yearning for another?

"There we are," she said, patting the strap and his chest beneath it. "After you."

Fenrir gripped the pack and started the climb. The attendant went back to picking the dirt from beneath his nails. Sophie followed Fenrir. After a few minutes, they were both catching their breath on the tower platform. Sophie helped Fenrir remove the pack then placed it beside her chair. There was the tea already steaming in mugs. They sat and drank and snuck glances at one another.

A pigeon landed on the railing near where the distortion

laid. It strutted and migrated closer to the foul mote, but the creature was like Sophie. It, too, seemed to sense the wrongness. It escaped the tug of the non-Euclidean in a flutter.

"It's strange, isn't it?" she said. "How animals can sense the distortions, but most people can't."

"Most?"

Sophie grinned, intertwined her fingers, and held them just hovering near her lips.

"There are always exceptions," she said. "And exceptional people. Like me. And you."

Fenrir's eyes flitted from side to side before settling back on her. He didn't deny her claim.

"Any theories on how such people developed this new, keen sense?" she asked.

Approaching the topic as idle curiosity. It was the right approach. Fenrir took the bait.

"Perhaps it's their way of responding to their environment," he said. "Those who have this sense are better able to avoid the danger, which is a useful skill for survival. They proceed to pass on such abilities to their children, and their children do the same."

Sophie tapped her fingers against her lips. "A fascinating hypothesis, but I suspect it doesn't capture the whole truth. There's so little we understand about the distortions."

Sophie freed her fingers, stood, and rummaged in her bag before hefting a massive text from it. She walked to Fenrir's side and cracked it open. Dust puffed out, and she waved it away with her hand.

"I promised a tome," she said. "This one is rather precious. Use care in turning the pages."

Fenrir drained the rest of his tea and slid the mug away. He moved his chair until he sat in line with the tome. Within seconds, he was engrossed. Sophie took the opportunity to do her measurements and touch up the ward. Even after twenty minutes had passed, Fenrir still devoured the contents of the book. He was voracious in his mind, more so than any of her peers. His hunger for knowledge drew her in. She leaned over his shoulder and glanced at what he read. Theorems and equations, obscure, ancient. She reached an arm out and tapped a line.

"Your lensing constant," she said. "This is the original calculation for it."

Fenrir nodded then seemed to take note of just how achingly close Sophie was. He avoided her eyes and tensed his shoulders.

"There are other texts I wanted to show you," she said, "but those are priceless and can't leave the confines of the Church."

"That's as it should be."

"Perhaps you go to them then?"

Fenrir turned, and his eyes shot to hers. He held her gaze, stern and quiet.

"I doubt I'd be welcome there," he said after a space.

"You're a toller. You already serve the Church, and you'd be my guest."

Fenrir faced forward again and stared down at the tome. He smoothed the pages with a soft touch.

"I'm afraid I have to turn down your gracious offer," he said, "but I thank you for it, truly."

The next day, Fenrir met Sophie at the interface between the upper and lower city and walked with her to the tower. She didn't comment on it beyond giving a wide smile, but it was enough. Every day thereafter, Fenrir was waiting for her on that cobblestoned street, and a steaming mug of tea did likewise on the tower's landing. Sophie was restless to uncover Fenrir's truth but knew he would tell her who he really was in time. A month passed in such a fashion. The distortion expanded.

PRAYER FOR THE ROT

Blessed is the Rot—the Rot of the Link, the Rot of the body, the Rot of the world.

The Rot of the Link is freedom, freedom from the tyranny the Others would thrust upon us.

The Rot of the body is comfort, comfort in knowing we are free of affliction.

The Rot of the world is purity, purity of space and time saturated in the laws of the Universe.

Blessed is the Rot for it signals the Euclidean reigns.

A TOAST

Fenrir dreaded the day he had to abandon the tower, not because of the distortion itself, but because of what else it signaled—the end of his time with Sophie. But it came nonetheless. A month they spent in each other's company. Every day lighter. A trace of joy creeping back into his hollowed heart. Then, it was over. She made her final set of measurements, touched up her ward, and stowed away her tools for the last time. Fenrir looked on with despair.

"The new tower is ready," she said, sitting at the little table they'd shared.

"So I was told," Fenrir replied. He dug in his pant pocket, fished out a letter, and laid it on the table. "A messenger dropped it off yesterday. Complete with directions for where it is. As if I couldn't see it clearly with my own eyes."

They both glanced at the duplicate tower not two buildings over. Sophie smiled and shook her head then leaned over and rummaged in her pack. She pulled out a cloth bag, a few objects wrapped in wax paper, and a wine bottle.

"We'll have to use the mugs," she said, nodding at the wine. "My housekeeper wouldn't hear of me taking proper glasses into the lower city."

Sophie was tight-lipped about her life outside of her work, but Fenrir had managed to piece together a rough approximation of who she was. High blood, which had been obvious from the outset, but also a member of a great family.

"What's all this?" Fenrir asked.

Sophie opened the bag and unfolded the wax paper. Rolls, cheeses, dried meats. Plus, the wine.

"We're celebrating," she said.

Sophie pulled a knife from her belt and split a roll open. She held it out to Fenrir, who reached for it. She let her hand brush his as she passed him the bounty. Then, she was working on liberating a chunk of cheese and a slab of meat. Fenrir took the wine bottle in hand and inspected it.

"It's my family's own," she said. "Fresh from the cellar where it's sat for probably decades. My father never liked wine so he didn't do much to decrease the hoard we have squirreled away."

"And your mother?" he asked.

Sophie's smile faded, and she focused on her cutting. "I don't know much about her preferences seeing how she died shortly after giving birth to me."

Fenrir winced at his misstep. "I'm sorry. I didn't realize."

Sophie glanced up. Fenrir still held the wine bottle with no proper tool to unleash its contents. She came to his side of the table and took the bottle from him.

"How would you be expected to know?" she asked. "There's nothing to apologize for."

Sophie placed the bottle on the table, held the neck in one hand, and used the other to jab the cork with her knife. She pushed. The cork fell through, but at the last moment, the hand on the neck slipped. The bottle tilted and covered the tabletop with its amber fluid. Sophie tried to correct her mistake, but most of the bottle was already lost. She sighed and flopped into her chair.

"Wonderful," she said. "Aren't I grace personified?"

Fenrir poured the remainder of the wine into a mug and handed it to her.

"We can't do a proper toast without two," she said.

She was sulking. Maybe he wasn't the only one tortured by this being their last day together.

"It's your wine," he said. "Besides, I have two more bells to toll before I can imbibe."

"I actually thought to come back in the evening for that very reason, but I have obligations tonight."

She looked down at her wine-drenched hands. Fenrir fetched the rag he used to clean the mugs and handed it to her.

"I have a bottle of spirits that I've been saving for a special occasion," he said. "How about I go home and retrieve it. We can eat this lovely spread, wait until I toll the last bell, and do our toast then. How would that suit?"

Sophie wiped her hands on the rag and smiled.

"It would suit quite well," she said, "but it's not the most practical suggestion. You would go all the way down the tower just to have to come all the way back up again? Why not enjoy our refreshments up here until you've tolled the final bell, then we both go to your home for that toast?"

***

Fenrir lived in a shack. Cramped, dark, dank, and in the most advanced stages of decay. So close to rot, it should have been a blessed thing. That's what the Church preached after all. That rot was a glory and a gift, but such dogma tended to stop at the domestic realm. There, cleanliness was godliness. So Fenrir couldn't help but be ashamed of his domicile when Sophie first stepped foot through its threshold.

They went there directly from the tower so he had no time to tidy the place. He apologized in advance, but it still couldn't prepare Sophie. She was a high blood. Besides dealing with the occasional distortion or afflicted, what did she know of how the other half lived? When he'd been better off, what had he known?

Sophie did an admirable job of concealing her shock, but he knew how she viewed the place. It was how he would have viewed it if he hadn't first laid eyes on it after living in a cell for five years. The framing was everything. To the Ashtin Broodfell of the time before the penitentiary, this place would have looked like the poorest pauper's darkest hole. To the Fenrir Mey that walked out of those iron-clad gates, this was a slice of heaven.

Fenrir beckoned Sophie in, pulled a chair out for her at his only table, and hurried to light an oil lamp. While he rushed about, illuminating the small space then searching for his special bottle of spirits, Sophie wandered. She peered at the trinkets he had arranged on a window sill, ran her fingers along the rim of a clock that no longer kept the time, and sniffed the dried herbs hanging from rafters. When Fenrir turned around with the coveted vessel, Sophie was holding a round metal disk. His heart stopped. Of all the things for her to notice, why had it been that? His sigil of the purge.

"Where did you get this?" she asked.

Fenrir put the bottle on the table and walked to her side. He gazed at the palm-sized silver coin bearing the word "purge" with a geometric form traced around it. He took the sigil from Sophie's hand and cradled it in his palm like the precious thing it was. Pure silver. He could have sold it and lived off the profits for many months, but he hadn't. Its preciousness stemmed not from the monetary value, but because it was all that remained of his old life. He still didn't know why they'd let him keep this, of all things.

"Only a surveyor would have such a treasure," Sophie said, "and not just any surveyor."

He felt her eyes fixed on him even though he still stared down at the metal disk. Fenrir sighed then met her gaze.

"You helmed a purge," she said.

The words brought those moments back.

Fenrir was Ashtin again. Twenty-six, fearless, proud. Only one year as a tier 1 surveyor and already bestowed the supreme honor of helming a holy purge. Twenty-odd lives resting in his hands. Forty-odd eyes locked on his as he explained their mission.

"We will split into two lances. One will face to the east and the other west as we exit Simetria from the south gate. We'll follow the city walls and scour the area for signs of distortion. When we find the foul motes, we contain them. If we encounter afflicted, person or beast, we end their suffering. Once we meet at the north gate, we'll advance two hundred paces away from the wall and again follow the periphery. We'll continue this routine until we've cleared the lands within a mile radius from our fair city's wall."

It sounded so simple, and the surveyors who hadn't yet taken part in a purge showed their naivety by smug smiles and too-eager head wags. The veterans knew it would be a veritable slaughter. If they were careful, the only dismembered limbs would come from the afflicted. More likely than not, it would be a smattering from both sides.

"Do not underestimate the afflicted," Ashtin said. "They'll be unlike any you've encountered within Simetria. These poor souls have lived with distortion for years. Their non-Euclidean parts are timeless so they don't age as we do. Many can barely even see our world as it is any longer. Their reason is gone, and the distortions have all but consumed them. They're monsters to behold. The mere look or smell of them can drive you insane if you don't steel yourself. So don your goggles, affix your beaks, and loft your polearms."

Ashtin did as he instructed, taking the tinted goggles and herb-filled beak that hung around his neck and moving them over his eyes, nose, and mouth. His surveyors did likewise. Now, they would be better protected from the foulness of the afflicted. But even with their facial coverings and leather-shrouded torsos and limbs, the distortions could still bring harm if they so much as brushed against one pulsing on an afflicted. And it could be so difficult to tell where the Euclidean parts ended and the non-Euclidean began. The most twisted of the afflicted could be so far gone that they were senseless masses of horror. It was always safer to keep their distance, and that was where the polearms came in. The weapon of choice for surveyors.

Some wielded voulges, others war scythes, but Ashtin preferred a fauchard. He marched toward the line of surveyors arranged in front of him, and they parted in his wake before pulling behind like a wave drawn in. Ashtin stopped at a rack and grasped his weapon, a wooden pole ending in a curved blade. The others did the same. One, two, and so on until all twenty were armed and eager to escape the confines of the armory.

"Forward," Ashtin shouted.

The lance did as he instructed. A horde of leather-clad men and women, bags dangling from their belts and nearly bursting with blessed chalk, polearms in hand, faces made to look like a strange form of bird, all belt and buckle and glassy round eyes. As they left the surveyor quarters and ventured through the corridors of the Church, clergyfolk stopped what they were doing and stared. A purge was a rare thing, a blessed one. Deacons and priests signed the Love of the Lady, the first two fingers of their right hands touching their forehead, trailing down to their sternum, then flicking off to the right. Bishops looked on, stern and noble.

When the surveyors made it to the main exit of the Church grounds, the Archbishop was waiting. He touched the forehead of each as they filed out. Ashtin lingered so that he was last. He stopped in front of Torrington, swung his fauchard into both hands, held it parallel to the ground, and bowed. Torrington sprinkled spore-laden waters on Ashtin's head and chanted his blessing.

"The Rot of the Link protect you. The Hand of the Lady guide you."

Ashtin lifted his head. "We go forth to bring rot to the undying."

Normally, surveyors didn't concern themselves with anything outside of Simetria. The other cities had their own sets of surveyors, and the spaces between said cities were dangerous and largely avoided. Out there, distortions had free reign, and they birthed noxious things. Any life that came in contact with them became afflicted. The non-Euclidean merged with the Euclidean in an unholy matrimony that cursed the host with eternal pain and, if left unchecked, unending life. There was too much world and too few surveyors to patrol it all. Instead, the Church prioritized its efforts on the cities, the last bastions of civilization after the fall of the Old World. It was only when the distortions outside encroached and threatened the cities that the Church called for a purge.

For Ashtin, the walk through Simetria was a blur. So too was the initial survey outside the city. A few distortions to contain. Nothing complex. But then, during their third circuit, many paces distant from the wall, they encountered the first cluster of afflicted. They tended to do that, stick together like molasses.

The surveyors struck. A sweep of a scythe. A slash of a voulge. Chunks of afflicted sailing through the air. Ashtin dodged the detritus. That too could be saturated with the non-Euclidean. Then a young surveyor mistimed her attack. Her scythe cut air, and the seven-handed limb she'd meant to liberate from the body it was attached to grabbed hold of her.

She yelped in pain and fear. She was doomed, and the only solution was a mercy killing by one of her comrades.

Ashtin sprinted into the fray and cleaved her head free of her body. She was spared the fate of affliction. Next, Ashtin turned to the horror that had gotten her and wielded his fauchard. He slashed in precise and efficient arcs, varying each successive one by mere degrees. The goal was to cut the afflicted into as many pieces as possible for that was the only way to free them. Complete and total dismemberment. Anything less thorough resulted in them rising again.

Ashtin lost himself after that, went deep into a fever trance. Others in the lance told him he had been elegant in his mercy killings, that his movements were a thing of beauty, that even the afflicted seemed transfixed by him. He pretended to be humbled by their awe and wonder. It was an act. Helming that purge only served to feed the swollen pride that eventually undid him.

"It was from the Purge of 523, wasn't it?" Sophie asked, forcing Fenrir back into the present.

Of course she would know which purge. It was the only one that had happened in the past decade.

"And if you helmed it," she said, "that means you're Ashtin Broodfell."

That name, spoken aloud, sent a shock through. No one was meant to apply it to him. He was Fenrir now.

"Ashtin Broodfell is dead," Fenrir said. "He was executed for his grave crimes."

"And yet, here stands a toller who knows the most obscure ways of the surveyors, who holds his mug like a high blood, and who owns a sigil of the purge. Top that all off with the fact that he resembles the man."

Fenrir's hand fell slack to his side, and he backed away from Sophie. It was the one secret he had to keep or truly face death, and yet she knew his name, the old name.

"Ashtin Broodfell is dead," he repeated. "Fenrir Mey is all there is now."

He dragged himself over to the table and fell into a chair. Sophie took the other seat, her eyes alight, boring holes into him. He would have given anything to have that look from her so long as it had come about in any other way. Why awe? If she knew Ashtin Broodfell, she knew the crimes that marred the name.

"You look pale," she said.

Sophie leaned towards Fenrir then glanced at the bottle of spirits and cups nearby. She stood and poured an ample amount for each of them. She set one cup in front of Fenrir then took up her chair again. She raised her vessel and cleared her throat. Fenrir forced himself to meet her gaze.

"This is the long-sought toast," she said.

He instructed his hand to lift, to drop the sigil on the table, and to take hold of the cup. He mimicked her posture, hand held high with vessel.

"It has been a pleasure working alongside you this past month, dear Fenrir Mey. I wish my visits to your tower could go on and on, but permanence is a foul thing, as the Church says. We now scurry back to our own lonely lives. I'm grateful that, for a sliver of an instant, I felt something like happiness. Cheers to the distortion that threw us together in the first place."

She lifted her cup then swallowed the contents in one draught. Fenrir stared with an open mouth. Everything was backwards.

"Did you toast to the distortion?" he asked.

"Just between the two of us. See, I have my own set of secrets. Maybe that helps put you at ease?"

Fenrir's initial shock was wearing off. He had to protect himself first and foremost.

"You can't tell anyone about me," he said.

Sophie reached across the table, grabbed the bottle, and poured herself another serving. She held the cup, nodded, and threw its contents back into her throat. She closed her eyes and shook her head before recovering.

"Didn't I tell you ages ago I would unearth your little secrets?" she said. "And that's all I wanted. Just to learn them, then let them lie."

Fenrir softened. Sophie knew who he was, what he'd done, and she wasn't spitting in his face. She sat across from him laughing and smiling and drinking. And she was a surveyor. Of all the people to understand exactly how heinous his deeds had been, she would know.

"Drink up," she said. "We have to celebrate. Today is more than our final farewell. Today is also my birthday. Twenty-eight years young, although not in the eyes of the great families. Here's another secret to balance the scales betwixt us. I ought to be wedded by now. I ought to have had children. I'm already betrothed and have been since I was a child, but something stands in the way. And that something, dear Fenrir, is a secret to put your own to shame."

Fenrir gulped his drink down and poured himself another. He waited for Sophie to say more, but she stayed quiet and thoughtful.

"Happy birthday," he said.

Her smile rebounded, and her laugh flitted through his small home. It felt so different with her here. For a fraction of a second, he could forget about everything he'd lost and instead exist in the present.

"Would that I could stay and spend my evening in your company," she said. "Alas, my life is not my own. Even on my birthday. There's a soirée at my home tonight, and so I'm forced to play the good host. Never mind that I don't care for my birthday considering it's also the day my mother died. That doesn't matter to the people I have to associate with.

What do they care how I feel? It's all propriety and rules and social protocol."

She went to pour herself another drink, but Fenrir grabbed the bottle. She looked up at him.

"Throwing yourself at the mercy of this poison won't do you any good," he said.

She released her grip and rose from her seat.

"You're right, of course. And on the topic of being a good little socialite, I really should head home to deal with preparations."

Fenrir rose and followed her to the door. Sophie reached for the handle then stopped and turned back.

"I'll miss our time together," she said.

"Me too."

Fenrir didn't know how much of it was the spirits or her agitated mood, but he liked to think maybe those simply gave Sophie the courage to lean in and plant a kiss softly on his lips. He was still trying to process what had happened as she slipped out the door, her hand waving through the crack before it closed.

SENTENCE

The Most-Holy Church of Impermanence
vs
Ashtin Broodfell

On this, the second day in the ninth month in the year of our Lady five hundred and twenty-four, the Most-Holy Church of Impermanence, in the form of the Judicial Council of Bishops, does hereby proclaim the results of the aforenamed trial.

The Defendant, Ashtin Broodfell, is CONVICTED of grave crimes against the Church and citizens of the city of Simetria, including failing to report an instance of distortion AND failing to report an instance of affliction AND laying hand to blasphemous objects in clear defiance of the Righteous Mandate for the Cleansing of the Synthetic. These crimes have been deemed especially unforgivable owing to the previous status of the Defendant as a tier 1 surveyor of our Most-Holy Church.

The charge is immediate IMPRISONMENT of the Defendant AND seizure of all assets AND revocation of all honors and titles bestowed on him. The Defendant will be transported to and held in the Most-Solemn Penitentiary of the Lower City of Simetria without delay until a suitable day and time is chosen for a private EXECUTION.

IN WITNESS, WHEREOF we have hereunto caused the Blessed Seal of Our Beloved Lady to be herein affixed.

Judicial Council of Bishops

The Rot of the Link protect us. The Hand of the Lady guide us.

THE BISHOP

Vergil's congregation gazed at him with love and all the many flavors of that intoxicating emotion. The love a proud parent might bestow on their favorite child. The love a man might have for his nearest and dearest friend. The love a woman might hold for a man she wished to wed. The assembly of devout, spread out before the pulpit, showed him all these facets of that coveted feeling. Vergil let it sink in. He lapped it up.

"Let us speak today of a timeless tale," he began.

Vergil closed the massive Axioms of the Euclidean and descended the steps of the pulpit. His fellow clergyfolk preferred to stand elevated over the masses they preached to, but Vergil was too aware of the symbolism of the act. He didn't need to lord over them. He just required their love, and for that, he needed to come down to their lowly level. He walked to the aisle, and the low bloods marveled at him.

He was the perfection of the male form. Tall and broad with a tapered torso visible through his flowing gray robes owing to the purple sash hugging his waist. His chestnut hair slicked back, reaching to where his hairline met his neck. He knew his deep set and piercing blue eyes alone were enough to command the attention he sought, but if he displayed a smile, his two dimples would undo the crowd, putting them squarely in his thrall.

The chapel was small and dark; the only light came through a rose window in desperate need of cleaning. It was just another reason he had to move closer to his congregation. True, being so near meant he would have to bear their foul scents, their unwashed rags, their matted hair, but it was a small price to pay for their adoration and loyalty.

"Let us speak today of the tale of the Most-Divine Saint Marcos Frenwith," Vergil said.

The congregation spoke in hushed whispers. This was a favorite of the low bloods, not simply because Marcos was the first Chosen of the Lady and the founder of the Church, but because of the simple fact that he had been a nobody. They saw themselves in him. To win a person's favor, to cement their undying loyalty, all that was required was to hold a mirror to their face. Show them the greatness they were so near. Make them feel remarkable even while they were the definition of mundane.

"Marcos Frenwith lived ages past, in the time of the Old World, in the city Simetria was built upon. Marcos was a simple man. A lowly clerk who smithed code for his masters. He never showed much promise. He never stood out in any way. Marcos lived his life simply until the Others came. When those deceptive beings first touched our world, Marcos felt dread. Many others did as well. These were entities outside of space and time come to our world with unknown aims. But as they spoke and expressed their desires, other people's concerns lessened, whereas Marcos's only grew the more potent. He did not trust their sweet words. He was skeptical of their delicious promises. He knew they came not for us but for themselves."

Vergil stopped, and the pause only served to draw his

congregation in. It was a tactic that never failed to work wonders.

"And in time, Marcos was proven right. But not at first. No, for many long days, his protests fell on deaf ears. His fellows told him he was being overly cautious and simply hated that which was different. Marcos felt powerless, so he turned to the collective voice they all shared and shouted his truth there. And in the realm of the digital, his words did reach others who were sympathetic to his beliefs. Marcos gathered an army of like-minded warriors, but they lacked a key ingredient for their cause—a plan. They wanted to strip the Others of their growing influence and, ideally, bar them from our world, but they had no means of achieving this lofty goal."

Vergil reached the end of the walkway that split the congregation into two sets of long wooden benches. He twirled around, his flowing gray robes trailing the movement. He touched his fingertips together and formed a down-pointed triangle with his hands. Then he strode forward with steps more akin to a march. Long and slow and solid.

"It was then that Marcos's words did reach Our Beloved Lady. She alone knew what was required to save our world. She alone could lead Marcos and his followers. And she did. Our Lady guided Marcos, and their efforts culminated in that most divine of all invocations—the Rot of the Link. When it was introduced unto the world, the voices of the Others faded. Marcos rejoiced, but the victory came at a price, for the Lady's voice too did diminish. With her last words, she told Marcos that this had been the only way. She gifted him with her wisdom and encouraged him to share it with the rest of humanity."

Vergil was back at the front of the chapel. He smiled and nodded.

"That was the birth of our Most-Holy Church of

Impermanence. And you, good, brave people of Simetria, are the successors to Marcos's calling. We all serve the Lady in maintaining the Rot of the Link, for if we were to lower our guard but an instant, the Others would use the Link to come flooding back in, hellbent on punishing us for ousting them in the first place. We know they are angry with us. The distortions are evidence of their rage and their attempt at castigation from afar, but we have weathered their attacks. Our brave surveyors contain the creep of the non-Euclidean, and your most hallowed rituals keep the distortions at bay."

Vergil sighed and placed his hands to his heart.

"You, good people, are heroes worthy of Marcos. If he were here today, he would weep in joy at the collective beauty of you."

Vergil bowed to the congregation, and while his head was lowered towards the ground, there were cries and shouts. He rose to a roar of clapping. That coveted feeling infused him as he walked down the aisle to the door. Vergil stood there and thanked each member of the congregation as they filed out. He always did this when he gave such sermons at these decrepit little chapels scattered throughout Simetria. He had done well. The low bloods would be satisfied for many days yet. If their bellies growled for bread or their parched throats clambered for clean water, they would recall his sermon and view their suffering as a noble thing. The poor would stay obedient.

Then it was off to the Church proper in the upper city. Discussions, meetings, a few new sermons to pen, some texts to read. The day got on, but Vergil only realized it when Nicolus arrived at his study.

"Bishop Holdsworth," Nicolus said, bobbing his head down.

Vergil glanced up and grunted in response. They were only six years apart in age, but in power and prestige, Vergil was worlds beyond the priest. Still, Nicolus was useful in many ways. He was popular amongst the high bloods. A beautiful face—the nose chiseled, the jaw sharp—with the body of a dancer. At least five women were vying for him at the moment, two of which came from great families. Nicolus was only twenty-four and already had fantastic prospects. He would wield power in short order. It was only wise to treat him with that in mind. So Vergil employed the tactic of never quite giving Nicolus what he sought. Both the carrot and the stick did their part in equal measure.

Nicolus carried three large tomes in his arms and looked around the study in search of somewhere to deposit them. Vergil lifted his hand and pointed to a desk set against the wall. It was already crowded with similar books, but Nicolus managed to make room for the newcomers. He was winded as he took a cushioned chair in front of Vergil's desk.

They were surrounded by the written word. Books on shelves. Books on desks, on chairs, on the floor. Vergil was in the midst of research and had been for years now. He was growing tired of the clutter, but his work wasn't yet complete. He still sought answers to impossible questions.

"Hand me that middle tome you brought," Vergil said.

He flicked his hand in the direction of the stack. Nicolus jumped from his chair and trotted over to the pile. He freed the tome then brought it to Vergil's side, where he stood closer than he needed to. Vergil grabbed the book from him.

"Shouldn't you be getting ready to depart soon?" Nicolus asked.

Vergil glanced at the clock set into the wall above the door. He balked at the time.

"So late already."

He stuck a parchment in the book he'd been reading and closed it, expelling a puff of dust. Nicolus stuck his thumbs into his green-gray priest's sash and waited.

"I rather regret coming up with the idea of the soirée to begin with," Vergil said, staying in his chair and slumping. "Sophie wasn't keen on it, but I pressed. Now, I wonder why I bothered. She doesn't want it, I don't, so who is it we're going to all this trouble for?"

"Why us guests, of course," Nicolus said.

He knelt down beside Vergil's chair and rested the tips of his fingers on the armrest, just barely grazing Vergil's robes.

"In any case, you must go," Nicolus said, "and the sooner you leave, the more time that gives us to stop by my house for a quick refreshment."

Vergil perked up.

"It'll give you the boost you need to make it through the tedious affair," Nicolus said before standing.

As they left Vergil's study and navigated the halls of the Church, Nicolus walked in front with Vergil behind, barely able to suppress his eagerness. A turn here, a twist there, then they were in the Church's grounds, the cobblestoned streets, and finally striding through Nicolus's door. The servants welcomed their master and his guest. Vergil gave his empty hello and followed Nicolus down the steps into the cellar.

Nicolus's home was modest for a high blood. He wasn't the eldest son and wouldn't inherit his family estate when his father passed, so this was the best he could do at the moment. But Vergil's underling was biding his time until he won the hand of a woman with wealth. Until then, Nicolus lived within his means, which translated to a stone rowhouse on a mildly fashionable street. It was maybe a third the size of Vergil's and not even a sixth of Sophie's. But for all its shortcomings, the house had a cellar.

Beige, brown, rust, white stones all kept in place with an uneven mortar. The smell of damp, the dewy air, the hint of traces of mold. A thrill ran through Vergil, less from the rot of the place and more from what came next. Nicolus pulled a metal key from the folds of his robe. Not even his servants were trusted to come to this sacred place. The key entered and thrust the lock aside. After Vergil slipped in, Nicolus locked the thick oak door behind them. A single beam of light filtered down through a shaft. It provided only meager illumination. Nicolus used a firestriker to light a few oil lamps hanging about the room.

Vergil untied his sash and removed his robes. He folded them into a neat pile and placed them on a table near the door. Nicolus did the same. Once the two stood in only their loincloths, Nicolus moved in front of Vergil, stared him in the eye, and spat in his face.

The spittle hit the cheek just beside the nose. It trickled down and left a slimy trail. Vergil grinned savagely. His arm shot out and grabbed Nicolus by the throat. The gasp and wheeze that issued set Vergil's groin alight. He strode forward, forcing Nicolus to backpedal until he hit the stone wall.

"You shouldn't have done that," Vergil whispered.

He threw Nicolus against the cold hard stones then grasped the leather cuffs that hung from the ceiling. Vergil thrust Nicolus's wrists into the restraints, pulled the clasps as tight as they would go, and secured them. He released Nicolus and waited for his prisoner to look up. Once he did, Vergil drew his hand back and slapped it across Nicolus's pretty little face. A bright red smudge appeared.

"Not the face," Nicolus said. "I have to go to the soirée too."

Vergil winced at his mistake then let his rage return.

"You dare tell me what I can and can't do? You?"

Vergil strode to a rack of tools set against a wall. He took a wooden paddle and slapped it against his open hand. The smack was undeniably satisfying. How much more euphoric would it be when it made contact with this delicate, effeminate creature helpless before him? Nicolus sagged on his ropes and struggled.

"Beg for mercy," Vergil said.

"Please, you don't have to do this. It was a mistake. I shouldn't have spit on you."

"No, you shouldn't have."

Vergil lifted the paddle high above his head then drew it down with force, square onto Nicolus's left thigh. His prisoner yelped, and pure ecstasy flooded Vergil. He waited for Nicolus to recover then repeated the movement once, twice, thrice, all on different limbs. Tears streamed from Nicolus's eyes.

Vergil wanted more. His loins ached. He could have tormented his underling for hours yet, but they had a soirée to attend. This was a refreshment, only meant to partly sate him. A proper meal would have to wait for another time. Vergil threw the paddle at the rack then released the clasps on his prisoner's wrists. Nicolus fell against him, weak from the pain and pleasure coursing through.

"Steady," Vergil said.

Nicolus grabbed Vergil's shoulders and laughed. Then he pursed his lips and tried to press them to his superior's. Vergil leaned away and held Nicolus back.

"Are you mad?" Vergil asked. "How many times do I have to say it? Nothing amorous."

Nicolus's eyes shifted from side to side, and a wave of red washed over his face.

"I'm sorry, Vergil."

Vergil pushed Nicolus away and moved over to his clothes. As he donned each article, his annoyance faded. Sometimes, he forgot who it was he dealt with. Nicolus was a poet at heart with so much feeling that he was forced to occasionally release his anonymous creations on the lower city. Little paper airplanes floating on the wind bearing poems. So ridiculous but also endearing. Was it any surprise that this artistic type would get caught up in the moment and let passion overtake reason?

By the time Vergil was dressed, Nicolus was nearly ready himself. They looked one another over to ensure nothing was amiss.

"How is the cheek?" Nicolus asked.

Vergil grabbed Nicolus's chin and turned his face to the side. He inspected his work.

"It will bruise, no doubt, but if you're lucky, it won't show until tomorrow. Now, we should be off. Sophie will be wondering what's kept me."

CAGED BIRD

Vergil was late. After all the fuss he made convincing Sophie to throw the silly soirée, he couldn't even be bothered to show up on time. Still, it was fortunate in some ways, seeing how Sophie had been running behind. Even after she flew through the doors of her estate, she took longer than usual readying herself for her guests. Her mind was miles away. Still sitting in a small dark house near the Most-Holy Southeast Bell Tower. Still digesting the truth of Fenrir Mey actually being the lauded surveyor Ashtin Broodfell. And that kiss she'd given him. Had she really been so brash? Yes, she had because she still smiled at the thought of it. And she wanted to do it all over again.

But now she had to focus. It was her soirée and her birthday. The house was decked out in standard fungal motifs—shapes reminiscent of the Amanita muscaria, the oyster mushroom, the shiitake. Hints of caps and gills and spores. A color pallet that strayed towards whites and browns and pale purples. Of course, just relying on the theme of rot alone was a bit prosaic, old-fashioned, traditional, so Sophie had instructed her servants to insert flares here and there. Dried flowers and grasses. Warm metals. Crisp ceramics. It had all taken far too much time and effort, and she took joy in none of it.

Even with the party underway and guests flooding her grand hall, Sophie had to stifle the grimace that wanted to adorn her face. Her duties were only starting. Now was the time to make her rounds, welcome guests, delight them with banal small talk. She laughed at awful jokes and pretended to blush at insipid compliments all while keeping an eye out for her betrothed. He finally strolled in half an hour later than they'd agreed on. Worse still, he was accompanied by that dreadful little priest who followed him everywhere he went. Sophie tried to quell her irritation. Nagging and badgering didn't work on Vergil. Bending him to her whim required a subtler approach.

Sophie slipped past guests with ease. She was an elegant dancer thanks in part to quick reflexes honed by her surveyor training. She managed to cross the ballroom in seconds to greet Vergil. His eyes lit up when he caught sight of her.

"Thank the Lady you're here," she said.

Vergil took her hand and pressed it to his chest. She did likewise. Nicolus offered his to Sophie, and she reluctantly performed the ritual greeting with him.

"Happiest of birthdays, Lady Roshem," Nicolus said.

"Thank you, Priest Yevin."

Nicolus lingered, and Sophie suppressed a scowl. She glanced at Vergil, but he was too preoccupied with his inspection of the room, wanting to see who was present, no doubt already planning who he would interact with and in what order. Sophie tapped Nicolus's arm.

"You know, so many ladies have been asking me where you were," she said. "You really ought to mingle."

Nicolus took the hint and excused himself while he got to work securing his future marriage prospects.

"Really, I don't know why you bother with that one," she said. "He's so blatantly false."

"As they all are," Vergil said. "He has his uses. But enough about Nicolus, how are you, my heart?"

Vergil peered at her, and she feared her face showed even a trace of her distraction. Vergil was exceptionally skilled at reading people, and he knew Sophie too well.

"Better, now that you're here," she said. "I can't weather these things like you can."

Vergil held out his hand, and she placed hers in it. His was gloved, of course. If it hadn't been, he wouldn't have dared touch her naked skin, although hers wasn't entirely lacking a buffer. Her hands had been dipped in black paint from the fingertips to past her elbows. All along her arm glyphs had been traced in white. Simple ones that Trisht, her lady-in-waiting, had been able to draw. This was all the rage in Simetria amongst the younger high bloods. Men and women alike. But of course, Vergil couldn't be seen following the latest fads in fashion. He was a bishop, and his role required him to maintain a sense of tradition.

Sophie looked him over to see what flares he had managed to sneak into the drab look the clergyfolk were stuck with. Gray robes with the purple sash. As always. Even on her birthday, he couldn't break with decorum. Meanwhile, she was dressed like a plaything, wearing what a high blood from a great family was expected to wear. A many-layered skirt, above the knee in the front but tapering in the back down to her ankles. Folds of fabric bunched together over the rump. White-laced boots reaching to just below her knee, stockings to cover the skin. Her neck adorned in the gilled collar meant to mimic an amanita. Topped off by a saucer of a hat reminiscent of mushroom caps. Even in their clothing, the citizens of Simetria harkened back to the rot. Their makeup too. Sophie's lip and eye shade were a dark purple underlain by a deep brown.

"Shall we dive in?" Vergil asked, holding out his arm.

"Just a few hellos, then we dance?" she asked.

"But of course."

Two hours they spent saying their hellos, and by the time they could have danced, Sophie was too spent to bother. This was how it usually went, these soirées, evenings with high bloods. With every empty statement, she found herself fading. After the last cluster they had chatted with dispersed to refill their drinks, she clutched at Vergil's robes.

"I can't do it any longer," she said. "Can't I go back to my room?"

"While you still have guests?"

Sophie glanced at the revelers, certain they would go on for hours yet.

"I did my duty," she said. "I said my hellos and talked and talked. It's my birthday. Is that not an excuse?"

Vergil looked at her. He would hold fast unless she uttered a specific set of words.

"I just want to be alone with you," she said.

Those were the magic ones. She and Vergil mounted the stairs then entered her bed chambers. The space was all white and lace and airiness. The bed was covered in a tent of translucent fabric, the wood painted in pale shades. Vergil closed and locked the door behind them before twirling to face Sophie. She kept her spine erect and her shoulders back. The raw desire writ on his face told her she looked stunning. He strode over to her, breathing hard, his hands hovering over her shoulders. He stopped himself and fumbled in his robes until he pulled out a pair of glyph gloves. White with gold lettering. He switched the ones he'd been wearing for this reinforced pair, flexed his fingers, then smiled at Sophie.

Vergil cradled the side of her face in his gloved palm and proceeded to trace his fingers along her jawline, removing her gilled collar, then continuing down her neck to the ruffles of her top. He plucked at the buttons until they opened and folded the stiff fabric back to expose her breasts. He continued to trace her form with the tips of his fingers. She slipped free of her top and let it tumble to the floor. Vergil pulled her to the rug near the dying fire then guided her down to the ground. She reached for his face, but his hand caught hers before it made contact.

"The paint is a mild buffer," she said.

"Mild isn't good enough, my heart. You know that."

She sighed and let her hand go slack in his. Vergil released it and continued his inspection of her body. He was at the waist of her skirt, and she hoped beyond hope that he would simply bypass her navel and move down into her thighs. But he didn't. He never did because his desire wasn't for the opening in her groin but rather the one set higher up.

Vergil unclamped her skirt and moved it down until her stomach was exposed. He trembled at the sight of it. His breath came out labored. Then he reached and traced a circle around the navel, further out then moving progressively inward. When his finger touched the ink set to skin, he hesitated. Every time, he did this. He wanted so desperately to migrate further in but was too terrified of what might happen. For, set back into the skin of Sophie's navel was a complicated movement, a roiling, a breathing, a rise and fall of forever.

A distortion.

Vergil sighed in frustration then jumped up from the ground. Sophie rose onto her elbows and watched him. He muttered to himself and swatted at the nothingness of the air. He was more agitated than usual. And so was she because, for all the qualms she had with Vergil or maybe precisely because of them, she did desire him in body.

"We could join," she said.

His head whipped to look at her.

"We could do it," she said. "We could keep a buffer between us. A thin layer of fabric perhaps. Even without it, the distortion wouldn't harm you. People have touched my skin. Trisht, my father, they were unaffected. My distortion is different. It hasn't afflicted anyone, myself included even after all these years."

"That would be the height of foolishness," Vergil said between clenched teeth.

Sophie stood and walked to him, but he kept her at arm's length.

"Please, Vergil, I'm begging you to touch me. I can't live like this. I can't keep waiting for a cure that doesn't exist."

Vergil went still, his frustration shifting into a blockade. He smiled and shook his head.

"Dear Sophie, I know the temptation is great, but we must be strong. We haven't withstood it all these long years to give in now. No, we maintain our course. I continue my research, while we bide our time and satisfy ourselves with what we have."

Vergil removed his reinforced glyph gloves and put on the pair he'd worn to the party. He wandered over to Sophie's dressing table and checked that his person was in order in the mirror. Then he turned to her. She stood where he'd left her, her torso exposed, the distortion twisting and turning endlessly. She wanted to shout and scream and strike him. He didn't dare touch her, and she was forbidden from touching him. It was beyond infuriating, especially because, just hours ago, she'd pressed her lips to Fenrir's. She'd had a taste of what Vergil denied her, and her hunger had only been awakened by it.

"You're leaving?" she asked.

"I have work to do still, work that I left undone in order to come here."

"Surely it can wait one night."

Vergil shook his head and smiled. She knew the look. He wouldn't budge, no matter what tactics she employed against him.

"Before I forget," Vergil said, "a little bird told me you visited the house of a low blood today. The toller whose tower you've been surveying. Fenrir Mey or some such name."

Vergil never did anything without reason. Him admitting he'd had her watched was purposeful, but to what end?

"A bird?" Sophie said. "Perhaps you mean a rat scurrying about, trailing my every movement. Are you having someone follow me?"

"I worry about you, Sophie. You have a dangerous job and a deadly condition on top of that. I do it because I care."

His words gave a part of the truth. This was his twisted way of showing love with the added bonus of keeping her in line. Sophie advanced on Vergil, her clothes still in disarray. His eyes flitted over her, and his hands turned to fists.

"How kind of you," she said, "but you need not worry. I was simply trying to unravel a few mysteries about this toller."

Vergil stepped in so that he towered over Sophie's already substantial height.

"And did you? Unravel his mysteries?"

She shook her head, orange-red curls brushing against her eyelashes.

"He's an enigma still, but that is that. Today was my last day working that tower. It's shuttered now, and I move on."

"Good girl," Vergil said. "Oh, and happy birthday."

Then he turned and slipped out. But Sophie wasn't satisfied with taking him at his word. He'd steered the conversation away from himself after saying he had work to do. He was lying, and she was resolved to get the truth, especially considering he was having his own spy on her. It made her blood boil and infused her with the daring to give chase.

As soon as Vergil closed the door, she threw on a blouse and cloak, slung a wrap over her hair, and ran after him. By the time she made it to the gate of her estate, Vergil was hurrying into the street. She kept back and followed. It was easy to keep sight of him given so few were out so late. The few footfalls that touched the cold cobblestones echoed against the stark stone buildings towering tall and thin. The lamplight cast strange shadows with sinister geometries, black fringed by a ghost green.

They moved into the lower city. Passing sewer gratings, Sophie caught whiffs of something sour. The scent of the old, of dust, of decay, blessed rot that she couldn't help but retreat from. Down there, fathoms below, the Old World slept, encased by the mausoleum of Simetria, a city built on the bones of the fallen, crushing it into the bedrock more with every year, holding so many delicious secrets.

Sophie caught a humming, barely perceptible, and glanced up at an attuner affixed to a building's corner. A distortion was nearby, but it wasn't the one embedded in her navel. Hers was invisible to the attuners. Sophie pulled the fabric shrouding her head tighter and focused on Vergil's figure. Her trailing continued for several blocks until he entered a two-story brick building.

Sophie lingered outside, trying to determine what kind of establishment it was. A business, clearly, given all the coming and going and noise issuing from within, but it sported no sign or other mark indicating its purpose. She didn't want to lose sight of Vergil, so she opted to take the risk and enter. When she did, its purpose was immediately known to her. Bare-breasted women, men garbed only in loincloths, laughing and drinking and touching. She gawked then felt a hand on her shoulder.

"Hello there, dove," a woman said.

Sophie shrank then reminded herself that she had as

much right as anyone to be in this place. Besides, she'd gone this far. She might as well learn exactly what Vergil was up to, although she didn't have to do much imagining to guess.

"Hello," Sophie said.

This woman had to be the madam. She was older than the others and much more clothed. She had dark red hair that was curled and expansive, with lip shade and a flowing dress that matched its hue.

"What can I help you with this fine evening?" the woman asked. "Perhaps you'd like to peruse the refined assortment we have on offer at my establishment? We have gentlemen as well as ladies. Whatever suits your fancy."

"I see," Sophie said.

She looked past the woman's head, trying to catch a glimpse of Vergil, but the room beyond the entrance alcove was too large and dark, and there were too many shadowy forms. Curtains covered nearly every surface of wall. A rich burgundy. Thick folds of fabric. It was meant to compliment all the wooden furniture with similarly colored cushions sporting elaborate, geometric patterns.

Sophie couldn't ask for Vergil outright. That would only tell the madam what Sophie's aims were, and Vergil would soon be informed of his stalker. No, Sophie needed to play along.

"What do you have on offer?" she asked.

The madam again touched her hand to Sophie's shoulder and steered her to a wall on the far side of the room. It was similarly covered in burgundy fabric but also sported several life-sized portraits. Sophie recognized the faces. Timor Shatterborn, Davon Fretman, Elizamet Horens, and on and on. There had to be at least a dozen images of high-blood men and women. Then Sophie spotted herself. She pulled the wrap more tightly around her face, grateful for the purple lip and eye shade that threw off the scent.

"These are lords and ladies of the great families," Sophie said.

"But of course," the madam replied. "That is our specialty here at A Taste of Refinement. These lords and ladies spend all their days following such mind-numbing rituals. They feel so constrained by social etiquette and desire nothing more than to let loose. That is what my fine establishment allows them to do."

Sophie squinted at her portrait. This was all news to her, and she was struggling to make sense of the madam's claims until she glimpsed a head of orange-red curls pop out of a doorway on the second-floor landing. The body associated with it wore a silk robe that left little to the imagination. The woman trotted along the landing until she descended the stairs and vanished from Sophie's view. Her doppelgänger. So that was the theme of this whore house. Look-alikes of the young and beautiful from the great families.

"There are so many options," Sophie said. "I simply can't decide."

The madam was getting impatient. Her clients likely knew exactly which of her workers they wanted to bed even before they stepped foot in the place. She was already eyeing other customers in need of assistance.

"How about you take all the time you need to think on it, little dove. Sit and relax, and when you're ready, just ask for Madam Gerton."

She didn't even wait for Sophie to respond before she was hurrying over to a male worker frantically waving. Sophie gawked. His only covering came in the form of a leather strip that cradled his groin. This place was doing little to appease the fire raging in her, and she had to remind herself why she was there. In one of these rooms, Vergil was up to something scandalous. The thought brought her doppelgänger to mind and the room she'd seen her issue from. Sophie migrated to the staircase, looking around to ensure the madam didn't spot her. She stole up the carpet-covered steps to the landing then counted the doors until she stood in front of the one the woman had exited from.

Sophie glanced over the railing at the chaos of the main room below. No one watched her. Everyone was too enthralled with their own illicit acts to give any heed to the fully-clothed woman. Sophie pressed her ear to the door, but she couldn't make out anything on the other side. She leaned down, pretending to lace her boot then peered through the keyhole. She could make out movement, but the finer details were lost to distance and the small aperture she was forced to view events through. She sighed in frustration then rose only to find her doppelgänger standing beside her on the landing, a wine bottle in hand.

"Sorry love, but peep shows aren't allowed unless the client is willing," she said. "And I guarantee this one won't be."

Sophie pulled back. "I thought I knew the man who went in there, and I was wondering if he'd spend the evening with me."

The doppelgänger grinned, and Sophie was shocked at how uncanny the resemblance was. The same shade of hair done in the same style. The eyes almost indistinguishable if not for the fact that they were nearer to a hazel than a green and were more narrow and wide-set than Sophie's own. Yet every other detail was fascinatingly close. The height, the build, the gestures and mannerisms. She could have been gazing into a mirror.

"I'm afraid the gentleman is a guest only," the doppelgänger said, "but perhaps Madam Gerton could suggest a suitable alternative?"

"Vergil Holdsworth, is it?" Sophie asked.

She needed to be sure he was the one behind that door. The woman's eyes widened, which meant Sophie had deduced correctly. A bubbling in her depths preceded the torrent of rage that cascaded through. First in her chest then fanning out into her limbs and abdomen before swirling around in her head. Vergil was a hypocrite. And a liar. Even if he refused to touch her, the least he could have done was spend the evening holding her through his glyph gloves. Instead, he satisfied his lust for her with a woman who played at being her.

Vergil likely saw it as just, that he only joined with someone who looked so similar to Sophie. He must have believed it was yet another sign of his unflagging devotion to her and her alone. Since childhood they'd been betrothed. Her father pledging her hand to Vergil via his father. Sophie's feelings towards the whole betrothal were complicated. Her instinct had been to fight, to demand she have some autonomy over her own future, but over the years, she'd been sucked in by Vergil.

There was something about him, a duality. He could be so sweet and so cruel from one moment to the next. He knew of Sophie's condition, and still, he hadn't turned away from her. He worshipped her, sacrificed so much for her. And yet, look at what he did. He refused to touch her. He had others follow and watch her every move. He chastised her for spending time with Fenrir all while he stuck his member in another woman's opening.

But Sophie refused to direct her indignation at this poor thing. The woman couldn't help that she resembled Sophie or that other high bloods used her to enact their fantasies. She was a victim of their perverse system. A low blood used and abused by the high bloods. The two forbidden from mixing through marriage but permitted to trade fluids. The thought sickened her, her hand cradling her stomach, hovering over the distortion that roiled under the fabric of her skirt.

Her distortion. Her condition. The thing that Vergil used to control her and as an excuse to deny her. Well, she would be denied satisfaction no longer. Twenty-eight years was far too long to go without passion. If he wouldn't give it to her, maybe another would, another who had horrid secrets of his own that would serve to keep hers intact.

"Actually," Sophie said. "I have a proposition for you, Ms…"

"Lady Roshem," the doppelgänger said.

Sophie smiled, leaned in, and removed her hood. She saw when the realization struck.

"If you're Lady Roshem, then you can just call me Sophie."

The doppelgänger gaped.

"My proposition," Sophie said. "I will pay you three times what that man has paid if you forgo your time with him and instead converse with me."

"But he's been promised my time."

"Three times the pay and you can't be bothered to craft a little lie? Perhaps your stomach suddenly ails you or your monthly blood came by surprise? In any case, that is my offer. If you accept, I'll be waiting down yonder." Sophie waved her hand at the room below. "Ten minutes. After that has elapsed, I'll assume you opted to snub my gracious offer."

The doppelgänger nodded. Sophie put her wrap back on and made her way down to the main room. She took up residence in a cushioned chair off in a corner. That way, she could spy Vergil departing without him taking notice of her. Within mere minutes, he appeared, face terse, lips pursed. Sophie knew that look. He was furious but trying to save face. The false Lady Roshem followed him to the staircase and wished him a fine evening. He threw his hand up and trotted down. Sophie kept her eyes fixed on him. The way he moved, his reactions, or lack thereof, to this environment implied he frequented the place. That thought alone cemented her plan into stone.

Once Vergil had departed, the doppelgänger waved to Sophie who quickly mounted the stairs and joined the woman in her chambers. It was fitted in a style not unlike the main room but adorned in forest greens with velvet cushions and pillows with tassels. Nothing like Sophie's own room. She took a seat in a chair along a wall. The doppelgänger simply stood in front of her guest, hands clasped in front, head bowed. But she wasn't penitent; she was beaming.

"It is such an honor to make your acquaintance," the woman said. "You don't know how pleased I am to actually be speaking with you. You."

"What's your name," Sophie asked.

"Why Lady Roshem, of course."

Sophie frowned. "I won't call you that. It's absurd. I have a serious matter to discuss with you, so I'd prefer it if we did away with the theatrics."

The woman stepped closer, nodding her head too many times. Suddenly, she was nothing like Sophie. The mannerisms were all wrong. Her movements too loose.

"Yes, ma'am, I mean, my lady. You are, of course, right. I go by Tillie when I'm not playing my role here."

Sophie softened then patted the seat next to hers.

"Tillie? Good. Well, Tillie, you made a wise choice in taking me up on my offer tonight because what I have to suggest could be a very lucrative agreement between the two of us."

"Can I just say something?" Tillie asked.

Sophie nodded. Tillie took the seat next to Sophie's. She sat on its edge, all nerves.

"I can't do what I just did again," Tillie said. "If the gentleman returns to seek my services, I can't deny him. Madam Gerton would throw me out on the street. The gentleman is quite powerful, and I am nothing."

"I don't care about all that," Sophie said, waving her

hand. "I know he'll be back. I could tell he's probably visited you scores of times already."

Tillie looked away.

"What I have to suggest is something between the two of us, something that would pay quite well."

Sophie stood from her seat then knelt in front of her doppelgänger, her hands on the armrests. Sophie had her locked in place but something more akin to an embrace than a caging. Tillie gazed back at her.

"What would it involve?" Tillie asked.

"Why playing me, of course. You seem quite adept at that already."

Tillie beamed and laughed. "Yes, my lady, I aim to emulate your most refined person. I spent many long hours learning about you, studying you, trying to become you in all the ways I could. I adore you. You are my muse and my art, all in one."

Sophie wanted to back away from the too-ardent fervor that emanated from Tillie, but that would only serve to wound the poor girl. So instead, she smiled and patted Tillie's hand.

"That's very good," Sophie said, "because I need you to channel your art to serve my ends. All it would involve is playing me. At my home. To my servants. Nothing more."

"I don't understand," Tillie said.

"I have eyes fixed on me. I can't do as I please because of it. You would simply stand in for me and allow me to spend a few hours in freedom. Could you do that? Would you?"

"So I just come to your home and pretend to be you?"

Sophie nodded and stood upright. "Tomorrow at the hour before midnight, we would meet in the alley four buildings over in the direction of my home," Sophie said. "You would wear your cloak, and I mine. We would switch, and you would go to my home and play as me. Perhaps sit in my room. Wait for me to return to the alley at a set hour. Then, we switch our cloaks again, and you go back to being Tillie."

"So you can have freedom," Tillie said.

"It would pay well," Sophie replied, "and you would be doing me a great favor."

"I would do anything in my power for you, my lady."

"I take it that's a yes?"

They shook on the deal, and Sophie again felt that lightness she got in Fenrir's company. Freedom. A taste of the limitless.

SOPHIE'S LETTER

15 October, year of our Lady 517

Dearest Papa,

Forgive me for writing to you rather than speaking with you. Every time I try to work up the courage to discuss this, I falter. Trisht suggested I pen this letter instead. Today, I am sixteen years of age, which causes me to reflect on my future, specifically my marriage prospects. You told me what is in store. I am to marry Vergil Holdsworth and bear an heir who will become the head of our great family. I have known this since my earliest years, and I have always taken that fact as immutable. But is it, Papa?

To be clear, I do not dislike Vergil. He brings me flowers every time we meet; he gives such a gracious bow; and he is the finest specimen of a man. More practically speaking, he has a bright future ahead of him, what with him only just being named a deacon and at eighteen years of age. He is everything a woman would desire in a husband.

And yet, something is amiss. There is a darkness in Vergil, well-hidden and masked. As long as his desires are denied him, he keeps up his fine act, but I see through it, Papa. The moment I wed him, I fear he will treat me more like a pet in the best case and a slave in worst. Perhaps you will laugh at my concerns and say they are only the silly musings of a woman with an overactive imagination, so let me provide you with evidence.

The day before last, when Vergil visited with his father, we took a walk in the garden. We wandered over to mother's mausoleum and sat on the stone bench there, shielded from prying eyes. Vergil spoke fine words, spouting compliment after compliment, lavishing me with adoration, more than the usual. Eventually, he got to the point. He asked me to show him my distortion. I was shocked and did not have the peace of mind to even deny the cursed thing's existence.

I wish you had told me that you told him of it. It was jarring to have my darkest secret shared without my knowledge. I understand that my betrothed would need to be privy to such information as we approach the age when two would normally wed, but still, Papa, how dreadful to be betrayed so. I will lay aside my admonishment for now and move on to what happened next.

As I tripped over my words, Vergil took hold of my hand and held it between his gloved ones. That was when I noticed the wards stitched into them. I tried to pull my hand free, but he only grasped tighter. He again asked to see my distortion, and what could I do but comply? Do you see what this moment was? Vergil knew my greatest secret, and he used that knowledge to pressure me to do something I did not want to do.

He wields immeasurable power over me now, Papa. I know what you will say in your defense. That Vergil loves me and will not wish me any harm, but what if he changes his mind one day? What if I do something to incur his wrath?

You have locked me in a cage, and it is one I see no escape from.

Your most distraught daughter,
Sophie Roshem

BROKEN TOOL

Amilia was so changed and yet not at the same time. That mane of black curls. Those soft eyes tapering at the ends. That rhythmic swaying she did when lost in thought. But the calloused hands were new as was the fadedness of her dress. The way she occupied her time too was wholly different. Always so soft-spoken but now shouting to passersby in hopes they would take notice of her goods. Amilia, once the daughter of a well-to-do merchant before becoming the proud wife of Ashtin Broodfell, now reduced to peddling flowers in the lower city's south market square. She was there every day. Fenrir knew because he'd taken to visiting. He stayed out of sight and never lingered long enough to draw attention to himself. Ten months he did this and, in doing so, learned a skeleton of Amilia's new life.

She lived in a shack not unlike his own but with her new husband and toddler daughter. She sold flowers while her strong-armed man broke his back transporting stones from the quarry near Simetria. Amilia had flowers like the ones she sold in little planter boxes outside her shack's windows. She hummed familiar tunes while hanging clothes out to dry in the alleyway that was the closest thing she had to a garden, her daughter sitting nearby in just a cloth diaper, tracing patterns in the dirt with a stick.

Her new life, except it wasn't new to her. She'd lived this sad existence for over five years now, ever since cuffs had been slapped on Ashtin's wrists, and he'd been carted away. His fall from grace coincided with hers because, as husband and wife, their fates had been intertwined. If Ashtin lost everything, including his name, so too did Amilia. And yet, she had escaped imprisonment and execution somehow. Perhaps her father had called in favors. Or perhaps the Church had decided to show her mercy. Whatever the reason, Fenrir was glad that she had been spared, but it pained him to see how far she'd fallen because of his own mistakes. And worse yet, he couldn't even tell her just how sorry he was. Even to Amilia, Ashtin Broodfell was dead and gone.

Amilia caught the attention of a lady wearing fine attire, a high blood on a trek into the quaintness of the lower city. This fine lady marveled at the hustle and bustle and viewed every mundane occurrence as a treat. The locals could sniff the naivety from a mile away. Amilia too. She pounced with four different bouquets in hand. After some haggling and chattering, the woman walked away with two of the bundles while Amilia smiled as she counted her coin. She'd worn that same look when running through the household finances, but back then she'd been counting silver coins rather than the coppers she now salivated over.

Fenrir couldn't bear to look any longer. He slunk back into the alley and walked with slumped shoulders to the newly constructed Most-Holy Southeast Bell Tower. He had another hour before he had to ring the final bell of the day and would while away the time sitting and staring out at Simetria.

Life was drab. Worse even than it had been before Sophie because she had been a splash of color that only served to show Fenrir just how monotone his existence was. Sophie had done more than please Fenrir's eye. She'd given him the contact he was lacking, that bond of the intellect, a shared fascination of the distortions. While Sophie had visited his tower, Fenrir hadn't even thought to watch Amilia. Now here he was, one day later and already falling back into old, bad habits.

After he tolled the bell and ran through the requisite rituals, Fenrir left for the day and took to wandering the city. He felt nostalgic and let his feet pull him along to places from his past. He replayed his fall from grace in reverse. From the new to the old tower, boarded up now with balustrades constructed to hold the distortion in. Then onward to the black, wrought-iron gates of the penitentiary deep in the lower city. Fenrir shivered at the recollection of all those long years spent in misery. Perpetual hunger and filth. Constantly battling illness or rats or other inmates. Not knowing if he would survive to spy the open sky again.

Fenrir moved on to the upper city, to where his crime had taken place. The Broodfell house. Now with a different family name gracing the bronze plaque out front and window dressings that were more garish than anything he or Amilia would have hung. Fenrir gazed up at the dormer windows set into the roof, and his stomach wrenched. He couldn't stand to recall what had happened in that attic. He tried to think back further to the time before his unforgivable act, before distortion had ever entered his home, when Trevon had been whole and happy.

There were flashes of his little round face laughing, of Amilia coaxing him step-by-step down the stoop to the cobblestoned street, of his small hand in Fenrir's. The ache eased, but Fenrir knew the relief would be short-lived if he lingered because, even with the distortion long gone, the house was cursed to him. He could feel the foulness emanating from it, despite the long still and silent attuner across the street.

Fenrir turned his feet to meet the slope that led to the Church, the apex of the upper city and like his second home when he'd been a surveyor. He didn't dare venture any further than the gate cradling the Church grounds, instead satisfying himself with gripping the cold metal bars and peering inward, picturing the scene eclipsed by shrubbery and white stone. Nestled deep in those hallowed halls, with floors so clean they were veritable mirrors, were the rooms dedicated to the surveyors' holy task. A library crammed full of tomes, a workshop concerned with crafting their tools, an armory that fashioned their essential defenses against the afflicted, both their polearms and the leather gear they garbed themselves in. Somewhere in there, Sophie did the duty he so craved to do. But there was no use sulking. It would do him no good.

Fenrir turned away from the Church and set his steps homeward just as night was falling. As he entered his shack, lit his oil lamps, and poured himself a drink, Fenrir told himself he had to accept that this was his new lot in life. After two glasses of an almost rancid ale, he was prepared to commit himself to this mindset. He spent the evening staring into his sad fire and almost reached a state of calm resignation.

Then, a knock sounded at his door, late in the night. Fenrir opened it a crack. The face peering back put him in a daze. Sophie. He opened the door but struggled with words. Sophie moved in and inspected her surroundings. She wore a cloak with a hood and seemed agitated behind her smiles.

"Would you like something to drink?" Fenrir finally asked, pulling a chair out and offering it to her.

Sophie retrieved a bottle from the folds of her cloak, deposited it on the table, then sat.

"We didn't get to properly drink any of my family's wine,"

she said, "and you sacrificed a special bottle of spirits for me. I thought I'd balance the scales a bit."

Fenrir fetched a cup and poured the wine for Sophie. He drained his own glass of its horrid drink before filling it with the gift she'd brought. They touched their vessels then sipped the amber contents. It had been ages since good wine had graced Fenrir's lips. He was almost stunned by the richness and warmth that cascaded down his throat. Hints of black cherry and cocoa.

"How was your birthday?" Fenrir asked.

"Dull, as those kinds of occasions usually are. But you know that well enough, don't you? Attended your fair share of soirées back in your heyday, no?"

Fenrir averted his gaze. It was bad enough she knew his old name, but recounting his history threatened to bring pain. Still, her coming was a god-send that he wasn't willing to toss aside.

"Broodfell wasn't a name that the great families saw fit to invite to those kinds of events."

"Maybe not before Ashtin took the Church by storm and dazzled them with his knowledge and skill," Sophie said. "A surveyor equally well-versed in the theory and practice of containing distortions and freeing the afflicted. Of course he'd be a much sought-after guest."

"Yet he chose to avoid such tedious affairs." Fenrir poured the rest of his wine down his throat. "He had a wife and young son that he preferred to spend his evenings with. Until he fouled everything up for the lot of them."

Sophie tilted her own cup back so that her wine was gone in of seconds. "I know what you did. In vivid detail. We hadn't met, but I was a tier 3 surveyor when it happened. Too lowly to associate with someone as skilled as Ashtin Broodfell but still very aware of the happenings within our surveyor ranks."

"And yet you choose to associate with me now, all while I represent everything you ought to despise."

Sophie rose from her chair and threw her hood back. Her hair was smooth and freshly curled. With her face no longer framed by shadow, Fenrir caught hints of lip and eyeshade. Deep purples and rich browns. Sophie moved to Fenrir's chair and planted her hands on his armrests. She leaned in and stared into his eyes, their faces only inches apart.

"No one knows what they'd do if faced with the decision you were," she said. "They can act disgusted and shocked, but the truth is, they might very well do the same. Ask any parent what they'd be willing to do to free their child from a fate worse than death."

Fenrir looked at her with a straight back and clenched jaw. "The difference is that I knew better."

"No, the difference is that you had the knowledge and skill to save him."

To mention Trevon was to plunge Fenrir into a torrent of emotion that threatened to rip him asunder, only Sophie seemed to anticipate this. Her hand gripped Fenrir's jaw and pulled his face in to meet hers. Their lips touched and stayed fixed on one another's. She tasted him with her tongue and teeth. Then she pulled him up from his chair and guided him to his bed before pushing him into it. Clumps of straw sewn into the mattress shifted with his bulk. Fenrir laid on his back and supported himself with his elbows, watching Sophie, waiting for whatever came next. She unclasped a broach that secured her cloak but held her hand in place to keep it from falling. She walked to Fenrir, step by step, until her legs grazed the bed's baseboard.

"They don't understand us," she said. "Special ones like us, ones that can feel the distortions, that have an innate understanding of them. Yes, I know you're like me. You couldn't have found that distortion in the tower otherwise. But I wonder, dear Fenrir, do you feel a distortion now? That discomfort like an itch that can't be scratched or an invisible lash irritating the eye?"

Fenrir was frozen. Expectant. Terrified.

"Do you?" Sophie asked.

He shook his head in what felt like slowed motion. Sophie smiled then let her cloak drop. Underneath, she wore only the barest of undergarments, lace and cream-colored. His eyes took her in. The beauty and symmetry of her. Pale and lean and lithe. Her hands rested on her stomach, elbows pointing out to the side like she was trapped in some strange funereal pose.

"I mentioned my betrothal last time I was here. To be honest, I don't dislike the man. I rather care for him, after a fashion, but he frustrates me beyond pale. He's controlling and jealous. He refuses to touch me, even while he fondles whores that wear my face. I try to be understanding, but it only goes so far. He's no simpleton. He knows as much as we do about the non-Euclidean, and yet he uses it as his shield."

Sophie stopped at Fenrir's look of confusion. She sighed.

"I'm talking in riddles, I know," she said. "Maybe I'm stalling. Maybe I'm trying to prepare you for something that nothing can prepare you for. So let me just take the plunge and trust in you, as you did in sharing your secret with me."

Sophie slid her hands aside and clasped them behind her back. Fenrir's eyes strayed to where they had rested and what she'd been hiding. That in and out, dissolution, melting, blossoming, window into the infinite. His mind couldn't process what he saw with what he knew. A distortion without that telltale unease was an impossibility. One embedded in someone far from affliction even more so. He gaped.

"It's not affliction," she said, "at least not like any we've encountered before. It doesn't grow or alter what it comes into contact with. It's a mystery, but one I'm loath to share with others, given what they'd do to me if they knew."

Fenrir leaned forward and peered at it. "How is this possible?"

Sophie turned and sat on the bed beside him, her hands cupped in her lap now.

"I don't know," she said. "I've studied it for years. It's why I became a surveyor in the first place, all in hope of making sense of what it is. In vain."

"How did you get it?"

"I was born with it. My mother became afflicted while she was pregnant with me. It must have been passed through the placenta. That's what the surveyor who helped my father said."

Fenrir moved to the floor, planting his knees on the wooden boards. He craned his neck forward and stared at Sophie's distortion. The lighting was no good. He rose and retrieved an oil lamp then moved back to inspect the impossibility.

"Look all you like," she said. "You won't find answers to your myriad of questions, I assure you."

Fenrir looked nonetheless from every angle he could. Yet Sophie was correct. He needed tools to study it, ones he was forbidden from touching.

"I find your reaction interesting," she said, "although I shouldn't be surprised you aren't terrified of me all of sudden. Just curious, no?"

Fenrir pointed to the ward writ into the skin around her navel. "You said it doesn't grow. Is that only because of the ward?"

"I don't know. They put the ward in place when I was a newborn. The surveyor who helped us would touch it up as I grew until I was skilled enough to do it myself."

"It seems some surveyors are quite open-minded," Fenrir said. "I would've expected them to turn you over to the Church once the distortion was discovered."

Sophie smiled and shook her head. "Coin has a way of opening minds and shutting lips," she said. "My father paid a small fortune to keep my condition a secret. The surveyor died several years ago, otherwise I'd be doing the same."

"Why did you share this with me?" Fenrir asked.

"To balance the scales, of course. I know your greatest secret, and now you know mine."

A JOINING

Fenrir was everything Sophie hoped he'd be. When she revealed her distortion, he didn't flinch like a typical Simetrian would or salivate at it like Vergil did. Fenrir looked at it with raw curiosity then to her with a softness that wasn't pity. More like understanding. There was a kindredness between them even deeper than their love of knowledge, more pervasive than their shared ability to sense the distortions. They were both horribly disfigured in the realm of the heart. Battered and beaten and broken by life and circumstance. Invisible scars made blindingly visible to each other now.

"We're not so different," Sophie said. "My mother suffered greatly because of me, not unlike the situation that got you imprisoned."

She opted not to elaborate because even behind Fenrir's hard lips and stern stare, she could feel him screaming. All these long years, and he hadn't let himself heal. He hadn't forgiven himself for what he'd done.

"So long as my father thought he could at least save me, he kept my mother alive. She was only six months pregnant when she came in contact with a distortion that had appeared in our wine cellar."

"Six months?" Fenrir asked.

He sat on the floor in front of her with the lamp casting wild shapes on his face.

"I came early, but not so early as you might think. She lived with affliction for two and a half months."

Fenrir's eyes bulged. According to the Church, the longest record for affliction without insanity was four weeks. Of course, countless souls had lived far longer than that, but those were the ones who had lost themselves. Affliction was a complex process. A distortion was agony, but it would leave the surrounding tissue intact for some time. And not all flesh would be converted to the non-Euclidean. Many afflicted who wandered the wastes outside Simetria were equal parts Euclidean and non, but there was a kind of threshold that was only poorly defined. At some stage in the process, the distortion reached the brain. That was when the afflicted's sanity left them. More research was required to understand that descent into madness, but the only way to study it was deemed inhumane. So they all lived with the ambiguity, but it was only temporary because, in the end, every afflicted lost themselves. There was no escaping their fate.

"My father paid the surveyor I mentioned to assist him in slowing the distortion on my mother. All in the hope that she would live long enough to birth me. And she did, but at a cost."

"The distortion spread to you," Fenrir said.

Sophie nodded and placed her hands around her navel, cupping it and caging it in at the same time.

"It's my bane and my boon. It doesn't spread, even if I or another touches it. I'm nearly certain it's what gives me the ability to sense distortions. And it keeps my womb in a state of timelessness, at least according to that surveyor. All the elements are there, but the cycle itself is halted, meaning I can't bear children."

Fenrir moved to sit on the bed beside Sophie. Her hips dipped towards his from the added weight.

"And that pains you?" Fenrir asked.

"I don't know. I don't know what it is to have had a mother, so how could I ever attempt to be one? Besides, motherhood seems like a convenient chain to shackle me to the home. I value my freedom too much to be satisfied with such an existence."

Sophie gazed at Fenrir over the side of her shoulder, a cluster of curls swaying into view. He reached a hand up and brushed them to the side, tucking them behind her ear.

"And yet?" he asked.

Sophie smiled at how easily he peered through her strong and proud words into the throbbing vulnerability of her.

"My life stands still. My betrothed refuses to wed let alone touch me without a progeny being a possibility. Even worse, my distortion is my ball and chain. He knows about it and could use it against me if I ever tried to defy him."

Fenrir went to say something, but Sophie touched a finger to his lips. She had come to Fenrir for more than sharing confidences. The night was getting on, and she'd waited ages for what came next. Sophie placed her hand on Fenrir's knee then let it stray up his thigh. He stiffened and held his breath.

"Are you afraid of me?" she asked.

"No," he mouthed.

Sophie leaned in until her lips tickled the hairs near his ear.

"Will you hold me?" she asked. "Touch me? Join with me?"

His reaction was instantaneous. It was clear Fenrir had been waiting on edge for her consent, and now that he had it, he dove straight in. His long and lean arms wrapped around her. His lips pressed to hers then strayed to her chin, neck, chest, and breasts. Fenrir's arms guided Sophie back until they lay on his bed, Sophie's face to the ceiling, Fenrir's buried in her skin. He moved back to her lips then let his hands explore her body. They brushed and stroked limbs and thighs then plunged into the region Vergil's would never venture near. Lightly caressing the hairs there, her loins aching in an expectation heightened by the promise that lingered so close.

Then, Fenrir touched her.

Fingers set to skin hidden by folds, rhythmic in their motions, riding the waves of her bliss. Fenrir moved his mouth to her ear and breathed into it through his nose. A jolt of ecstasy shot through her. An urgency ramped up. Sophie was getting what she longed for, but it wasn't enough. She wanted more. She wanted him.

Sophie pulled back from his kisses, and Fenrir gazed at her.

"I want to join," she said.

"Tell me exactly what you desire."

He was teasing her. He knew. And yet she reveled in this willful side of him, so unlike the timid toller who had stood with a hunched back and averted eyes so many weeks past.

"For you to enter me," Sophie said.

And he did. Gently, waiting until her body was truly ready to receive him. That feeling. That release. That moment of expectation relieved, but even then it wasn't over, because it'd only just begun. Fenrir joined with Sophie in countless ways for what felt like ages and seconds at the same time. She could have let it go on all night, except he seemed to need this joining as much as her. Fenrir held out for as long as he could, but even his seemingly limitless stamina was no match for the primal drive to spread his seed.

After Fenrir let out his moan of release, he held Sophie, arms and legs wrapped in hers. They lay like that and watched the flame from the oil lamp fade. No words. No movement. They were still and silent, fearful of what reality might do to this moment. Shatter it with its ugliness. Make practicality rear its hideous head. Sophie didn't want that, not after the beauty of her night with Fenrir.

She let him fall asleep cradling her. Was this what losing yourself in someone meant? She already sensed the pull, that dizzying inertia, that fear and hunger of the unknown. Was she falling for him so easily? Was one joining all it really took? No, it wasn't just that night. Sophie had been sucked in by Fenrir slowly and stealthily these past weeks. Tonight was just the culmination of her descent into another kind of madness. She was tired of fighting it. Rot wasn't blessed, but the life that preceded it was. She only had the one chance at it, and she'd be damned if she wasted another second.

CORRESPONDENCE

The text herein is meant for the eyes of Our Beloved Lady's most devout servants. Only clergyfolk with sufficient learning are prepared to read the words writ in these sacred pages. What follows is a correspondence, transcribed word-for-word, between Reya Dunham and our Most-Divine Saint Marcos Frenwith. Some archaic terms are used and obscure references are made. When possible, explanations of these are included.

Marcos,

I don't like that I'm only now sending you a message. I like even less the context of why I'm obliged to send it. I'm sure you've heard things about me[1]. I'm certain your eager little followers are desperate to win your approval in any way possible, including disgracing your former friend.

[1] *This letter is assumed to be dated circa February, the year of our Lady 2. Reya Dunham is most likely referring to activities at odds with the Cleansing of the Synthetic.*

Before I dive into the heart of the matter, just let me be clear—I'm sorry that life worked out like it did for the two of us. I wanted you to go to Oxford[2] too, but in the back of my mind, I was also relieved you didn't. You had a way of holding me back at UoB[3,] and it wasn't just me having to explain the concepts while we crammed for exams or debugging your code for you[4]. You just didn't have the hunger that I did. You were perfectly content to sail through life being as unremarkable as possible. I wasn't[5].

[2]*Oxford University, a well-lauded institution for higher education.*

[3]*Abbreviation for the higher education institution known as University of Birmingham, where Reya Dunham first made the acquaintance of Saint Frenwith.*

[4]*Before turning to the wisdom of our Lady, Saint Frenwith was trained as a codesmith. It is why he was able to assist our Lady in developing the Rot of the Link and understood the dangers of the realm of the digital.*

[5]*Reya Dunham was an adept codesmith. She received certificates from institutions for higher education and served as a scholar at one such institution before the Old World fell.*

I should have kept in contact, but after a while, I just lost steam trying to keep a dying friendship alive. Getting together with Thomas[6] was the nail in the coffin. Yes, I always knew you cared for me as more than a friend. I don't really know how I felt about that. In any case, I doubt us still being friends would have stopped you from going on your crusade against the alfom[7].

[6]*Thomas Pierson, husband of Reya Dunham.*
[7]*A heretic's term for the Others, one condemned by the Church.*

I know why you did it. I didn't trust them either. I was highly skeptical when they finally made themselves known[8]. I also believed that we needed to treat them with caution and avoid becoming overly reliant on them. But here is where we differ, Marcos. I know that we did become reliant on the alfom, and that means we can't just shut them out of our world[9] and continue to function as we did before. It's too late for that. They infiltrated our systems and rewired the lot of them. The world is falling apart without their oversight, just like they designed it to.

[8]When the Others first arrived, they covertly built a movement and influenced humanity via individuals who tended to be forgotten and ostracized by society before making themselves known nearly two years later.

[9]This refers to the Others being barred from our world owing to the Blessed Rot of the Link.

There's so much I could say related to how you're handling the new world order, but let me be brief and blunt, just like the old days. You're mucking it up. You have to stop this borderline religious fervor of hating all tech. You were always an atheist's atheist, so I have to assume your word choice and use of iconography is purposeful. Which leads me to some worrying rumors I've heard.

People say you want to pull the plug on the Digisphere[10], but I know that can't be true because that would mean all those minds that exist in it, all those people who went digital[11], would die. This is murder, plain and simple. That's three quarters of the world's population, Marcos. Do you really want to go down in history as the enactor of humanity's worse instance of genocide?

[10]The archaic term used for the realm of the digital.

[11]Individuals that uploaded their minds into the realm of the digital. Reya Dunham's belief that these individuals were still people is inaccurate as later established by Church scholars in their determination that the soul is not captured in the process of the digital uploading of the consciousness.

I'm sure at this point you're feeling particularly annoyed

with me, so I'll shift my tone from indignation to grave concern. Something is happening, and it's related to your Linkrot virus[12]. I've seen data that show a worrying trend. The laws of physics are acting up. Strange pockets of distorted space[13] are appearing and disappearing. We need to study this, but researchers can't do that without their tech. Please make an exception to your "synthetics" ban[14] and let them make sense of these strange occurrences, for all our sakes.

[12]*The archaic term used for the Blessed Rot of the Link.*

[13]*This is the first known mention of distortions. Reya Dunham's use of the term "distorted space" likely influenced Saint Frenwith to adopt it for Church parlance.*

[14]*The early iteration of what would later become the Righteous Mandate for the Cleansing of the Synthetic, which included banning the use of all synthetics and powering down the realm of the digital.*

Sincerely,
Reya

Addendum: There are no records of Saint Frenwith having deigned to respond to Reya Dunham. He clearly received the letter, given its inclusion in the Church Archive and the fact that he tasked his devout servants with the study of the distortions around this time. The fate of Reya Dunham is murky. She was executed for crimes against the Church not one year after penning this correspondence, but the details of said crimes are not recounted anywhere in Church documentation. Her death marked the end of any meaningful resistance to the blessed tenants of our Church, paving the way for the marvelous reign we are now blessed to find ourselves in.

RENDEZVOUS

The heart was a strange thing. Resilient. Tenacious. Treacherous. Fenrir had thought his was dead and gone. He'd imagined that his yearning for Sophie was limited to the carnal, but one night was all it took to convince him otherwise. His days passed in a daze. He waited impatiently for the sun to drop below the rooftops and chimneys of Simetria, to flee and take its revealing rays away with it. Night was beauty now. The darkness coddled them. Sophie could use it to shroud herself and move unseen from the empty and silent streets of the upper city into those of the lower one right to Fenrir's door.

Four taps. Long, short, short, long. That was their signal. He would unlatch the door. She would take a lap around the block, return, and slip in. They'd repeated their joining as often as they could. With each rendezvous, Fenrir waited for his desires to ease. He didn't like this feeling of powerlessness. He'd known it before, with Amilia and others who had preceded her, but he'd made the mistake of thinking himself resistant to it now. Of time and circumstance having worn the edge of feeling down. He'd been a fool to imagine a fundamental part of himself, of his very biology, so changed.

But he fought it nonetheless. He ignored it as he could.

He let Sophie suggest her visits. He demanded nothing of her. Expected nothing. But still, she came. And he came to expect her whether he meant to or not. Then, there was a stretch, five days, where she couldn't risk her forays into the lower city. There was some kind of gathering of the great families that absorbed her time. Her absence gnawed at Fenrir. He sat in his shack, elbows on his table, chin in hands, staring at the cobwebbed, fogged window. Those five nights of solitude told him everything he'd been denying. He was a slave to his feelings for her.

Tap, tap, tap, tap.

He rushed to the door. His hand hovered over the latch. He stared at the metal, the iron worn silver on the edges but stained black elsewhere. If he kept his door locked, would she return to try it again? How long would she persist before moving on?

Time passed, enough for Sophie to take a circuit around the block. The handle jangled, but the lock prevented the door from swinging in. Fenrir held his breath. Why resist? He had nothing else. So what if he lost himself? What good did control do him? He grabbed the iron, squeezed, and pulled. The door cracked. He peeked out. A cloaked figure was retreating but turned on hearing the creak from the ungreased hinges. Sophie hurried back to him and slipped inside.

"Did you not hear me?" she asked.

She untied the knot under her chin and peeled her hood off. She twirled and removed the cloak, holding it out to Fenrir. He took it and hung it on a hook near the door. He avoided her eyes.

"I'm just out of practice," he said then regretted.

Had it come out with a trace of bitterness? Sophie patted her hair, taming the stray locks that had clung to her hood. She looked as she always did—stunning. Too at odds with Fenrir's shack and, worse, his person.

"Would you like some wine?" he asked.

"I just came from the last of those dreadful soirées. Wine is the only thing that gets me through them."

The flush on her cheeks had been lost in the wavering candlelight of his room, but it was visible now. Eyes not as alert as usual, softer, more relaxed, her movements too, smoothed out. She pulled a chair from the table and sat.

"So that's a no?" he asked.

"It's been five days," she said. "Wine is the last thing on my mind."

Fenrir was beside her in an instant, stroking her bare shoulders, drawing her lips to his. They didn't even bother with the bed. The chair and table were sufficient for their needs, an abatement of a different kind of hunger. It was only afterward that they wandered over to his hay-stuffed bedding, stray stalks poking Fenrir through the threadbare sheets. He didn't care. His body was numb and tingling. Sophie rested her chin on his chest and ran her fingers through the sparse hairs there, fair and soft. A smile danced on the edges of her lips, and a light flickered in her eyes. Was this the bliss to her that it was to him? He didn't dare ask.

Sophie turned her face to the ceiling and rested her head against Fenrir's breast. It rose and fell with his breath, a cluster of orange-red curls bobbing in perpetuity. Sophie sat up, extended an arm towards a beam set into the wall, and retrieved a silver object from it. His sigil of the purge. She inspected it, one side then the other, over and over again.

"Would you ever participate in one?" Fenrir asked.

"Heavens, I don't know. It sounds exciting but also terrifying. I have no idea if I'd be up to the task."

"You're tier 2. You would be fine."

Sophie turned to face him, her head pressed against his skin still.

"So you think the tier system is fair?" she asked. "No room for favors or partiality?"

"Did you give favors to get where you are?"

She moved the coin to his breast, balanced it upright, one finger at the apex, and spun it in circles.

"It's not about consciously asking for or receiving favors. I'm Lady Roshem, the head of a great family. I get privileges others don't without even trying for them. I could be a tier 2 surveyor in name only, and I'd only learn of my inadequacy in the heat of a purge. Far from ideal."

She released the coin and let it fall flat then hoisted herself up on her elbows. She was nude still, and Fenrir let his eyes take in the impossibility of her.

"Why did the Church spare you?" she asked. "Favors?"

The question was like a slap in its abruptness. Sophie was normally coyer. She wasn't bothering to hide behind fine but empty words. Did that mean the nature of their relationship was changing?

"I don't know," Fenrir said.

"They didn't offer any explanation? They just released you from the penitentiary, and what?"

"They told me I was free to go as long as I became Fenrir Mey entirely. I was a toller. I lived in this shack. I would never again touch surveyor's gear. I would leave my old life behind. That was all."

Sophie tapped her chin. "Why do you think they did it?"

Fenrir didn't want to leave this moment. He didn't want to revisit that pain and uncertainty, that loss of what little he'd been left with, his name. But how could he deny those green eyes that peered at him with such vivacity?

"The only thing that makes sense to me," he said, "is that they didn't want to lose a valuable asset. My expertise could come in handy to the Church."

"Ashtin Broodfell was remarkably skilled."

Sophie moved in, her breasts resting against Fenrir's chest. He was spent, but even so, lust was stirring.

"Ashtin was skilled," Fenrir said, "but not so much so. Not to justify this ruse."

"What else then?"

"Someone was looking out for me."

Sophie crept in further. Her face was nearing his.

"Did you have any sway with the bishops or other influential high bloods?"

Fenrir shook his head. He'd been awful at playing those kinds of games. Too honest for politics. Too proud to give praise that wasn't warranted.

"Your wife then?" Sophie asked, her lips brushing his chin. "Amilia Broodfell, wasn't it? She had clout back then. Maybe it was her."

For all the connections Amilia had had, mostly through her father, she hadn't wielded enough power to save Ashtin from his doom, unless there were things he hadn't known about her.

"You're still married to her, aren't you?" Sophie asked. "I mean, technically speaking."

"She was married to Ashtin, and Ashtin is dead."

Now, Sophie's hand was exploring. His leg to inner thigh to groin. The want was returning in full. His body, too, was responding.

"Well, Fenrir seems very much alive," she said, "and Fenrir is all I care about."

She pressed her lips to his, her hand more adventurous in its forays now. Fenrir was ready. He grabbed her and showed her just how alive she made him, how he could give, how she infused him with a longing that he'd thought was dead. When they were short of breath, their passions appeased for the moment, Sophie nestled into the nook between his arm and side.

"I'm glad you've put the past behind you," Sophie said, "but I wonder, where does Fenrir go from here?"

"Where am I to go, a toller with no other lot in life than ringing a bell?"

The flood of angst and bitterness surprised even him until he understood where it originated from. Sophie had done more than awaken his lust. She'd made him want again, want in all ways.

"What do you long for?" she asked.

Fenrir laughed. "A series of impossibilities. To be a surveyor again." He hesitated. "To share more than scattered nights with you?"

Sophie stiffened, forced a laugh, and rose. She slipped over to her things and threw her robes on, quickly, expertly. Fenrir watched, well aware of his misstep. He shouldn't have said that. He should stop the want while he could. Be grateful for what he had. Even if desires were stealing back into his heart, that didn't make him whole. He was still just a shell of a man. No good for anyone. Barely himself.

HOLY RELIC

Theopold scurried into Vergil's office just as the bell towers finished tolling. It was time for the start of the second set of daily rituals. The bishop frowned as the dark-skinned man dropped into one of the two chairs set in front of Vergil's desk. No smile, no ducking of the head, no sign that he respected Vergil and his position in the least. Of course, that's because he didn't. Theopold despised the Church, but he could have at least pretended it was otherwise when he found himself in its hallowed halls.

"You shouldn't make a habit of openly flouting the rituals," Vergil said. "It looks bad for me to be meeting with someone so sacrilege."

His graphite stick was poised, ready to kiss the achingly empty parchment set beneath it.

"But that's why I came when I did," Theopold said. "Everyone is too preoccupied to notice the scraggly old man come to visit Bishop Holdsworth."

"Since you're here, you'll humor me, heretic or not."

Vergil pulled a piece of parchment from his desk drawer along with a spare graphite stick and pushed both towards Theopold. The old man blinked and stared at the writing utensil and medium as if they were drenched in poison.

"Go on," Vergil said.

He got to work writing, starting with the Divine Equation of the Quadratic. After a few seconds, he glanced back at Theopold, still and stiff.

Vergil frowned. "It's every citizen's duty."

Theopold sighed and shook his head but grabbed the graphite stick and drew a diagram of a cone, marking its height and radius, then noting the formula for its volume.

"They do nothing, you know," Theopold said. "These rituals. Dig into the archives. There's a definitive work by surveyor Thatchhold proving the uselessness of them."

"I don't doubt it," Vergil said, "but that isn't the point."

Theopold stopped writing. Vergil glanced up and found the old man staring at him.

"Appearances," Vergil said. "They're everything, especially here."

Theopold mumbled and got back to work. They continued in silence until the second bell sounded, releasing them from their duties. Vergil took the two pieces of parchment and laid them aside then he opened one of his desk drawers. His fingers brushed against a smooth casing.

"I have something special to show you today," Vergil said, "but I really must know that I can trust you completely with it. It's not like the other trinkets. This is a relic."

Theopold's blank stare transformed into a mania bordering on frenzy. Eyes bulging, lips licking, nostrils flaring. Vergil grimaced at the look of him. It wasn't just the deep wrinkles set into his forehead or the too-shiny head or the rail thinness of him poorly concealed by tattered, beige robes. It was how hopelessly blatant Theopold was about his perverse beliefs. A cultist through and through.

"You can trust me," Theopold said. "I've been true to my word thus far, have I not?"

Vergil was going to show Theopold his find regardless. He didn't have another option. Only a cultist would know how to make sense of its contents. Still, Vergil enjoyed seeing the spindly fellow squirm. He waited ten seconds, Theopold's eyes shifting from Vergil's own then down to his outstretched arm then back, over and over again. Finally, Vergil deposited the relic on the desk, and Theopold sprang to hover over it.

"I found it in the Church Vault a few days past," Vergil said. "It's different than anything I've laid eyes on before, which suggests it comes from the Old World. What can you tell me about it, Mr. Cromford?"

"Can I touch it?" Theopold asked, already reaching for the treasure.

Vergil waved. Before the bishop's hand had even settled back onto his chair's armrest, Theopold cradled the relic. He held the object up to the light streaming in through the windows set behind Vergil. The relic was composed of two parts—a clear casing of some Old World material and a disk of many hues, changing as the light struck it in different locations and creating a rainbow arc.

"It's a synthetic, clearly," Vergil said, "but what is it besides?"

Theopold nodded and laid the relic back on Vergil's desktop with the utmost care. He wore a grin that threatened to split his face in two.

"It's a type of compact diskette."

"I thought those had all degraded ages ago," Vergil said. "This looks intact."

Theopold leaned over the desk and peered at the relic again.

"It could be what was called an M-disk. Archival quality to store data for the long term."

"Could be or is?"

Theopold moved back to his chair and stared at Vergil. His mania was still there but hidden now beyond a mask of stoicism. That's how these heretics always were. A tiresome lot that Vergil was forced to work with to achieve his loftiest of goals.

"I couldn't say without the proper tools to read it," Theopold said. "And if you wanted to know what code was writ on it, I'd need those same tools, ones I don't have access to."

Vergil had suspected as much and was prepared for this eventuality. He grabbed the diskette, tucked it into his robes, and rose from his chair.

"Follow me."

Theopold jumped from his seat and trailed behind Vergil. They went from narrow to grand corridor then into winding hallways before plunging down a stone staircase, poorly lit and seldom used. The rot was making inroads in this part of the Church, and Vergil had to remind himself not to pinch his nose and to maintain a neutral expression. Even in the company of a cultist, he had a role to play and appearances to keep up.

After several minutes of navigating tighter and tighter spaces that only grew damper and darker, Vergil and Theopold came to a junction that contained a heavy wooden door. Lamps were lit on each side, and the door bore a plaque, weathered to a blue-green, that read "Vault."

"The Church Vault?" Theopold asked, his tongue darting out and licking his lips.

"You requested tools to retrieve the contents of the diskette. This is the only place with such equipment."

"You have access?"

Few did, but Vergil was one of those few. He pulled a ring of keys from his robes and ran through them until he found the one he sought. The long metal rod went into the hole set below the doorknob, and with a turn, they were granted admittance.

The Church Vault was a small space encased by gray stones and mortar, overflowing with the forbidden. Although Saint Marcos had championed the Cleansing of the Synthetic from the world, he also knew the value of such tools. Only the most learned of clergyfolk were allowed in this hallowed room. Most never bothered to visit, but Vergil had a goal that required exploring unorthodox solutions. Frequenting the Vault was one half of that, associating with Theopold was the other.

As soon as they entered the room, Theopold began investigating every object. He muttered to himself and gasped with wonder. Fingers running over cables, hands patting housings that sounded with a hollow thud, eyes jumping from synthetic to synthetic, his body barely able to keep up. He shuffled from one side of the room to the other three times before Vergil's patience was at an end.

"Is this piece of equipment what you require?" Vergil asked.

He stood beside a table that held another relic of the Old World, orders of magnitude more forbidden than anything else in the Vault. A console, a tool for codesmithing, a fundamental part of the realm of the digital, now lonely and inert and isolated from any network. Theopold scurried over to Vergil's side and nearly drooled. He caressed the console like it was a woman's body.

"Well?" Vergil asked. "Is it sufficient for the diskette?"

"Yes, yes," Theopold said, "so long as it's powered."

Vergil pulled the diskette from his robes and handed it to Theopold.

"Work your magic, and tell me what's on the thing."

Theopold took the diskette in both hands, deposited it

on the table, then searched on the black box of the console. He shouted in pleasure and pointed to cords that snaked out of it and plunged into a large metallic closet in the corner of the room.

"That must be the power source," he said.

Theopold pressed his forefinger to a button on the black box, and the machine came to life. It whirred and clicked and put on a show of lights, green and red and white, on and off in time with the sounds, then the reflective surface set next to the box blinked and showed a sequence of words writ with light.

Vergil moved closer and peered at the horrid thing. It was beautiful in its blasphemy, like any sin could be.

"It's working," Theopold said, vibrating with excitement.

"What about the diskette?" Vergil asked.

"We must wait for the screen of home. The console thinks just now."

They both stared at it as it ran through mysterious routines, displaying a blue background with white text that meant nothing to them—CMOS Setup Utility, BIOS, CPU, Boot Device. Theopold stared at it and murmured to himself. He pulled a rectangular object towards him. It held dozens of buttons marked with letters and numbers and symbols. Theopold proceeded to touch his fingers to them in a sequence that Vergil couldn't follow. The screen flickered then threw up small pictures, Old World hieroglyphics, before showing a life-like image of rolling hills of green with a blue sky flecked by clouds. Theopold took the diskette, opened the casing, and lifted the delicate saucer. He peered again at the black box then touched his finger to a different button set into it. A light flashed, and a horizontal surface popped out. Vergil started and took a step back.

"That's meant to happen," Theopold said, depositing the

diskette into the tray-like piece then turning back to look at Vergil. "Let us see what we can find on this relic of yours."

Theopold pushed the tray in, and they waited as the console digested the contents. A rectangular surface appeared on the reflective screen. It contained one small icon with text below it. Vergil moved to stand just behind Theopold who lowered himself onto a stool stored under the table. Vergil squinted at the text, but it was just a string of nonsensical letters and numbers: RD_QuarantineProtocol_v5.3.4.

Theopold used the buttonpad to interact with the object. A new rectangle showed itself and eclipsed the previous one, but this one was far from sparse. It was filled with text, and even Vergil, with his limited knowledge of the Old World, knew code when he spotted it.

"A program," Theopold said.

"For what?"

Theopold held up his hand then read through the contents displayed. His brown, bloodshot eyes shifted back and forth, tracing line after line. Theopold gasped then hurried to hide his surprise. Vergil moved closer.

"What is it?" he asked.

"I would need more time and my notes to be sure," Theopold said, before trailing off.

"Well, give me your best guess. Clearly, you have one based on your reaction."

Theopold pointed to the text at the beginning.

#Developed by Reya Dunham. Do not pass on to others not initiated into the Distortion Purge Effort. Do not enact the code until it has been approved by all researchers. For direct upload into any Link node containing the Linkrot virus. Any other attempt to deploy the package may result in the system flagging it.

Vergil knew the name, and although the rest of the text was peppered with jargon he didn't understand, he could make out what it entailed.

"This was an attempt to stop the distortions," Vergil said.

Theopold nodded and watched Vergil as he spoke his next words with care.

"It seems to be the work of Reya Dunham, and I would surmise that this was the crime that resulted in her execution."

"But it was to stop the distortions. Surely, the Church wasn't against such a noble cause."

Theopold tapped the text that read "Linkrot virus." "It would be if such a tactic meant disrupting the Rot of the Link in any way."

Vergil felt his lips begging to pull taut into a smile, and this time, he let them. He was willing to have Theopold see a portion of his true intent because he would need the cultist's assistance moving forward. Only Theopold had knowledge of the Old World, and only he would be willing to do unspeakable acts in the name of his beloved Others.

"Well now," Vergil said, patting Theopold on the shoulder, "isn't that a fascinating turn of events. It just so happens that I've been meaning to find a way to undo distortions myself."

Theopold looked back in shock then let his own face settle into a grin that mimicked Vergil's. Without words, they established an understanding. A bishop and a heretic—an unlikely alliance but one that just might lead to where they both so ached to go.

PROMISE MADE

Vergil never summoned Sophie to his study at the Church. Their betrothal was still unofficial, with Vergil loath to announce it so long as Sophie suffered from her condition. Him requesting her presence in this manner meant she went in her role as a surveyor. She was grim when she entered, not least because of the guilt that accosted her every time she found herself in Vergil's presence.

Three months she'd lain with Fenrir as often as Tillie's schedule would allow. Sophie had initially viewed joining with him as a kind of itch to be scratched. She imagined that once the deed was done, she would be satisfied for a long while yet. How naïve she'd been. She ached for him, and him her. They couldn't have enough of one another both in body and mind. Sophie was intoxicated by Fenrir, and she was terrified that Vergil would sense her addiction. Thus far, he hadn't, but this overly formal meeting put her on edge.

"Surveyor Sophie," Vergil said as she entered, "please come in."

A woman stood beside Vergil's desk. She was older, dark-skinned, and wore her black hair in a tight bun. Her searching eyes were set behind square eyeglasses.

"Thank you for your time," Vergil said to her. "I'll be in touch."

She gave him a brief nod then did likewise to Sophie as she passed by on her way out. She was familiar somehow, but Sophie couldn't place her.

"I know that woman from somewhere," she said.

"She's a scholar at the university. You probably heard a lecture by her."

"No, that's not it."

"Well, it hardly matters," Vergil said. "Now, come to my side."

Sophie advanced into the study and gazed at its contents. She'd known Vergil was an avid reader, but his hoard of books was bordering on excessive. She peered down at the titles of ones that looked to have been read more recently, and a common theme emerged—distortions. So this was for her? Her guilt heightened and planted a fluttering in her chest.

Vergil stood behind his desk, arms clasped behind his back, a hint of a smile on his lips. It was the pose he used on his congregation, at least the handful of times Sophie had gone to one of his sermons. Sometimes, she forgot just who Vergil had become. When she looked at him, she often saw that serious little boy that her father had introduced her to when she'd been just five years of age and him seven. Other times, he was the awkward but budding adolescent of fifteen. Rarely was he the influential bishop she now found herself before. She suspected this was because, to her, his role as a clergyfolk felt somehow false. Vergil was too big a fish to happily swim in the crowded pond of the Church, but where else was there for him to go? Simetria was the largest and most powerful of all the cities, and the only rank higher than a bishop was Archbishop, the Chosen of the Lady. And there could be only one of those.

"You never invite me here," Sophie said.

"I like to keep my work and my personal life neatly separated, but I have something to show you that I'd rather not risk transporting away from Church grounds."

Vergil beckoned her closer, and Sophie moved to his side, trying to think how she would have acted before she'd taken up with Fenrir. Would she have stood so close? Would she have smiled and gazed at him through partly closed eyelids? She settled on standing at an appropriate distance and acting as her surveyor self. It was the safest path to take.

Vergil opened a drawer and placed a strange object on top of his desk. Sophie peered down at it but couldn't match it to anything she'd seen before. It had colors that didn't belong together and a foreign sheen.

Vergil tapped it with his forefinger. "This diskette is the answer to all our problems."

Sophie's heart raced. Had he really done it? After all this time, had he found a way to cure her? She tried to dampen the hope that surged. She had to manage her expectations or risk the disappointment that was sure to follow.

"Our problems as in?" she asked.

Vergil nodded and grinned. "Our best hope of curing you of your condition, but even more of riding the world of its greatest evil."

Sophie couldn't take in the meaning. For over five centuries, they'd lived with the threat of the non-Euclidean. For equally as long, countless scholars, far more brilliant than Vergil, had attempted to find a solution, to no avail. Now, here Vergil was claiming he'd done the impossible in the form of this strange, shiny, round object.

"I don't understand," she said.

Vergil's smile faded. He was disappointed by her reaction. He came so close his robes brushed against her leather coat. Then he plucked her tricorn off her head and tossed it on his desk. He dug into his robes, pulled out his pair of reinforced glyph gloves, and donned them. Vergil took Sophie's chin in his safely buffered hand and forced her to stare back at him.

"Soon, I'll be able to touch my lips to yours," he said. "Soon, I could ravage you on this very desk."

Sophie's face burned. She went to pull free, but Vergil's grip tightened.

"Listen to me," he shouted.

Sophie went stock still. Vergil had never raised his voice to her. Her mind went back to Fenrir and what Vergil would see as a betrayal. She hardened and glared at him. He grinned at her defiance.

"Do you hear what I'm saying, dear Sophie?" Vergil leaned in and whispered in her ear. "I'm going to rid you of your distortion. We have the means now."

He pulled away and released her chin. She continued to glare at him.

He tapped the object on his desk. "This holy relic is that."

To be rid of her distortion and cleanse the world of them. Without her distortion, Vergil wouldn't have a hold over her. She could find a way to escape. To be free. Sophie grasped her hands together and even went to embrace Vergil before he held out a hand to keep her back.

"Sorry," she said. "I forgot."

"The only catch is that the task will be fraught with danger. It will require a trip to the Old World, deep into it. You'll have others to assist you, the best that I can find, those who know that place and can predict the dangers you'll encounter."

"I'm honestly surprised you'd let me go," Sophie said.

Vergil picked up the diskette. "If I could trust anyone else with this task, I'd keep you here, but this is too valuable a find to hand off to another. It has to be you, my heart."

Sophie knew her strengths and her worth. She could descend into the Old World and likely survive some regions, but Vergil had said she would have to venture deep into it.

She didn't trust her skills enough for that. Even if she was a tier 2 surveyor, she had never faced an afflicted in a non-controlled setting. She'd performed a mercy killing here and there to be sure, but the Old World would be brimming with afflicted long lost to their distortions.

"And what of other surveyors?" she asked. "Will you have a tier 1 accompany me?"

There were only two such persons in Simetria at present, and she couldn't imagine either agreeing to such a reckless adventure, not to mention the fact that Vergil had no influence over either of them.

"I had assumed you would be sufficient for any work requiring a surveyor," he said.

She wouldn't be. She needed another with skill that rivaled, if not surpassed, her own. She had to approach the request delicately. Fenrir's name was already known to Vergil thanks to that little bird that had chirped about her months past. She couldn't appear too eager.

"I don't trust my own abilities," Sophie said. "I haven't even been in a purge, and you're talking about me diving into the Old World. No, Vergil, it would be the height of carelessness to send me as the sole surveyor. If you can't secure the assistance of a tier 1 surveyor currently serving the Church, I happen to know of one who was forced into retirement."

"Oh?" Vergil asked, tilting his head.

"Ashtin Broodfell. He's alive but living under a different name and forbidden from using the tools of his former trade. I suspect a high-ranking bishop such as yourself could make an exception for the noble and essential work we aim to undertake."

Vergil craned over Sophie. "And how-oh-how did you manage to unearth such a delightful secret as Ashtin Broodfell still being alive?"

"You know me and my lust for such things," she said. "Do you recall that toller I had to interact with because of the distortion in his tower?"

"Fenrir, was it? Although, I thought you weren't able to unravel his mysteries."

Now would have been the time for Vergil to admit that he knew of her rendezvouses with Fenrir, but he only looked back at Sophie with a frank stare. He had no idea. Her trick with Tillie had worked.

"Well, sometimes I can't let go of such things," Sophie said. "I discovered the toller's true identity a few months past but promised to keep it to myself."

"I understand the importance of keeping promises, but I'm a bit hurt that you would hide such a fascinating find from even me."

"I didn't think you would care. Back then, it was just an interesting little fact, but now that it has bearing on the situation—"

"I don't like it. How could we trust him, a disgraced and morally corrupt former surveyor?"

Sophie moved in close, gazing at Vergil through softened eyelids. "Oh, but that's the beauty of it and precisely why we can trust him. He has his own secrets to keep, which means he'll be more obliged to keep quiet on the whole thing."

Vergil laughed, his eyes alight, hungry. A schemer appreciative of a fellow sly mind. Sophie always knew how to sway him.

***

Sophie leaned against Fenrir's shack just next to his door. He'd tolled the day's final bell nearly twenty minutes past, but he still hadn't returned home. Then again, she never risked visiting him so early. She had no idea what he got up to in the hours they didn't share, late into the night. Sophie shifted her weight onto her left leg and recrossed her arms. Low bloods glanced at her as they passed, their downcast eyes likely taking note of her well-made leather boots. Despite the winter chill, most hobbled along in sandals or bare feet. Sophie put on an air of indifference towards them. The truth was, she was afraid of them. They were so many, and her kind so few. If one day they decided they'd had enough of being treated like dirt underfoot, all they had to do was rebel. The Church would bend then break. It had happened in other cities. Not many, but some. Simetria had been fortunate thus far, but from what her eyes spied when she frequented the lower city for her work, it was only a matter of time until a spark took and ignited into a veritable inferno.

This was another reason why she had to undertake her quest into the Old World. The distortions were a large part of their collective suffering. True, the non-Euclidean didn't discriminate between the lower and upper city, between low and high bloods, but the have-nots tended to lack many of the resources or services that the haves benefited from. A stroll along her street showed as much. For every block near the Church, attuners were affixed to buildings at ten-foot intervals. Down here in the heart of the lower city, there might be one attuner for a stretch of road that ran for five hundred feet. And besides the infrastructure, there was also a distinct lack of surveyors. All the looks she got standing against Fenrir's shack proved that her kind was rarely present here.

Sophie started to debate returning later in the evening when Fenrir's form appeared around the bend of a building. His eyes looked through the others crowded around him then settled on Sophie just as he stopped at his door.

"Oh," he said, nearly dropping the keys he pulled from his pocket. "Surveyor Sophie, what a pleasant surprise."

She stood stiffly and gave him a hard nod. "Toller Fenrir."

Passing low bloods eyed the two of them. They were

both painfully aware of just how exposed they were out in the open street.

"I have surveyor business to discuss with you," Sophie said.

Fenrir looked at her, the keys still in a confused tangle in his hands. She glanced at his door and jerked her head at it.

"Would you like to talk inside?" he asked.

She smiled and nodded. Fenrir hurried to find the right key then flung the door open for her. He followed and shut it. The formality and stiffness they'd projected towards one another in the street faded. There were in their sanctuary now. Free to be their true selves. They stood in the one room that made up Fenrir's home, his bed tucked in one corner, the fire that served as his kitchen in the other, the table dominating the central space.

"Did something happen?" he asked.

"I have news, but it's not of the bad variety."

Fenrir relaxed and sighed. He moved to his table and flopped into a chair. His breath came heavier than it should have just from a simple walk home.

"Goodness, did my coming upset you that much?" she asked.

She removed her hat, set it on the table, and took the seat next to his.

"I thought we'd been had," he said. "I never really considered until now what would happen if our rendezvouses were made known to your betrothed. I honestly tried not to think of him at all, but this episode reminds me of the dangerous game I'm playing."

"Dangerous?"

"Bishop Vergil Holdsworth," Fenrir said. "That's your man, is it not?"

She'd never told Fenrir her betrothed's identity.

"Our betrothal isn't public."

"The lives of the great families are the only entertainment we lower-city dwellers get. Your love lives are of special interest."

Sophie huffed and crossed her arms. She didn't like being watched. Learning that the masses whispered of her comings and goings, of who she would wed and bed, of all the heartache and drama of her high-blood life, it was infuriating.

"In any case," Fenrir said, "Holdsworth is influential. From deacon to priest in five years then priest to bishop in another six. His ambition rivals that of Ashtin's. He is powerful."

"Your concern's wasted. Vergil knows nothing about us, and soon, it won't matter at all. That's what I've come to tell you. There's a solution to my condition."

Sophie rose from her chair, pulled a parchment from the pocket that lined her coat, and unfolded it on the table. She pressed her fingers to the creases to force it to lay flat. Fenrir's home was dark, and he set about lighting the oil lamp. Once he'd finished, he returned to the table and loomed over the parchment.

"Do you know what this is?" she asked.

Fenrir inspected it. "A map, but of where, I'm not sure. It's not Simetria but…"

Sophie waited for him to see it, the reflection of the surface into the deep, the symmetry of the thoroughfares with the streets above. His eyes widened.

"This is the Old World," he said.

"And do you know why I've brought it to you?"

Fenrir shook his head and sighed. He knew, and he didn't like it one bit. "You want to go down there."

Sophie moved to his side until their arms touched. She tapped a finger to the map in time with her words.

"'Want' doesn't capture the necessity of the expedition I must go on. 'Need' would be a more apt word. Or, even better, 'desperately need.' The solution for my condition is below, deep in the Old World."

Fenrir shook his head more forcefully and frowned. His fingers pressed against the wood grain of the table until they showed white.

"It's suicide," he said.

The Old World had been walled off years past, even before Ashtin's supposed execution, but there were rumors of quiet expeditions approved by the Church. Sophie had never been approached for such a task, but that didn't mean others hadn't been sent. The Church had a Vault and an Archive teeming with items and information on the Old World. Some of that came from the distant past, but some had been more recently discovered. There was only one logical place to retrieve such treasures.

"You've been there before?" Sophie asked.

"No, but I've read accounts from those who have back when the Church was foolish enough to think they could contain the distortions down there. There's a reason they gave up on it long ago. Hordes of afflicted. Distortions so thick they saturate the air."

"Well, I don't have a choice."

Sophie raised her hand to Fenrir's face and brushed his straw-colored hair back from his emerald eyes. It was difficult to be around him and not join. This place, his presence, it all brought the carnal to mind for her, but she couldn't let herself get distracted. She'd come here to recruit Fenrir.

"This is how I remove the distortions," she said, "mine and all the others."

Fenrir's mouth opened. "How?"

"Vergil found a relic that requires access to a specific object in the Old World. I don't know the details, but there will be others that join me who do. The one thing we're sorely lacking is a competent surveyor to help me."

Fenrir's brow furrowed, and his fingers curled to form fists still planted on the table.

"Just one?" he asked. "Why not a lance of them? If this mission of yours is really what you say, why wouldn't the Church do everything to ensure it succeeds?"

"Because our expedition is meant to be a quiet affair. Vergil doesn't want others to know, else we risk them discovering my motivation for going. I need someone that I trust completely."

"Me?"

Sophie wanted to reach out and hold Fenrir. She wanted to pour her raw emotion into him so that he could understand just what it was she felt, but the flesh would always be a hindrance. Even in joining, the body blockaded the union of the mind. It was humanity's perpetual plight. Wanting to be one with everything but holding on dearly to oneself. Balancing the ache for belonging with the selfishness of the ego.

"I don't trust my own skills," she said, "not for dealing with the afflicted. Like I said before, I don't know how capable I really am. I suspect my odds of surviving in the Old World aren't as good as I'd like. But with a tier 1 surveyor at my side?"

Fenrir looked away from Sophie and down at the map below his fists. "I haven't touched a polearm or used my tools in nearly six years."

"You would have some time to hone your skills," Sophie said. "Not much, a few days perhaps, but from what I've heard, your aptitude came more from natural talent than training. You'll pick it back up quickly."

Fenrir shook his head and pushed himself away from the table. He paced the room from the door to his fire and back, avoiding looking directly at Sophie.

"If we go down there and somehow manage to succeed,"

he said, "your distortion will be gone, and then what? You'll wed your betrothed at long last, and what we have will end?"

Sophie intersected this path, forcing him to stop his marching and look at her. She held out her hands, and he placed his in them. She pulled Fenrir in until their bodies touched all along the front. Their hands stayed clasped together down at their sides. She turned her face so that her cheek touched his.

"Ridding myself of my condition is the first step in breaking free from Vergil," she said. "As long as I have my distortion, he owns me, but the moment it's gone?"

"You would break away from him?"

Sophie saw what Fenrir asked between his words. He wanted to know where he fit into the picture. If Sophie didn't wed Vergil, what did it mean for him?

"I'm not making any promises," she said. "I'm simply saying this would give me options, ones I don't have at present. My current future is no future. You think what we have can go on indefinitely? Neither of us is so young and naïve to believe that. Help me get my agency back, and let yourself be a surveyor one last time, before we remove the very reason for the existence of our order in the first place. If we succeed, the world will change. For good."

Fenrir released his grip and pulled his fingers free from hers. They moved apart, stern and grim.

"I'd need armor, a weapon, tools," he said.

Sophie dug in her coat pocket, pulled out her notepad and graphite stick, and handed them to Fenrir.

"Write down as much detail as you can about each item you once called your own. I'll scour the armory's storage to see if your old things aren't still there. My understanding is that the Church is loath to part with any essential tools, even those used by one disgraced."

Fenrir moved back to the table, took his seat, and

scribbled away. Sophie was silent for a space. Once Fenrir had stopped writing, she moved to his side, one hand on the back of his chair, the other on the table's edge.

"And the tolling of the bell? What will happen if I disappear into the deep for days on end?"

"Fret not. I'll talk with Vergil about finding someone to step in for you. Those involved in the expedition will meet to discuss the details in the coming days."

Fenrir closed Sophie's notepad and handed it and the graphite stick back to her.

"To be clear," Fenrir said, "I won't be punished for acting the part of a surveyor, correct? This is all happening under the auspices of the Church?"

Sophie leaned over and retrieved the map. She folded it then tucked it, her notepad, and graphite stick into the various coat pockets they'd issued from.

"Yes, dear Fenrir, your secret stays safe. I give you my word that no harm will come to you from the Church. I can't do the same in the case of whatever we find in the Old World, however."

Fenrir let his severity ease into a small grin. "The latter is my role, is it not?"

Sophie nodded and made her way to the door. She glanced over her shoulder at him.

"It would be ill-advised for me to return here," she said. "And perhaps it would be best if Toller Fenrir was to stay holed up in his home while he battled the illness that kept him from his toller duties? Come late tonight, to my home. The servants will provide you with a place to sleep, food, whatever else you need. Until we return from the Old World, you are my guest. Covertly."

Fenrir grabbed her arm.

"If we succeed and come back from the Old World," he said, "and you want to break away from Vergil, I'll help in any way I can. No expectations. I'd simply do this for you, Sophie."

"One thing at a time. First, we tackle the distortions. Vergil comes after."

THE EXPEDITION

Fenrir had known Sophie was wealthy, known she was the head of her family, but he hadn't quite grasped the extent of how privileged she was until he wandered the halls of her home. He came under the cover of deep night, as she'd suggested, then stayed indoors thereafter. He didn't know what she'd told her servants, but they didn't seem at all concerned with this stranger in their midst. To be fair, he wasn't entirely out of place. Once he'd traded his worn and tattered tunic and pants for a fashionable doublet, he slipped back into being a high blood. How he held himself, how he walked, even how he spoke. He thought the transformation unsettling and strange.

His time in Sophie's estate was lonely. The only servant that interacted with him was an older woman named Trisht. She brought him three meals and switched out his clothes while he slept. She didn't talk much, only answering his questions with the least possible configuration of words. Fenrir let her be. He ate his meals then devoted the rest of his waking hours to training.

True to her word, Sophie retrieved his old armor and weapons. She'd even found his glyph gloves. He was glad to first lay eyes on them in solitude because, at the sight of them, Fenrir nearly wept. Once his emotions settled, he tore off his fine attire and donned the garb of a surveyor. The leather fit looser than before. He had lost a fair amount of bulk owing to his time in the penitentiary and the meager fare he could afford on the salary of a toller. But when he finished dressing and inspected himself in a mirror, Fenrir gawked.

Black leather with red threading for the coat that reached to his ankles. Pants tight but allowing an ease of movement. Boots high and sturdy. Last was his hat, tricorn with a tuff of red ribbon sticking out. That had been a gift from Amilia. The only difference from his days as a surveyor came in the empty epaulets, no longer bearing the purple hue that indicated tier 1 status. This was as it should be. Safer to be anonymous. Even without the rank, Fenrir was so changed simply by this set of clothing. Dashing, striking, almost adonic. Sophie seemed to think so too when she came to him that night.

Fenrir was wielding his fauchard in the cellar. The wood of the pole as smooth and soft as he recalled. The heft of it balanced. Clean strikes. Smooth transitions. Sophie was right; it all came back so effortlessly.

"Muscle memory," she said, startling him from behind.

He hadn't even heard the door open, yet there she was standing before it. In her own surveyor gear with her voulge in hand, two little hooks at the rear facing away from the axe-like steel piece fitted to the end of the pole.

"That's how it all comes back," she said. "Your muscles are embedded with the memory of your movements. As I told you it would be."

She walked into the wide and dim room, especially cool in the winter night, and looked him over, blatantly eyeing every inch of him. She smiled at what she spied.

"My goodness," she said, "you look incredibly delicious

in your surveyor gear. No wonder I was so smitten even back then."

"Smitten?"

"Everyone wanted a piece of Ashtin Broodfell," she said, coming up to his side. "Women, men, silly little lovestruck surveyors."

Sophie grabbed his fauchard, but Fenrir was loath to part with it. She tugged, and he relaxed his grip. She carried both their polearms to a table set against the wall and laid them down. Then, she advanced on Fenrir. He waited for her. Let her run her fingers all along the smooth black that covered his shoulders, arms, chest, stomach, groin. She lingered on the latter and pressed up against him.

"We only have a couple of days," she said. "Let's make the most of them."

Fenrir guided them to his cot. It was small but sufficient for their needs, especially considering they didn't spend very much time splayed on it. He joined with Sophie against the wall, the table, a chest his gear had been delivered in, the cold stones of the floor. They moved in a myriad of ways, took positions neither had tried before. It was like a part of him that had been sleeping was awakening from the mere presence of his old identity. He was energized and eager and reckless. Sophie seemed to like this side of him too. They ended their dance on the cot with arms and legs intermingled, sweat disappearing in the chill air, chests rising and falling slower and slower. Sophie laid her head on Fenrir's chest and ran her fingers through the few tufts of hair there.

"I think I might just love you, Toller Fenrir," she whispered.

He held his breath, and she glanced up at him.

"I needed to say it," she said, "in case I don't get a chance to again. You don't have to respond. In fact, it's better if you don't."

Sophie jumped up and started to dress. Fenrir rose on his elbows and looked at how the shadows played on her thighs and back. Of course he loved her too. Desperately. But she was right. It was better if he kept that to himself. There was so much at stake in the days ahead, and he had to focus on the task he'd been assigned. Loving her and protecting her didn't always go hand in hand, especially when it came to affliction. He'd learned that the hard way with Trevon.

"Well, come on," Sophie said, lacing her boots. "I didn't just come down here to join. You need a proper partner to train with. Cleaving the air will only do so much to prepare you for the Old World."

Fenrir jogged over to the bundle of leather that was his gear and dressed. Then, Sophie handed him his fauchard and readied herself for an attack. She was fast and strong. A horizontal strike from the side that Fenrir dodged shifted into an overhand crossbody slice. Fenrir opted to parry that one and in doing so disrupted Sophie's balance. She recovered but not quickly enough. Fenrir was in too close for her to properly defend herself. She settled on planting a kick into his stomach. It knocked him back a few paces, giving her the time to reset her stance. They stopped, leveled their weapons, and circled one another in an arc.

***

This routine repeated for the next four days. Fenrir alone until Sophie visited late in the night. Them joining then training. He made great strides in that time both physically as well as in the ways of the wards and other tools. He would need every option at his disposal. He had to be honed to a startling sharpness.

On the fifth day, he woke to Sophie stroking his hair, sitting on his cot.

"Is something wrong?" he asked.

"It's time to meet the others that will join us on our

expedition. Get dressed in your doublet. We're going for a stroll in the upper city."

Sophie wore typical high-blood attire as they walked side by side along the cobblestoned street. It was the first time Fenrir had seen her dressed in such a way. Normally, she was either garbed in her surveyor gear, as he'd seen her at the tower, or in the cloak she wore when visiting him at night in his shack. The lace and silk and ruffles suited her. How could she seem so perfectly at home in both hardy leather and this fine dress? He'd always hated the doublets he'd had to wear as a high blood. Even more so now that he was out of practice weathering their discomfort.

"Where are we going?" he said.

It was midday, and he felt exposed even under the thick winter cloud cover. The only coat that Sophie had for him had been her father's, and it smelled of smoke and dust.

"To Priest Nicolus Yevin's home," she said. "The man reminds me of a weasel, but he's loyal to Vergil. No tongues will wag about us visiting for a quick afternoon tea."

"Why not the Church? You said our expedition was approved by them."

Sophie glanced at Fenrir with just her eyes, her head erect and facing forward. "You walking out in the street is one thing, but entering the hallowed halls of the Church is asking to be recognized. There may be other considerations too. You can ask Vergil for further clarification when we arrive."

Fenrir's legs stopped responding, and he found himself stranded by their treachery. Sophie went a few steps before realizing she walked unaccompanied. She turned, and her look of confusion shot life back into Fenrir's immobilized limbs. When had he gone so soft? Terrified by the prospect of meeting her betrothed when he'd faced scores of afflicted throughout his life? Maybe he wasn't ready for this expedition after all. Then again, the dangers of the non-Euclidean were something he was well-versed in. These complex games of the heart were an entirely different matter.

"He'll be there?" Fenrir asked.

"This expedition is his brainchild. He's the one who organized it. Only he knows all the ins and outs."

Fenrir was silent.

"We'll be fine," she said. "He doesn't suspect a thing."

"Maybe not yet, but seeing us together might give him some hints."

Sophie sighed and bundled herself tighter in her winter cloak. "Just pretend we only know one another from our time in the tower and haven't spoken in months," she said. "Channel your old self from your surveyor days. Be arrogant and bored, and Vergil will believe it to be you."

"Arrogant and bored?" Fenrir said. "That wasn't how I used to be."

Sophie turned to look at him through the bundle of fabric shrouding her. She smiled and laughed. "Well, that's certainly how you came across."

Memory was a strange creature, hazing out the past, twisting it into a facsimile of itself. So much had happened to him since then, but more than that, it was perspective. On the outside, Ashtin had seemed aloof, while inside his head, he'd been filled with doubts. Confident of his abilities one minute, terrified it was all a lie the next. Rash in his desire to prove himself to himself. Look at where it had gotten him. A former high blood, playing a low blood, playing a high blood. The shift was dizzying.

Not a block later, they ascended a set of steps that led to a stone rowhouse with a forest-green door and a brass knocker in the shape of a lion's head. Sophie rapped it, and within seconds, it opened. A slight man with brown skin and shoulder-length, slicked-back, black hair let them in.

"Priest Yevin," Sophie said.

She offered her hand, and he put it to his chest. She repeated the ritual with him.

"Thank you for having us," she added.

"You're always welcome here, Lady Roshem," Nicolus said. "But please, let me take your coats and follow me to the cellar. The others have already arrived and are waiting."

Besides Sophie's, Fenrir hadn't been a guest in a high-blood home in years, yet he found the current situation odd. Nicolus shouldn't have answered his own door. He had servants for that. And he certainly shouldn't have been the one to take their coats. The whole affair was more secretive than Fenrir would have expected, and it couldn't have been just on his account. He wasn't that recognizable, and besides, as far as Simetria was concerned, Ashtin Broodfell was long dead.

Nicolus led them down a hall to a thick oak door. It opened to a landing followed by steps. Another door stood at the bottom.

"It's unlocked," Nicolus said.

Sophie moved past their host and descended. Fenrir trailed her. The door above closed. After the past few days, Fenrir ought to have been comfortable in subterranean spaces, and he did find Sophie's cellar calming in its stillness and silence. But this space felt mildly hostile. He suspected at least a part of that had to do with the knowledge that Vergil was just a few short steps away. Sophie reached the door and waited for Fenrir to come to her side. She glanced at him, nodded, and turned the knob.

Four figures were waiting. Four sets of eyes settling on them. Sophie went in first, leaving Fenrir to close the door. When he turned back around, Sophie was standing in front of Vergil. They kept their greeting professional, simple nods of their heads, hands clasped behind their backs. Fenrir ambled up to Sophie's side and locked eyes with Vergil's. There was a true and proper rival. Both men were tall and appealing in their own ways, but where Vergil was broad with an overt masculinity to him, Fenrir was lean with sharpness.

There was a moment, a twitch of Vergil's lip, a minuscule twist and strain of his neck, but then it was gone. He beamed at Fenrir and reached for his hand. Fenrir let Vergil take it and press it to his heart. The grip was strong but not to the point of discomfort. Fenrir repeated the greeting with Vergil, doing his utmost to match the strength of his hold as precisely as possible. He wanted to signal that he was on a level plane, neither bowing before the bishop nor holding his nose up at him.

"Why did you choose this dreadful place to meet?" Sophie asked Vergil.

Fenrir took in their surroundings for the first time, letting his focus shift from the arresting man to the room. It was well-kept with fresh mortar and stones in some places. The lighting too was good, nary a shadow to be found, but the various furnishings were mostly draped in cloth more for shielding from inquisitive eyes than protection from the elements.

"It's private," Vergil said, "and we have private matters to discuss. Since everyone has arrived, let us begin."

Vergil advanced to a table set against the wall. He leaned against it, facing his guests.

"You all know a rough approximation of the expedition that I have planned," he said. "You will be going into the Old World to find and interact with a relic there. You will know just what each of your roles demands, nothing more. If you have qualms with that, you are free to step away, but before I go any further, I require each of you to set your name to this contract."

Vergil tapped the parchment laid out on the table behind him. An ink well and pen sat adjacent.

"It's a binding agreement between you and the Church. Feel

free to read the actual words, but to summarize, it simply says that you release the Church of all liability should you come to harm. It also states that you will keep anything you see, any truths you learn, to yourself. To do otherwise is to risk imprisonment, up to and including execution. Once you sign your name, you will have no choice but to go on the expedition. Understood?"

There was a shifting and restlessness to the movements of the others. Fenrir was perfectly still, as was Sophie. She had no choice but to go, and if she went, he did too.

"Before everyone makes a decision," Sophie said, "perhaps we can introduce ourselves to set our minds at ease with the knowledge that we stand with the best of the best here, and our expedition is no fool's errand?"

Vergil smiled and pushed himself away from the table. "That's a fine idea. Please, Lady Roshem, you begin."

Sophie nodded and smiled. "I'm Lady Sophie Roshem, head of a great family and a tier 2 surveyor for our Most-Holy Church of Impermanence. As my rank implies, I'm skilled in the theory and practice of containing distortions and dealing with the afflicted."

Sophie's eyes moved to Fenrir, and she nodded to him. He was caught off-guard.

"I'm Fenrir Mey," he said then dropped off, unsure of what to say and not say.

Sophie swooped in. "Fenrir is a former surveyor who was forced into an early retirement owing to complex Church politics. His skill surpasses my own, and his inclusion in the expedition is an invaluable asset."

Fenrir glanced at the others to gauge their reactions. There was a middle-aged woman with darker skin and eyeglasses who wore her hair in a tight bun. Her garb and look implied she might be an academic, but her physique clashed with that interpretation. Sculpted arms, square shoulders, a muscled neck. Her expression was reminiscent of a sphinx.

The boy beside her acted as her foil, his amber eyes wide and his mouth still forming an "o." He couldn't have been more than seventeen years of age with pale skin, ashen brown hair kept short, and a figure that was more limbs than anything else. The third and final companion lingered back against the furthest wall. He wore tattered robes with a hood shrouding his head and bathing his face in shadow.

"As for the others," Vergil said, gesturing to the middle-aged woman first.

She gave a curt bow to each of them in turn. "Dr. Leida Kristopherson. I work at the university—"

"Close-combat training," Sophie said.

Everyone looked at her in confusion.

"That's where I know you," Sophie said. "During my surveyor studies, you were a guest trainer. Apologies, I saw you in the bishop's study a few days ago and just couldn't place you."

"I see," Leida said. "Yes, I've lived a few different lives in my time, but I'm on this expedition in my academic capacity as an archaeologist."

"What a pleasant surprise that Dr. Kristopherson also happens to be a scholar who can hold her own," Vergil said. "She's well-versed in the ways of the Old World and the Bygones. However, she hasn't actually visited it, so Phelp here will assist with navigating that labyrinthian jungle of ruins."

The boy stepped forward and gave an overly formal bow. A low blood attempting to emulate a high blood, but even his garb gave him away, ill-fitted and worn. Fenrir softened to him. They were inverses of one another—a high blood living the life of a low blood and a low blood striving to be a high blood. Yet, they shared the plight of inhabiting worlds they didn't belong to.

"Does Phelp have a family name?" Sophie asked.

The boy threw a disarming smile. "It's just Phelp, my lady. I like to keep things simple and such."

"Phelp is a skilled cartographer," Vergil said. "Despite having had no formal education, he was able to pass the civic examination and is certified by Simetria to draw maps."

"And I've studied the Old World like no other," Phelp said. "It's a passion of mine, you might say."

Vergil turned his attention to the robed man lurking in the back. He waved a hand, and the man reluctantly stepped closer.

"Lastly, we have our practical expert on all things Old World," Vergil said. "The other half to compliment Dr. Kristopherson's theoretical knowledge."

"Theopold Cromford," the man said.

The name reverberated in Fenrir's ears and instigated a violent reaction. Before he even knew what he did, Fenrir rushed the man and had him pinned against the stone wall. His hood was knocked back in the process, and the visual cues reinforced the verbal ones. Fenrir knew this man and despised him with every fiber of his being.

Theopold gasped for air, the collision stealing it from his lungs. Sophie ran to the pair and pulled Fenrir back. Vergil stood between the two men, an arm pinned against each chest.

"Fenrir, stop this," Sophie shouted.

Her words brought him back to himself, and he arrested his struggles. Fenrir moved away, and Vergil's hand lost contact.

"If that man goes on this expedition," Fenrir said, "I do not." He pointed to the subject of his words thick with hate.

The look of the older man forced horrid memories to come crowding back. Fenrir's mind swam in misery.

Trevon was wailing and holding out his arm. Amilia inspected the cause of his distress. Her face lost a few shades of color. She retreated from the son she adored and gave Ashtin a blank look of disbelief when he came to her side. Ashtin glimpsed a foul movement on his son's arm. That in and out, that rise and fall, that torment of forever that had slithered its way into the sanctity of his home and embedded itself in his most precious creation. A distortion. Trevon, an afflicted.

It was a tasteless jest by fate. That his home, buffered by wards writ by his hand into the very walls, brimming with attuners, made a veritable bastion against the non-Euclidean, his home had become tainted with the curse of the Others. They must have been laughing at his misfortune and carelessness because, even in that moment, Ashtin had the clearness of mind to see his missteps. The only way distortion could have entered was through him. A tiny speck of detritus on his armor from a mercy killing the day before. Him the fool to have brought the very foulness into his sanctuary. Now, Trevon was paying the price.

A desperation and hunger to save the boy consumed Ashtin. He tossed aside his pledge to the Church in an instant. He bowed down in worship instead to his hubris. He would do the impossible and save his son. Not free. Not perform the requisite mercy killing. No, he, Ashtin Broodfell, so skilled and blessed and leagues above his peers, he would do what no other had done. He would cure an afflicted.

Weeks he spent trying every variation on every obscure ward and ritual. Trevon's cries and whimperings grew more frequent and strained. Amilia stood by in the doorway of that blighted attic room, her face an inert mask floating in the dust-choked air.

"I'm close," Ashtin said.

"He suffers," Amilia replied.

"I can save him. I can do this."

"This can't go on."

"I just need more time."

"It's torture," Amilia pleaded.

"I can save him," Ashtin shouted.

Amilia stared at Ashtin with hard eyes but eventually retreated, leaving him to combat an indomitable evil on his own.

The weeks stretched. The distortion grew. Trevon's wails faded. The pain was so intense and pervasive that it became the boy's world. His look was glazed and distant. When Trevon entered more lucid phases, he would sing in his high-pitched voice of the wonders of the world he glimpsed. A realm of impossibility. Of angles and planes and shapes and forms that could not be understood. Of colors beyond sight. Of sounds beyond hearing. Of an essence that tasted of something both sweet and bitter. The end was drawing near. The distortion crept to the boy's brain.

Ashtin was desperate. His grave crime was too far gone to admit. He had one last route to attempt, and it was one that put him squarely in treacherous territory. He would use synthetics, that most forbidden of relics treasured by the Others and banned by the Church. In his dealings with folk in the lower city, Ashtin had heard whispers of a cultist more brazen than others of his ilk. This one was no mere mindless husk. He was knowledgeable enough to venture into the Old World and retrieve scores of relics. Ashtin loosened tongues by slipping silver into palms, and soon enough, he had a name. Theopold.

And here he was again. Those same partly closed eyes stuck in a perpetual squint. That incessant licking of the lips. Older and more wrinkled than when they'd last met, but the cultist nonetheless.

Fenrir lifted a finger and directed it at Theopold, the movement more like a casting of a curse than a simple gesture.

"This man is not to be trusted," Fenrir said. "He's the one who turned me in."

Vergil cleared his throat and turned to Leida and Phelp, who both looked on in bafflement.

"Perhaps we should take a moment to sort out this matter," Vergil said. "Dr. Kristopherson, Phelp, would you be so kind as to wait upstairs with my colleague?"

Leida nodded and headed for the door. Phelp took a few seconds to process the request then trotted after the archaeologist. He looked over his shoulder every few steps.

Once the door to the cellar had closed, Vergil sighed and shook his head. "What a lovely little mess we find ourselves in."

"Let's have some clarification," Sophie said. "Fenrir, what is your history with Mr. Cromford?"

Fenrir grimaced and spat. He clenched his fists and ground his teeth. This flood of anger was new. In all the long years he'd spent bearing all manner of humiliations both in the penitentiary and as a low-blood toller, never had this righteousness gripped him so. He had been broken and shamed into submission, but one look at the man who betrayed him was enough to usurp the natural order that had become his norm.

"This man and I had an arrangement," Fenrir said. "He was to provide me with equipment that I would use to save my son from affliction. He sold me such tools at exorbitant prices, squeezed a small fortune out of a desperate, grieving father, then earned yet more coin by making my transgression known to the Church."

"That's not true," Theopold stuttered.

He was no longer cowering but stuck his chin out in defiance. Fenrir glared at him.

"So you never met this man before?" Vergil asked Theopold, pointing to Fenrir.

"I didn't say that," Theopold said. "He tells a partial truth."

Sophie put her hands on her hips and tapped her foot against the stone floor.

"Let's move past the riddles," she said. "What do you claim is true and what a lie?"

"I sold him relics," Theopold said, "but I didn't turn him in. Why would I? It's bad business getting your customers imprisoned."

Fenrir saw red and would have lunged at the cultist if Sophie didn't seem to anticipate him. She laid a hand on his shoulder, and the contact cooled his blood.

"Did it ever occur to you that another disagreed with your methods and turned you in?" Theopold asked.

"No one else knew," Fenrir said. "He's lying."

Vergil shook his head, moved to Fenrir, and led him aside by the arm.

"It seems we find ourselves in a pickle," Vergil said, "as a low blood might put it." The bishop lowered his voice to a whisper and talked into Fenrir's ear. "See, the expedition needs the two of you. The other ones outside, I could find suitable alternatives for, if they decide not to join, but you and Theopold are essential. There are no others to fill your respective shoes, so I can't simply scrounge up another heretic more to your tastes."

Fenrir went to interrupt, but Vergil squeezed the arm still in his grip until it radiated pain. He'd found some kind of pressure point on Fenrir and was wielding it to great effect.

"But how about this?" Vergil said. "You put your hatred of him aside, suffer his presence for the duration of the expedition, then after you all have done what needs to be done and his expertise is no longer needed, you can enact your revenge."

Vergil released Fenrir's arm and watched him closely. Was this the kind of man he was allying himself with? One who tossed lives around like playthings? But the offering Vergil held out was tempting, and what choice did Fenrir have? He had promised Sophie he would protect her. Theopold or not.

"Fine," Fenrir said. "I'll do it."

Vergil grinned, the dimples that appeared contrasting with that dark side lurking.

"Trust me," Vergil whispered again in Fenrir's ear, "it'll be all the sweeter when you finally get to plunge a knife in and watch the light fade from his shifty little eyes."

Vergil made his cruelty and violence known almost as a taunt or warning. Then, he turned back to Sophie and clapped his hands.

"Very well, everything is sorted," he said. "Now, let's invite the others back in and get everyone to set their names to the parchment. Afterward, we can dig a bit more into the details of this most sacred mission."

Fenrir watched Vergil after that. As the others scrawled their names in ink, as Phelp used the maps he'd brought and explained his proposed route, as Leida and Theopold chimed in with their assessments of where their goal might be, as Sophie explained the threats they were likely to encounter and ways for combating both distortions and the afflicted, as all these happened, Fenrir kept his eyes almost leashed to Vergil. He studied how he moved, reacted, gestured, and, most significantly, how he hid himself so effortlessly.

Did Sophie really know the man she was tied to? He suspected not because if she had glimpsed the vileness so painstakingly obscured by fine words and elegance, she would never have dared defy him as she had by laying with Fenrir. Or even worse, mulled escaping his grip altogether. It would be a herculean effort, her breaking free from Vergil, maybe even rivaling their expedition into the Old World. But what could Fenrir do? He had promised to aid Sophie in the Old World and after. Let Vergil think Fenrir was just another fly caught in his elaborate web. Vergil's arrogance would be his undoing. Just as it had been Ashtin's.

OLD WORLD

"Here is the precious relic," Vergil said.

He held the diskette in his palms like an offering. Sophie gazed down at it. So small and unassuming, and yet this was the thing that she'd been waiting for. It would free her from her distortion, put her life back in her own hands.

They were alone in Vergil's study at the Church, the expedition set to start in short order. But first there was this relic to pass off and their goodbyes to say. In private. Away from prying eyes. Sophie reached out and grabbed hold of the diskette. She treated it with the care befitting its holy role and stowed it in an inner pocket of her pack.

"Theopold will know what to do with it," Vergil said. "Ensure that he survives, at least until you find the console, but don't let him touch the relic until then."

"Yes, yes, I know," Sophie said. "He's a heretic and not to be trusted."

Vergil frowned.

"I'm not taking this lightly, if that's your concern," Sophie added, "but you're repeating yourself unnecessarily, my dear. I hear all you say. My ears are wide open in these pivotal moments."

"Would that I could go with you."

Vergil cradled Sophie's face in his reinforced glyph gloves. He touched his fingers to his lips then hers. A kiss by proxy. Even now, it was all he would give. Her about to face the hell that was the Old World, and him cowering in fear of her distortion. So unlike Fenrir.

There was no point in delaying the inevitable. Vergil took Sophie's hand in his and led her to the door. Once outside, visible to all again, their hands were their own. He was a bishop and she a surveyor. They walked the hallowed halls of the Church, stained glass throwing colors along their path, incense and a droning hum hanging in the air. Sophie let her feet take her on a route ingrained in her soles. First, through the central hall, where the Archbishop conducted the thrice daily rituals, the enormous chalk board he employed being cleaned in preparation for the next tolling of the bell. Sophie moved through an arched opening set in the rear of the hall, which granted access to the rooms reserved for her kind. Spaces for the mind and the body of the surveyor. Tomes in the former. Polearms and leather in the latter.

Vergil waited while Sophie retrieved her voulge and small tools that she affixed to her belt. She already wore her armor, but to face the horrors of the Old World, she would need more than simple leather. She moved to a chest with a plaque that bore her name, used a key to open it, then pulled out a beaked mask and goggles tinted with dark glass. Both had been specially fitted to be flush with the geometry of her face. They would protect her from the sights and smells of the afflicted. She'd rarely had to make use of them in her routine surveyor tasks, the afflicted she dealt with being newly affected by distortions. It was only those who had lived long years with the non-Euclidean that were of concern. Those could be nightmares to behold, and any they encountered in the Old World were likely to be veritable horrors. Sophie stored both protective devices in her pack, already overflowing with food and bedding. There was no knowing just how long the expedition would take, but several days was a conservative estimate.

Now that she was properly fitted for the expedition, Sophie was ready to join the others. Vergil led her to where they waited, at a junction in a narrow and dark set of corridors deep in the Church's bowels. Nicolus was there, torch in hand, along with Fenrir, Leida, Phelp, and Theopold. The others were prepared, packs on their backs, weapons or tools in hand, faces set and stern. Vergil took Nicolus's torch then beckoned all to follow. Sophie lingered in the rear, where Fenrir plodded along. He glanced at her and nodded.

They'd shared what could have been their last night together. It had been a melancholic thing. Pain interspersed with pleasure made all the sweeter by the fact that it might never come to pass again. Sophie had held back any outward signs of grief. But even with dry eyes, she knew that Fenrir saw her anguish. They'd lain together that morning on his cot, arms wrapped tightly around one another. She'd pressed her face into his chest and tried to soak in the essence of him. She needed the scent ingrained in her memory. It might be all she could have of him moving forward.

After many more minutes of narrowing halls and stairwell after stairwell, they reached their destination. A round room with an arched opening and a vaulted ceiling, far more spacious than anything they'd seen in several thousand steps. Vergil touched his torch to sconces arranged along the dark gray stone walls. They stood at a threshold. The opening they'd come through on one side and a massive door etched with faded markings on the other. Nothing hinted at the true purpose of this place, and that was what the Church wanted. No one was allowed to descend into the Old World, and what better way to discourage the practice than making the few entrances unremarkable and obscure?

Sophie had never been to this place. She'd never even gotten so close to the ruins that slept below Simetria. A kind of rush surged through her at the thought of what came next. She gripped her voulge and moved ahead of her companions. Only Vergil stood between her and the door.

"This is your way into the Old World," he said. "It's one of the few that's still accessible, and the one mostly thoroughly mapped, to a point."

Vergil nodded to Phelp, who held a thick roll of parchment bound in leather under one arm. Sophie prayed that the boy was as skilled a navigator and cartographer as Vergil claimed.

"I'll unbar the lock, then you're free to enter," Vergil said. "But we can't leave the way open, per Church ordinance. To ensure you can return, Nicolus has graciously offered to stand watch. He'll camp here until then."

What would happen if they didn't return, if distortions or the afflicted got to them? How long would Nicolus wait? How long would Vergil grieve for her?

"Three loud taps on the door," Nicolus said. "That's how I'll know it's you and not another."

He demonstrated the rhythm he would listen for.

"I wish you all the best of luck on your most holy endeavor," Vergil said. "The Rot of the Link protect you. The Hand of the Lady guide you."

Vergil gave the sign of the Lady. Phelp signed it back. Leida, Fenrir, and Sophie nodded. Only Theopold grimaced, as expected of a heretic. He didn't believe in the Church's teachings. He cursed Saint Marcos and the Lady and the Rot of the Link because, to a cultist like Theopold, those only served to sever him from his source of worship—the Others. But Sophie took care not to show her distaste for the man. He was essential to their mission, after all. Only Theopold knew what to do with the diskette. It was of the Old World, and knowledge of its workings, like so much from that time, had been lost with the Cleansing of the Synthetic.

Vergil pulled a metal key from his robes, inserted it into a large lock affixed to a bar on the door, and granted them access. As he and Nicolus pushed, the massive slabs of the door groaned on their decaying hinges. The air that issued forth was stale and musky. The scent of the old. Of the still. Of that blessed rot.

But if so blessed, why did it mingle so closely with that which was most foul—distortions and the afflicted? So much of the Church's teachings were paradoxes like this. The clergyfolk claimed this duality was a sign of the divine, and that only the most learned could understand why the rot would associate itself with both sides.

After the gust of air had passed, they were free to take that first step into the unknown. Sophie led. This was her expedition, and whether her companions knew it or not, they faced danger for her. They walked through, one by one. Sophie, Phelp, Theopold, Leida, then Fenrir. Once they were all past the threshold, Vergil and Nicolus pushed the doors back into place. The light and sound and air were cut off. They were alone in the Old World.

Leida and Theopold carried torches so that the surveyors' hands would be free to make use of their weapons and Phelp's for referencing the maps he carried. Sophie turned back towards the others. They formed an arc with her as their center. The wavering flames of their light sources made their faces look grotesque. Even Fenrir was nigh unrecognizable in the foul airs of the Old World.

"Prepare yourselves," Sophie said.

She set her pack on the ground, pulled out her mask and goggles, and hung them around her neck. Fenrir did likewise.

"What are those for?" Phelp asked.

"To protect against the afflicted," Sophie said.

"Don't we need them too?" Phelp asked.

Sophie smirked at his ignorance. Here they were, living in a world constantly threatened by distortions, and yet so actually knew anything about their greatest nemesis. It was easier to pretend distortions didn't exist and live your life in careless bliss, at least until the non-Euclidean encroached and forced itself forefront into your mind.

She understood the mentality. You couldn't constantly be on guard. That tension and perpetual anxiety would wear a soul down, grind it into nothingness, leave a shadow of a person in its wake. But there was a balance that could be achieved, where you knew enough to protect yourself but weren't overburdened with the bane of existence. That was the line surveyors walked. Perhaps it was asking too much for the average Simetrian to emulate them.

"If you're close enough to need these," Fenrir said, pointing to his mask and goggles, "your fate is already sealed."

"If we encounter afflicted, keep your distance," Sophie said. "That's all you can do."

Phelp gripped his maps tightly.

"Fret not," Leida said. "We have two highly skilled surveyors protecting us."

"We all have our roles to play," Sophie said. "Focus on the task you were assigned, and we'll fare well enough."

She wanted to believe her own words, was desperate to, but Sophie had no concept of just what it was they were attempting. Was it the suicide that Fenrir had called it? Or was there a chance of success? She had to hope it was the latter. Why else would Vergil have suggested it? Why else would a cultist, who alone knew this world and its dangers, have joined them?

Sophie hoisted her pack and moved to Phelp's side.

"You know where to take us?" she asked.

Phelp nodded. They had gone over his maps for hours already, but now that they were in danger's way, she had to make sure Phelp could keep his wits about him.

"Like I said to the bishop," Phelp said, "I have good confidence in my maps up to a point. After that, it'll be some guesswork and making sketches as we go."

"Let's go forth," Sophie said. "The longer we linger in any one place, the more likely we are to attract attention."

They set off, arranged as they'd entered. It was the marching order they'd settled on. Sophie watching their front, Fenrir their back, Phelp whispering guidance on their route, Leida and Theopold lighting their way. Their path was nothing remarkable at first, just less well-hewn stone tunnels, still too tight and cramped, damp, chill. It went this way for the first hour of their trek. There were only a few points on their path that diverged, but Phelp's maps were clear on the correct route to take. They stayed alert, but their caution was wasted. Nothing of note occurred. Even distortions were lacking. Sophie didn't feel that tug of unease that so characterized their presence. Had the stories of the Old World been exaggerated?

The second hour into their trek, the tunnels widened. Stray bits of light leaked from cracks overhead. Water trickled. The air freshened ever so slightly, then they stumbled into an open space. It was low-ceilinged but wide with a sizable body of water dominating the area. Sophie instructed the others to wait with Fenrir while she and Theopold inched ahead to scout.

They came to a narrowing of the path, wherein half of it plunged into the black water. Sophie didn't like the feel of it. Too still, too silent. The trickling was gone now. Even the echoes of their footfalls got caught in a too-thick air. She found it hard to catch her breath, and each movement was like wading through molasses. She glanced at Theopold.

"What is this feeling?" she asked.

"A miasma of some kind?" he said. "From distortions?"

"It's not distortions. This feels different."

"You can say that without a detector?"

"I can," she said.

There was no use hiding her abilities on this harrowing journey. She'd decided that ahead of time. Both she and Fenrir had agreed to make use of their unique talents openly. They couldn't afford to waste time and energy keeping it secret.

"Should we press on?" Theopold asked.

Sophie had to exercise extreme caution. No one else would be coming down to save them. Vergil had never admitted it, but Sophie saw the truth clearly enough. The secrecy of their meetings, the lack of fanfare as they set off, the use of experts who had little to no connection to the Church. Vergil was operating outside the Church's blessing on this expedition of theirs. He couldn't have risked them denying his request and damning Sophie's one chance at a cure.

"We'll go back to the others and explain what we found," she said. "Maybe Phelp will have an alternate route."

Phelp sat cross-legged on the ground and laid a map across his lap. Leida leaned in to provide light. Fenrir kept his eyes trained on their surroundings, while Sophie and Theopold explained what they'd encountered.

"Miasma?" Leida said.

"A pocket of foul air," Theopold said. "There are all manner of relics with noxious gases trapped inside."

"But we're nowhere near signs of civilization," Leida said. "What relic would be emitting such vapors?"

Theopold pointed to the black waters not three steps distant. "Something submerged. You can never anticipate when you're near a relic. Signs of civilization or no."

"Well, Phelp," Sophie said, "do you see a way around this pool?"

Phelp used a glass eyepiece to investigate the finer details of his map. While he pondered their options, his tongue peeked out from between his pursed lips.

"There's one," he said, "but it would set us back a few hours at least."

"We're not in a race," Sophie said. "It's better to be cautious, especially while we adjust to the environment down here. Take us this other way."

Phelp tucked his eyepiece in his vest pocket, rolled up his map, and jumped from the ground. The lot of them were back to wandering through curving corridors. This went on for what seemed like thrice as long as before, then the hall opened into a cavern. They all gaped at the sudden change. There was natural light, but it didn't emanate from shafts overhead. It was an eerie pale glow that came from a thick growth of fungi. The irregular walls were covered by a mat of them, a plethora of hues—blues and purples and greens and browns—all soft and muted. Larger ones, more akin to the size of shrubs, extended from the ground with caps as wide as three hands and gills as thick as fingers. They were everywhere, covering nearly every surface in an area the size of a modest chapel. This felt like a place of worship in other ways too—a ceiling stretching impossibly high, rhythmic dripping of water reminiscent of a distant hymn.

"Such blessed rot," Phelp said.

Sophie wasn't religious. Her role as a surveyor was mostly born from necessity. Yet even she could feel a righteousness saturating this place. This was where they would camp. She checked her pocket watch. They'd only trekked for four hours thus far, but time in the world above was a foreign thing already.

"We stop here for the next several hours," she said.

The others turned and looked at her in confusion.

"We're making camp already?" Leida asked.

"We're taking rest," Sophie said. "Understand that your usual sleep-wake cycle is a thing of the past whilst we're in these depths. We rest when we can. We eat when we can. If we find a safe space, we make use of it. It could be days before we find another such as this."

"The longer we linger, the more likely we are to attract attention," Theopold said, harkening to her words from earlier.

Sophie let her pack fall to the ground and put her hands on her hips. "I wasn't aware that this was a debate. Last I heard, I was leading this expedition."

"What says the other surveyor?" Phelp asked.

Sophie clenched her jaw. The audacity of the boy to question her judgment. Fenrir had been eyeing their surroundings. At mention of him, he half turned towards the others. He took his pack off and dropped it.

"This surveyor serves at the pleasure of Surveyor Sophie," he said. "If she says we take rest, then we take rest. Don't you dare ask my opinion over hers again."

Phelp ducked his head. The others fell in line after that. Sophie tried not to dwell on the injustices leveled at her, but the sickening pit in her stomach lingered. Why was her life always like this? Being a surveyor had made no difference. Becoming the head of her family, too, didn't matter overmuch. She was simply viewed as a placeholder. Her primary role in life was to produce a male heir who would proceed to take what had been hers as his own. As long as she had the distortion, that wasn't a possibility, but after it was gone, what then? She wouldn't accept the life that was waiting for her, the life Vergil wanted to force on her.

The others unloaded their packs, took food, laid down blankets, milled about. Sophie wandered over to Fenrir.

"How would you like to split the watch?" she asked.

"However you prefer," he said. "This is your expedition, after all."

"The others seem to forget that."

"Try not to take it personally. You're as much of an unknown to them as they are to you. It's hard to trust a stranger, and this place is brimming with dangers. They're on edge."

Sophie ripped the tricorn from her head. It was constraining. The place, their situation, all of it, was increasingly claustrophobic. She wanted to hold Fenrir instead of stand apart and act distant and aloof.

"We should converse with them," he said. "Build a sense of comradery."

"Even the cultist?" she asked.

Fenrir frowned, and a muscle in his neck twitched. He took his hat off too and set it on his pack. "I'll leave that to you, and I'll take the first watch."

Sophie went to Leida first. The archaeologist had a notepad and graphite stick out and was scribbling away. Sophie sat down across from her on a larger stone in one of the few areas not covered by fungal growth. Leida glanced up, put her writing utensil between the pages, and closed her notepad.

"Yes?" she asked.

The interaction felt forced. Sophie despised these surface-level exchanges that precipitated more meaningful ones, but Fenrir was right. She needed to connect with these people. They could be down here for many days yet and would likely face hardships together. Sophie had to ensure they were a cohesive whole. That was the burden of leadership.

"Are you taking notes on this place?" Sophie asked.

"On what we've encountered thus far, yes," Leida said, "although my interests lie in the more human-centric aspects of the Old World. A pool of water and a cave of fungi are hardly fascinating to me."

This woman was an enigma to Sophie. She hadn't had

much time to dwell on it, but with Leida now sitting in front of her, the oddness of her history came forefront to Sophie's mind.

"You work at the university now?" Sophie asked.

"That's right."

Sophie didn't know much of the place except that it mostly existed to distract Simetrians that would otherwise devote their time and effort to causing trouble for the Church. The professors taught the more intellectual high bloods who then went on to become professors themselves. It was a closed system that only served to sustain itself. Worse still, it operated at the pleasure of the Church, which meant any meaningful findings about the past would be buried.

"But you used to offer lessons in close-quarters combat," Sophie said. "How on earth did you end up as a scholar?"

Leida placed her notepad on the ground next to her and squinted at Sophie. She had an interesting face. Square and harsh. Utterly unfeminine but appealing in its inherent strength.

"I was born a low blood," Leida said. "I learned many skills in the lower city. I did what I had to do to get by, but I loved learning and found my way to the university, thanks to the priest at the chapel my family frequented. I went to the university, distinguished myself, was offered a position on completing my studies, and work there now."

"How did Bishop Holdsworth settle on you for the expedition?"

"I'm well known amongst my peers for my work on the Old World. I suppose he found me through word-of-mouth, but you'd have to ask the man yourself. Now, if we're done with the interrogation?"

"Interrogation? Heavens, I was just trying to learn more about you."

Leida stifled a sigh and tapped her fingers against her knee. She was using hostility as a shield. It wouldn't work on Sophie, however. In fact, it simply told Sophie that Leida had a secret to hide, and Sophie was so very fond of unearthing secrets. Her interest in the woman was only heightened.

"In truth, I have scores more questions for you," Sophie said. "For instance, why go on this perilous journey when you seem to have such a lovely life waiting in the upper city?"

Leida smiled without her eyes. "Why, for the sense of adventure, of course. My days are filled with reading and lecturing. It's safe but tedious." Leida paused, watching Sophie closely. "Or something like that. Now, if you don't mind, Surveyor Sophie, I'd like to take the rest that you suggested. Idle chit-chat doesn't qualify as that for me."

Leida picked up her notepad, opened it, and resumed writing. There was no use in pestering the woman further. Sophie rose and glanced around. Fenrir stood on watch. Phelp was already curled in his blanket. Theopold lingered in the shadows. She'd leave the boy for Fenrir to talk with once he was awake. Theopold was her obligation. Sophie approached the heretic and forced her lips into a smile.

"It's not safe to be on the outskirts of the camp," Sophie said. "It makes Fenrir's and my job more difficult."

Theopold had his back to her. At the sound of her voice, he fumbled with something. When he turned around, there was a trace of an indentation set between his eyebrows, circular and no larger than a pinky nail, like something sharp had been there and left a ghost of itself. Theopold clasped his hands behind his back and nodded to her.

"Your words ring true," Theopold said. "But the other surveyor poses a risk of his own to my person, such that I'm forced to weigh the dangers against one another. Which is worse? The non-Euclidean or a surveyor seething with hatred towards my person?"

"Fenrir won't harm you," Sophie said. "He's given his word."

"As he gave his word to the Church before betraying them?" The old man grinned, exposing a haphazard set of teeth.

"I thought you'd appreciate anyone working against the Church, given your own allegiances," Sophie said, "which does raise the question, why are you helping the Church with this expedition?"

Theopold stepped out of the shadows and closer to Sophie. She had to force herself not to grimace or retreat. This man was a traitor to their people. He bowed down to that which would enslave them, the very source of the distortions in the first place—the Others. She could never understand heretics like him. Yes, there was much that was wrong with the Church, but the one thing the Church had gotten right was ousting those foul creatures. If Theopold and his kind had their way, they would welcome the Others back with open arms.

"Even a heretic like me would help the Church if it meant stopping the distortions," Theopold said.

So Vergil had told him the goal of their expedition then. But of course he had. Theopold had to know their aim. His role alone required it.

"But the distortions are a gift from your lords and masters," Sophie said. "Would you reject their oh-so-blessed offering?"

She couldn't avoid making this one jab at him and his hypocrisy. And yet, despite her words, Theopold's smile didn't waver.

"Oh, child," he said, "you have so much to learn."

Theopold brushed past her and moved towards the others. He found an open area on the ground, unfurled his mat, and laid on it facing the ceiling, hands with fingers intertwined and resting on his stomach, eyes wide open, lips forming inaudible words in an endless train. The only one Sophie could make out by sight was "link." He prayed to it, that severed string that once tethered their world to the one the Others hailed from. To the Church of Impermanence, the Rot of the Link was holy. To heretics like Theopold, the Link was the blessed thing and the Rot most foul.

MEMO

Recipients: employees@list.server.TheLink.co.uk

Subject: *PLEASE READ* Increase in Malicious Activities at the Birmingham Link Node

==

Dear Employees,

We have received troubling reports that suggest a heightened risk of malicious attacks directed at our Link Node. Anti-Link activity has spiked in the Digisphere within the past week, and our node is the locus of the efforts of bad actors.

If you receive a suspicious email, do NOT open any attachments. Do NOT reply to the sender. Immediately flag the email and inform your supervisor. The methods of bad actors have become remarkably sophisticated in recent weeks. They have been particularly adept at phishing campaigns. The data breaches from last month appear to have been perpetrated by the same individuals, so be aware that even your personal accounts may be targeted.

We will be implementing new security protocols, and we ask for your patience. Understand that your workflow may be interrupted, but the stability of the Link is of paramount importance. It supersedes all other duties in the company.

We sometimes forget the incredible significance of the work we do. Let this serve as a reminder that we are the custodians of the Link to the alfom. We must act accordingly and treat our work with the care and attention it necessitates.

Best Regards,
Greg West
CISO The Link, PLC

MEETING OF BISHOPS

"Right this way, Bishop Holdsworth," the deacon said.

They had already climbed three flights of stairs, and Vergil was beyond winded. He cursed under his breath but outwardly smiled while dabbing his sweat-speckled brow with a handkerchief. Sophie's initials caught his eye, embroidered in a yellow-gold thread. Gifted to him back when he was a mere eighteen years of age and her sixteen. Somewhere deep below the city, she wandered the Old World. One day past, and already Vergil was impatient for her return. In the meantime, he had to act as though nothing was different, as though he wasn't about to change the very fabric of society.

"You can sort yourself on this landing, Sir Bishop," the deacon said.

They'd reached the top of the tower, one of the three that sat adjacent to the Church's massive dome. On top of it was that light that forever shone, the one synthetic they allowed, the one that told them the Rot of the Link held. Vergil smiled at the thought that soon, so soon, it would go out.

The deacon ducked through the arched opening and moved across the platform. Vergil hung back in the stairwell, swallowing air, gazing at the gray sky that threatened rain. Within minutes, the man ducked his head back in.

"The Archbishop will see you now," he said.

Vergil nodded and moved past the deacon onto the platform under an open sky heavy with dark clouds. So high above Simetria, Vergil almost felt as if he could reach up and touch the ominous clusters of vapor. He resisted the urge and instead walked solemnly along until he came to a cage-like structure and a man tending to the pigeons within it.

Vergil bowed, and as he rose, he eyed the Archbishop. He saw the man regularly from a distance, during his sermons, as he walked the halls of the Church, at the occasional bishops' meeting, but it had been many weeks since Vergil had stood so close to the man and scores more since they had talked in private. In that time, the Archbishop had aged. The tufts of his white hair were thinner. The dark brown eyes had sunken back further. The wrinkles were more deep set. Torrington wasn't a day over sixty-five, and yet he looked almost a decade older than that. The weight of Simetria on one's shoulders was a burden to be sure, but the Archbishop did more than oversee the city their Church resided in. Torrington was the head of the Church, which meant all the Churches in all of the known world.

"Your Eminence asked for my presence," Vergil said.

"Eminence is such a strange honorific, no?" Torrington asked. "It implies I emanate something, but I wonder what that would be. Empathy? Grace? Wisdom?"

Eminent or emanate, two decidedly different words. Torrington was the head of the Church, meant to be the wisest of all the bishops, and yet he didn't even grasp the basics of language. So emblematic of the Church at large. Still, it wouldn't serve any purpose for Vergil to correct his superior.

"Perhaps all of the above?" he suggested.

Torrington smiled and stroked the head of the pigeon he held. "You were always such an effective flatterer. Did the Church or your father teach you that?"

"Most likely both," Vergil said.

He clasped his hands behind his back and stood upright. He had no earthly idea why the Archbishop had asked for this meeting, but he suspected it was a bad sign. He was playing with fire using the relic and sending Sophie into the Old World, but he'd been careful. Painstakingly so. The only one who knew a shred of anything related to the expedition was Nicolus, and Vergil trusted the priest with his life. The carrot and the stick ensured that, and Nicolus reveled in both.

"It's a shame your father can't see what you've become," Torrington said. "He was always quite severe with you, but look at the fruits of his labors. To be a bishop so young. It makes me wonder what you would have from life in the coming years."

The Archbishop opened the cage and put the bird back inside. Then he pulled a sliver of paper from the folds in his robes and flattened it out using his fingers.

"I haven't mulled it overmuch," Vergil said.

"A wife? Children?"

"Of course."

Torrington clicked his tongue and shook his head. "Then you take a strange route for such things. Thirty years of age and not even courting. I've heard that, instead, you frequent a place where there are no marriage prospects."

The whorehouse. Vergil tried not to react to the reference. Someone was wagging their tongue about him and his private habits. It was a bad sign, but then again, if this was all this meeting was about, luck was on his side.

"Why waste your time?" Torrington asked. "Why not focus on that which is before you? Sophie Roshem perhaps?"

"You asked me here for gossip about my love life?" Vergil asked.

"I asked you here to talk about your future. Part of that is continuing your family line. This," Torrington held up the slip of paper, "is the other half. I've received word that Scalium is turning against us. Breaking away from the Church proper."

"They're mad," Vergil said. "They'll just go the way of Rotatia. None of us can survive on our own. We can only fight the non-Euclidean with harmonious unity."

Torrington smiled at the righteous words. "And yet their Senior Bishop is resolute. I could take the route of Archbishops before me—bring a lance of surveyors and visit Scalium. It would show my presence and make the point that I can and will march against them if need be. But I wonder, Bishop Holdsworth, would that be the tack you'd take if you were in my place?"

Vergil gave himself a few moments to think. It was always better to avoid answering right away, even if he knew what he would say in an instant. Being overeager gave the impression of recklessness and naivety.

"I wouldn't send anyone outside the city walls," Vergil said. "I wouldn't bother with anything so overt or dangerous to your Eminence or the surveyors."

"Then, what would you do?"

Vergil had to tread carefully. There was a fine line between cunning and ruthlessness, and he sometimes made the mistake of showing himself to be squarely situated in the latter.

"Perhaps attuners in Scalium are damaged," Vergil said. "Perhaps many of the detectors are faulty too. The clergyfolk there have been negligent in their duties. The surveyors too lax. From this carelessness, distortions spread. It would be a sign that the Lady had turned her back on the Senior Bishop and left Scalium at the mercy of the Others' advances."

"An interesting idea to be sure but far too sacrilegious to employ of course." The Archbishop stroked his chin.

"You know best, Eminence," Vergil said.

"It is good to hear you say that," Torrington replied. "But I wonder if you mean it or it's just another example of your effective, albeit empty, flattery."

Vergil frowned and gripped the hands still clasped behind his back.

"These pigeons are fascinating, are they not?" Torrington asked.

He turned to the cage and ran his fingers along the metal wires. The pigeons cooed and hopped closer to their master. They tilted their heads so that an eye of each was angled at Torrington. He smiled at them. Vergil wanted to ask what pigeons had to do with him, but he knew from experience that the Archbishop would eventually get to his point. In the meantime, he had to be patient and act the part of a star pupil. It was tedious.

"They can sense the Earth's magnetic field," Torrington said. "That is how they can fly so far and yet always make their way back home."

"A useful skill."

"But that in and of itself is useless. Without me to send them hither and thither, they'd lack purpose. Much like the clergyfolk."

Vergil held back a laugh because he knew exactly what Torrington implied. He saw it day after day without fail. How vacant and petty his fellows were. How their uselessness only served to weaken the Church. But he suspected Torrington didn't understand that a strong leader wasn't always enough. Sometimes, the rot encroaching on their sacred communion was not blessed. Sometimes it hinted that a fall was imminent.

"But not all the clergyfolk are so helpless," Torrington said. "Some can envision a better future. Even fewer have the skill to lead us there. I'd wager you are one of those rarities. Like me."

Torrington couldn't have been more wrong. The man was as obsolete as the clergyfolk he scorned. The fact that he didn't even see that made it all the more tragic.

"Such kind words that I hardly deserve," Vergil said.

"I don't use them lightly. I say them for a reason. You have a mind well-suited to be Archbishop."

The statement was a shock. Vergil's star was rising, but he never suspected that he was being considered for such a holy role at so young an age. For a fraction of a second, he debated if he hadn't made a mistake sending Sophie into the Old World with the relic.

"Your Eminence thinks far too highly of me," Vergil said, bowing and using the moment to recover.

"Well," Torrington said, "that's an interesting lead into what I really asked you here to discuss. I need you to reassure me that I don't, in fact, think better of you than you are."

Vergil waited for more. Which of the scores of his questionable activities or habits was the old man referring to?

"Troubling rumors have come to my ear," the Archbishop said. "Some claim you're associating with low bloods and, worse, a heretic. You're frequenting the Archive and Vault more than necessary. Is there any truth to these?"

Someone was most definitely watching him, taking note of who he met with and where he went. Of course they would. Vergil was growing more powerful and influential with each passing month, and the older bishops didn't take kindly to being overshadowed by a newcomer. Vergil knew how to get Torrington off his back with ease, and it had the added benefit of shoving the old fool's failings into his face.

"I've noted a troubling trend," Vergil said. "The distortions seem to be increasing. I was trying to determine if this was part of a larger pattern. That required me to talk with experts that the Church might not choose to associate with and to make use of the historic writings and objects in our hallowed Archive and Vault."

"I see."

"My investigations show that the distortions are indeed increasing and have been for a long time."

Torrington nodded and turned back to his birds. He grabbed some seed from a sack, tossed it into their cage, and whistled at them.

"It's a concerning find, is it not?" Vergil asked.

The Archbishop pulled his eyes away from the pigeons and back to Vergil. Exhaustion was writ on his face. Every crevasse seemed darker and deeper. The skin looked slack and pale. Blue veins shone through.

"It's as concerning as it's always been," Torrington said. "And yes, before you ask, the Church knows this and has for a long while."

Vergil feigned surprise. "And what are we doing to resolve this threat?"

"A problem for future generations," Torrington said, waving his hand.

"Perhaps if there was a way to stop the distortions?"

"There is none."

That was the lie that had broken Vergil's faith. A few strings of words in a weathered tome from the Archive undoing all the long years of his service to the Lady. Vergil knew whence the distortions came. And he knew how to undo them. The relic Sophie carried was the key, and even now, every step she took was bringing them closer to their collective deliverance.

"If the Others created the distortions, perhaps we could reason with them," Vergil said.

"To commune with the Others is to break the Rot of the Link. It's blasphemy. No, Bishop Holdsworth, don't be tempted by a seemingly simple solution. We must take the hard path, for it is what leads to salvation. Put these poisonous musings aside. Come back into the fold. Do that, and one day you'll be Archbishop."

Vergil smiled and nodded and ducked his head. He gave the sign of the Lady and turned away from Torrington. As he walked down the staircase, Vergil found that the meeting had only bolstered his resolve. He had made the right choice. The Church was in its death throes. It was nigh time for a change, and Vergil was only too eager to be the harbinger of a new age. Indeed, who better than he? If a fool like Marcos Frenwith had altered the course of history, why not someone many times his better? All that was left was for Sophie to save herself and, in the process, the rest of the world.

THE AFFLICTED

Fenrir didn't like the look of the place. It was too open and wide and dim. After spending the past two days in winding tunnels punctuated by the occasional cave, this vastness was unnerving. The party stood on the edge of a cliff and gazed down at the ruins of the Old World. They'd come across it suddenly. Even Phelp's maps had failed to predict the sights that met them. A ceiling that stretched up what seemed like leagues, so high that Fenrir almost thought he could spy vaporous clouds in the uppermost reaches. Then there was left to right and forward to back. The view was lost in the murkiness of the diffuse lighting from the fungi that flourished.

The scale was one thing, but the ruins themselves were another. Fenrir knew the Old World had been different, had been a place saturated with the synthetic, but he hadn't really pictured what that might translate to in terms of the city itself. Metal and stone and brick, which weren't entirely unexpected, but oh, the height and breadth of them. Whole blocks occupied by a single structure and that towering up to the ceiling itself. So massive. Even after all the long years since that world had ended and given way to theirs.

"How does it not collapse?" Phelp asked, pointing to the ceiling of the cavern. "I mean, Simetria lies above, doesn't she? So how come it doesn't all come crashing down into this cave?"

They looked to Leida, who had spent her life studying such mysteries.

"The Church entombed this place," she said, "and it loves its symbolism. It was a deliberate act to bury the old beneath the new. As for how, well, they still had the benefit of various tools of that time before the Cleansing of the Synthetic."

"But like, how did they make the ceiling solid?" Phelp asked.

Fenrir smiled at the boy's tenacity.

"We can talk about the marvels of the Old World another time," Sophie said. "Let's use this vantage point to make sense of where we're heading next. Phelp?"

While the boy fumbled with his maps, Fenrir moved to Sophie's side.

"What exactly are we looking for down there?" he asked. "I'm assuming you at least have some idea."

"A console," she said. "A very specific one that will allow us to retrieve information on a diskette I have."

"And that will tell us how to stop the distortions?"

"So Vergil believes."

Theopold was loitering nearby. He usually tended to avoid Fenrir as much as was possible in their small group, but for once, the cultist was inching closer.

"Theopold will know more, I suspect," Sophie said, noticing his encroachment, "given the console is why Vergil had him join us in the first place. Or do I misspeak?"

Theopold nodded, watching Fenrir through the corners of his eyes like an animal afraid a predator would pounce. "You speak a partial truth. It's not so much that the diskette contains information we wish to obtain, but rather it acts as a key to that which we seek."

"We?" Fenrir asked. "We aim to end the distortions, whereas your kind worships their makers. I don't see how our goals would align."

Sophie tapped Fenrir's arm, and it brought his blood down to a gentle simmer.

"The point is, we seek a console," Sophie said, "and to find it, we must scour the ruins."

"Scour?" Phelp asked. "See, I remember the bishop saying he'd narrow the options down a bit after our last meeting."

"A console will need to be fed," Sophie said, "and we can follow the trail of the lifeblood of synthetics."

"That's not entirely true," Leida said. "The system you speak of is unlikely to still be active after all these years."

"This console will be powered," Theopold said.

"It sounds to me like all we have to go on is that our prize is somewhere in a big swathe of buildings?" Phelp said, pointing to his collection of maps spread out on the ground.

A pendulum. That's what the boy reminded Fenrir of. He swung from elation to despair minute to minute. Young and filled to the brim with emotion. It brought Trevon to mind. If Fenrir's son was still alive, he would be about half the age of Phelp but still prone to those same turbulent episodes.

A rustling sounded, Theopold pulling a parchment from his robes. The cultist went to Phelp's side and tossed it in front of the boy. "Perhaps this will be of use."

Fenrir's eyes darted to Sophie, and he managed to catch a trace of annoyance before she wiped it clean from her face. So Vergil had kept secrets even from her, secrets he'd opted to share only with Theopold. Phelp unrolled the paper and used rocks to hold the edges down, prone as they were to curling up.

"What is it?" Phelp asked.

"It is of the Old World," Theopold said.

"I can't make sense of it," Phelp said. "It's like a map but unlike any I've laid eyes on."

The boy tilted his head from one side to another as if the change in perspective might infuse him with the insight he so sorely needed.

"Perhaps our esteemed archaeologist can decipher its contents," Theopold said.

Leida handed her torch off to Sophie then moved next to Phelp. She inspected the parchment, and her brow furrowed.

"It's for synthetics," she said. "A schematic of the network the Bygones used to commune."

"But that's long still now," Phelp said, "and if it doesn't work anymore, why would it be any use to us?"

"Think about it a moment," Theopold said. "Once upon a time, the console we seek was special and connected to scores of other such devices. This allows us to follow that trail, inert or not."

Phelp's eyes lit up. His frustration turned to excitement, and he started to compare his own map of the Old World with the one Theopold had provided. Leida and Theopold chimed in with suggestions, and as the minutes stretched, Fenrir became more fixated on the cultist. He knew far too much and had been entrusted by Vergil more than anyone else. There was some other aim to their expedition. There had to be, otherwise the cultist wouldn't be here. What did he care of distortions? Why would he risk life and limb to end them?

Fenrir moved close to Sophie and spoke in hushed tones. "What exactly did Vergil tell you about our mission?"

Sophie kept her eyes on the others and whispered back to Fenrir. "We have to take the diskette to this console, and Theopold will handle it from there."

"Theopold said the diskette was a key, but to what? How does Vergil know the things he does? The diskette, the console, this map of synthetics. Where does he find these objects and this knowledge?"

"He's a bishop," Sophie said. "He has access to everything the Church does."

"Why then didn't he share the whole truth with you? Why trust the cultist more?"

"My thoughts exactly."

"What have we gotten pulled into?"

Sophie extended a hand so that the back of hers touched his. Her pinky finger reached for Fenrir's, and he held it in turn. This was all they would have. This pale and paltry substitute at intimacy while an unknown future stared them down.

"There," Phelp said, jamming his finger onto the parchment. "That's it. It's got to be."

Sophie's hand slipped free of Fenrir's, and she moved over to their companions.

"Good," she said. "Now, find us a way down this cliff."

Phelp led them to a slope, too regular not to be man made. It felt as though it were stone, but it wasn't hewn from a solid piece nor composed of cobblestones. Some other kind of synthetic? Or a stone that wasn't true stone? As they descended towards this buried city, an unease crept up on Fenrir. When they came upon the first building, the distortion let itself be known. Sophie's rigid posture told him she sensed it too.

"Nobody move," she said, holding up her hand.

"Distortion," Fenrir said.

Leida, Theopold, and Phelp went stock still. Fenrir scanned their surroundings for any sign of roiling or disturbance, but the lighting was too irregular with the fire dancing wildly on Leida and Theopold's torches. The surveyors inched forward, honing in on the foul mote.

"We can't be bothered to contain it," Fenrir said. "We'd waste too much time doing so for every one we come across."

"We'll erect a basic ward," Sophie said. "If we do it together, it won't take more than a few minutes. We'll contain just enough to provide us with a path through the maze and make it easier to sense them. Right now, it's like a thousand little voices merging into a roar."

Sophie was right.

"Follow us," Sophie instructed the others, "but stay back a few paces."

Leida, Phelp, and Theopold trudged behind the two surveyors as they moved their heads this way and that.

"There," Fenrir said, pointing to an alcove in the building.

The structure was only a few stories tall, not unlike some of the houses in the upper city. It was made of stone, again like the houses of the well-to-do in Simetria, but these looked false somehow. Too similar, too smooth, too flush with what was meant to be mortar. Fenrir ran his hand along the stone. It was covered in a thin layer of dew but didn't feel as weathered as one might expect for the centuries it had sat entombed.

Sophie advanced, and he followed, honing in on their quarry. Once they were satisfied that they'd established the extent of the distortion, they pulled out their blessed chalk and began to scribble the most basic of all the wards. A triangle of equals with each side marked by a single tick and each vertex notated with a partial arc. All sides and angles symmetric and whole. They didn't have time to truly refine the ward and make it a thing of perfection, but it would do the job they required of it. Within seconds of finalizing their work, the unease from the distortion faded into a faint throb. Sophie smiled and nodded at Fenrir before dusting the chalk from her gloves.

"Onward then," she said.

They followed the street. Buildings of brick lined their way with sizable gaps in between. The petrified corpse of a tree implied greenery had once filled these spaces before the sunlight from above had been cut off. Now, they were empty pockets of stone or groves ripe with fungi. As they passed the buildings, Fenrir peered in through walls of windows, glass long shattered. He tried to guess what these places had been used for, but so much of the Bygones was a mystery. Like the strange carriages that sat alongside the road, with four wheels of synthetics but no space for a horse or man to pull from. Eventually, Phelp led them down a crumbling staircase that deposited them on a walkway along a dried canal.

"This isn't ideal," Fenrir said. "We only have two directions to make use of—forward and back."

"It also means we only have to watch those two directions," Sophie said.

Fenrir stayed in the rear while she took the lead. They passed under a bridge and encountered another distortion. The surveyors used the same basic triangle of equals ward to contain it. Fenrir felt the tugging and discomfort of distortions above them on all sides, but as they advanced, a flood of dread pulsed from one direction in particular. It was where they headed. He had to silence the screaming of his psyche telling him to "run run run."

Terror was a part of a surveyor's job, but Fenrir's familiarity with the sensation had long since faded over the years. And besides that, there was another concern that lingered in his subconscious and was now making itself known in his waking mind. The last afflicted that Fenrir had faced, the last he'd given a mercy killing had been Trevon. The hand gripping his fauchard trembled, and Fenrir squeezed it tight.

Two more distortions and another bridge. The buildings flanking the old canal rose in height. That awful unease steadily increased. The path hit a sharp bend to the left. On their right and across the canal, a marvel of a structure showed itself to them. It was battered by years and the elements—the colors faded, the glass shattered, cladding fallen off in chunks—but despite that, it had a beauty unlike anything Fenrir had ever seen. Its exterior was decorated with numerous geometric forms composed of squares. The most common manifestation of that exalted polygon was the symbol for addition. A holy sign.

A flood of foulness filled Fenrir. He whipped his head away from the architectural wonder and watched the bend in their path. A lumbering form emerged. It was humanoid but so far removed from its origin in all ways. Iridescent in color with lumps and bumps covering it. It moved in grotesque starts and stops, rolling forward then shooting growths outward to advance. It detected them, the whole mass going taut and a thousand eyes reflecting the torchlight.

Sophie was ready. She sprang forward and sliced the creature clean through. It howled in anguish, the sound a complicated mix of high and low frequencies. Sophie was close and took the brunt of the auditory attack. She shouted in pain and dropped her voulge to cover her ears. Fenrir gasped at the fatal error; to lose your polearm was akin to death.

He wasn't letting her go so easily. Even with ears aching, with the sound muted and distant, Fenrir rushed forward. The creature reintegrated itself and lifted a limb to strike Sophie down, but Fenrir was too fast for it. He severed the member from the main mass. Sophie recovered, retrieved her voulge, and joined Fenrir in the dance of a mercy killing. The two of them moved in concert, and within seconds, they reduced the afflicted to a pile of inert hand-sized pieces.

They gasped and wheezed and looked at one another. They smiled. Then, the torrent came. A wave of impending doom barreled towards them. Their eyes widened in horror. There was sloshing and groaning, sucking and yelping. Wet masses slapped the ancient stone of the path. Neither surveyor waited to behold what was bearing down on them. Fenrir pointed to the building with the geometric forms on its exterior. Sophie nodded and sprinted back to the others. A wooden pole extended part way over the dried canal, and she hopped across it to the other side. Leida, Phelp, and Theopold followed.

Fenrir went last and, after crossing, thrust his leg against the makeshift bridge with all the might he could muster. It shifted then tumbled down. Just as he moved to dive into the safety of the building, he caught a glimpse of the horde on their trail. It was bedlam. Even if he'd given himself the time to take in their pursuers, he wouldn't have been able to make sense of what he saw. These things had no beginning or end. A senseless mass of various appendages. Lidless eyes. Mouthless teeth. Handless claws. Heads and necks and flesh on flesh on flesh, all intertwined with those foulest of motes—innumerable distortions.

If Fenrir had given the afflicted more than the briefest of glances, he would have been undone. Instead, he threw himself inside, stumbled after the others, and fixed his mask and goggles in place with hands that wouldn't stop shaking. Sophie led the charge, taking only a moment to orient herself in the maze. They stood in a space enclosed on all sides but open to what was once the sky and now only the packed earth of the Old World's sarcophagus. Fenrir pointed to the complex array of crumbling staircases and walkways that stretched upward. Sophie seemed to take note of his mask and moved hers into place as she sprinted to the nearest means of ascent.

Fenrir tried not to think about how unsound the structure had to be after all these years of neglect. He forced himself to focus on the tangible. Each foot thudding against the cracked stone. The sweat trickling down his brow from the too hot mask. Hands still vibrating against the wood of his polearm. But no matter how hard he tried not to think, his thoughts jeered at him.

Where are you running to? You have nowhere to go.

Fenrir almost tripped over a chunk of cladding in one of the walkways, and for half a second, he wondered if those blessed Euclidean forms might shield them in some small way. One look down the central well of the building told him how wrong the Axioms of the Euclidean were. That mass of horrors moved unimpeded. In some cases, the afflicted even climbed on the very geometries they were meant to curse. No amount of wards would save them. They were doomed.

Fenrir stopped on a landing at the top of a narrow set of stairs. The perfect bottleneck. The party was about halfway up the structure, and he hoped that if he distracted the horde, the others could find a way out. The afflicted were unlikely to comprehend how many trespassers there were, what with their minds being all but overtaken by the non-Euclidean. What was a human form to them? Senseless and incomprehensible in their blessed geometries.

As the crawling mass of chaos approached, Fenrir's panic escalated, but when it should have reached a peak and forced him to abandon his post, a kind of calm washed over him. This was what he was meant to do. This was why he'd been spared from his execution. It had been a source of constant shame and loathing. Why had he been allowed to walk free after all he'd done wrong? What purpose did his freedom serve? No longer permitted to be a surveyor. Forced to exist as a toller. To what end? This second chance of his hadn't been a conscious choice made by another, but rather a random series of them that culminated in that vague but potent word. Fate.

Fenrir's hands stilled. His mind went quiet. He took a wide stance and waited for the afflicted. The first one rolled forward, seemingly oblivious to the threat that Fenrir represented. One upward slice split it clean in half. The two sides went limp and tumbled down the steps. The next afflicted vaulted over its wounded kin and shot a gnarled arm towards Fenrir's face. He side-stepped and liberated the creature's head from what only loosely passed as a body. The flood of afflicted abated a moment. They seemed to register that something was fighting back and dispatching their companions with ease. Fenrir didn't give them a chance to react. He tore down the steps, severing the writhing masses of afflicted struggling to reintegrate. Then, he charged the ones standing by in uncertainty.

It was the purge all over again. He was sucked in by the carnage. Of how a simple sweep of a hand through space could somehow end a life. Of how with each mercy killing he made, the unease lessened and let him breathe again. He was cleansing the world. He was saving them from the fate he hadn't saved Trevon from. The thought of his son, normally a form of paralysis, had the opposite effect in the heat of battle. Fenrir was spurred on with renewed frenzy. A savage beast, a whirlwind of gore, a focus of devastation. When he came to himself again, an arc of viscera coddled him. Beyond, a veritable mob of afflicted seemingly watched.

They parted in an undulating wave, and from that baffling movement, a more familiar form emerged. Strikingly humanoid. Asymmetric with odd growths on the face and neck and hip but human. Two eyes, a nose, and mouth. Jet black hair almost reaching to the ground. Dark skin with only a peppering of foul motes. Fenrir could even see that this had been a woman before her affliction.

"You are not meant to be here," she said in a whisper of echoes sounding just next to the ear. "You enter our domain. You dare strike one of us without cause. When we come for retribution, you persist in laying such waste."

She threw her hands out and scores of arms joined the primary ones to point at the gore on the ground. Fenrir was frozen. Afflicted weren't supposed to be aware, let alone capable of speech.

"Blood for blood," she said.

The afflicted lifted her countless arms, and on the hands were claws that could rend Fenrir in two. His fauchard was no match. This was the end.

"Stay your hand," Sophie said.

Fenrir glanced back in a panic. Why hadn't she run? Why was she wasting his sacrifice?

"I drew first blood," she said. "I'm to blame, not he."

Sophie descended the stairs until she reached Fenrir. She placed her free hand on his arm as she slipped past.

"Sophie, no," was all he could get out.

"I attacked," she said. "This is my expedition. The blame falls on me."

The afflicted woman's hands hovered in expectation. One swoop, and those claws would ravage Sophie's lovely form. Instead, they dropped.

"I sense likeness," the afflicted said. "A familiarity in you. A song of beauty and horror intertwined. A stillness. A being trapped in time. One of us."

"One of us," the other afflicted murmured. "One of us. Of us. Of us. Of us. Us. Us us us us usususususssssssssssssss—"

The afflicted woman raised a hand, and her fellows fell mute.

"You have a distortion," she said to Sophie.

"I do," Sophie said.

There was a suck of breath from behind Fenrir. A quick glance over the shoulder, and there were Theopold, Phelp, and Leida at the top of the stairs. Spectators to it all.

The afflicted woman moved closer. Halting step by step. Fenrir mirrored her advance. Sophie stood firm. They were within an arm's reach of one another now, and the true extent of the afflicted woman's condition was revealed. She was far gone. Even if she retained many of her human characteristics, she had to have been afflicted for years. Her skin was infused with distortions, and the deep lines set into her face told of her constant agony.

"We do not harm fellow afflicted," the creature said. "So Mother says."

"So Mother says," the afflicted mass repeated. "Mother says. Mother says. Says. Says. Says. Says. Sayssayssayssaysssssssssssss—"

Again, the afflicted woman raised her hand, and the creatures went silent.

"I am Mother," she said. "I say you come to no harm, and so it is. But lives were taken. The scales must be balanced."

"Balanced. Balanced. Balanced. Balanced. balancedbalanceddddddddddddd—"

Sophie removed her mask and goggles then laid her voulge on the ground.

"And so they will be," Sophie said. "That's why we're here. Allow us to continue our trek, and we will rid you of your distortions."

"You seek the Source?" Mother asked.

"The Source?"

Mother turned back to her horde, tossed a cluster of hands at them, and they dispersed. Within seconds, the afflicted were gone. The roar of fear shifted to a distant tugging, and Fenrir's frenzy abated.

"Follow," Mother said.

LINKROT VIRUS

"Are we really just going to trust an afflicted?" Phelp asked.

He was almost hanging onto Sophie's coattails with how close he followed behind. She couldn't blame the boy. She was equally as terrified as he, but she didn't dare let it show.

"She's not like a typical afflicted," Sophie said.

"Much like you," Leida said from behind.

Their normally linear train had turned into a haphazard cluster while they followed Mother. Everyone was on edge, suddenly having to trust a creature that was supposed to represent everything they loathed.

"You've really got a distortion?" Phelp asked.

"I do," Sophie said.

"I'd never have known. Does it hurt? Is it getting worse? When did you get it?"

Sophie waved her hand to stop his ceaseless string of questions. She needed to think. Finding an afflicted who was aware flew in the face of all the Church's teachings. Sophie watched the form in front of her. Mother moved like a human and not. She looked like them and not. She was between two end members, trapped in a kind of stasis. Much like Sophie.

"Are we going to this Source?" Sophie asked.

Mother plodded along for several steps before she seemed to register the question. She stopped and turned. The face that peered back was unnerving in its duality.

"First, rest," Mother said. "You are not prepared for the Source."

She turned and continued her slow and steady lurching with legs shrouded by tattered fabric and growths.

They all walked through the ruins. Skirting towering structures that threatened to crumble at the subtlest touch. Plunging through tunnels bored through solid rock. Scampering over the detritus of the Old World. The things Sophie saw, mysterious and incomprehensible, much of it made of synthetics. She'd known the Bygones had coveted the false and scorned the natural, but she'd never quite grasped just how all-consuming their fixation had been on that made by man.

The egotism. Narcissism. Hubris. They'd been so proud of themselves. They'd believed they had the Midas touch, but it hadn't been gold they'd turned their world to. Just rot. Everything they made, all they'd done, here it lay disintegrating with the eons that slipped by. Their descendants cursing them. Their names forgotten. Their memories unhonored. Fools. The lot of them. And would Simetria's own descendants do the same? Would the Church of Impermanence stand the test of time if they persisted in perpetuating the sad and tired repetition of humanity's folly—that lust for power and the lies it coated the tongue in?

An afflicted who was aware.

Mother stopped and pointed to a stone building that stood in their path. It wasn't nearly as tall as some of the other structures, but it felt massive somehow. Perhaps it was the spire set off to one side, tall and thin. Or the thick growths of moss on the roofing that contrasted with the red-brown of the stone. Or maybe the round clockface that was triple the height of any woman or man.

"St. Martin's," Mother said.

Sophie knew no saint who had borne that name.

"Who's Martin?" Phelp asked.

"The structure was named for him," Leida said. "It's a church."

"Looks a bit too asymmetric for that, no?" Phelp asked.

"The Bygones had their own religions," Leida said. "They knew nothing of the Axioms."

Fenrir came to Sophie's side and gazed up at the architectural wonder. His mouth hung open. She watched him, hoping to peel back the layers of stoicism he shielded himself with. He was rattled, more so than even her, as his shaking hands had implied while he cleaned the afflicted's detritus from his armor. But his sudden tendency to avoid her gaze stemmed from something other than shock. She checked that the others weren't looking in their direction then brushed her hand against his. He flinched.

"Are you alright?" she asked.

"Adrenaline," he said.

She pretended to believe the lie. It wasn't the time or place to push for more.

"You will take rest here," Mother said.

She lumbered around the side of the tower to a massive wooden door. It swung to as she approached, a wall of afflicted hovering beyond. Sophie's companions hesitated. She led by example and strode after Mother with her head held erect and her footfalls steady and solid. The afflicted retreated into the depths of the church, hiding amongst the shadows. Discomfort gripped Sophie. She would find no rest in a place this thick with distortions.

Still, Sophie followed Mother, who led them to the end of the long hall with a vaulted ceiling. It was reminiscent of the

Church and chapels Sophie was accustomed to but lacking in the holy symmetries. There was a pattern to the place. Mirror planes abounded. Rotation axes too were common. But the formulas that had been utilized in constructing it were not those approved by the Church. Too many lines and arches and flourishes that managed to blend together to weave a tapestry of wonder. There was a kind of beauty to the almost chaos.

Mother stopped at a table and lifted a jar filled to the brim with phosphorescent fungi. She pointed to the torches that Leida and Theopold gripped and tossed several hands at a bucket sitting near the base of a column. The torchbearers looked in confusion at Sophie. She leaned her voulge against a decrepit bench, moved to her companions, and grabbed the torches from their hands. She strode to the buckets that gave off pungent odors and plunged the torches into the liquid. The flames hissed as they died, and their corner of the church was bathed in a soft fungal glow.

"Better," Mother said. "Flame is too bright. Fast. Unsteady. No good for seeing distortions."

Sophie scanned their surroundings and detected multiple instances of the foul motes, but their immediate vicinity was safe.

"Sit," Mother said, pointing at the steps that led up to a platform.

Sophie complied, and her companions did likewise. They sat in a row, still uneasy but with the bulk of the initial shock wearing off. They hadn't died. They had somehow survived what should have been their final moments. Mother stood in front of her guests, and even from that vantage point, there were parts of her that were impossible to comprehend. Warped and roiling and breathing in and out. Sophie avoided fixating on them for fear of getting lost.

"I want to apologize for my actions," Sophie said. "I

didn't know that afflicted could be aware. The Church doesn't teach us surveyors that such a thing is even possible."

"We are all here and not," Mother said. "Some more present than others."

"You seem remarkably present," Sophie said.

"It comes at a cost."

"What do you mean?"

Mother sighed, but the sound shifted into a scream at its end.

"We are lulled by a song nestled in the non-Euclidean," Mother said, "but to give into the song is to lose oneself. To retain identity, we fight against the song, but it is perpetual pain. A difficult existence. You see?"

"Why not embrace a mercy killing to end your suffering?" Fenrir asked.

His voice quivered with each syllable. He sat next to Sophie, the tension radiating from him.

"No such thing," Mother said. "Afflicted do not die. Ever."

"But the dismemberment—"

"Does not end our suffering," Mother said.

Sophie's eyes shot to Fenrir's face, and she caught the moment the blood drained from it. Even his lips lacked color. She knew where his mind had gone, and why he looked like he'd been dealt a mortal blow. His son. When Fenrir had been Ashtin, he'd been forced to give his son a mercy killing. That alone had to have been brutal, but now to learn that the carnage served no purpose? That the pieces of his son languished in agony for all these long years? Sophie placed a hand on his, but he didn't seem to register the contact. His eyes were glazed over, staring into nothingness.

"How will you end the distortions?" Mother asked.

Sophie tore her attention away from Fenrir and back to the afflicted and their predicament.

"We have a relic that is said to be the key to stopping them. We just need to find the console the relic is designed to interact with. Could that be this Source you mentioned?"

"The distortions can only be ended by going to the Source," Mother said. "The Source of the Link and the Rot that befouls it."

"What does the Link have to do with this?"

Mother swayed then looked at Theopold. "This one knows. I can sense it."

The entirety of the party turned to the cultist. Even Fenrir had been brought out of his daze. Theopold smiled and licked his lips.

"That I do," he said.

"He's a heretic," Phelp said.

"A label," Mother replied. "Meaningless. He knows."

"What's she talking about, Mr. Cromford?" Sophie asked.

Theopold wiped the saliva from the corners of his mouth and groaned as he stood. He looked down at his companions and shook his head.

"You won't like to hear it," he said.

Sophie frowned, and he sighed.

"The Rot of the Link is the source of the distortions," Theopold said.

"Bollocks," Phelp said. "Everyone knows that the Others caused the distortions as punishment for us ousting them."

"That's a lie concocted by the Church," Theopold said. "The distortions come from the Rot of the Link itself, the Linkrot virus as the Bygones called it. Its sole purpose is to sever the Link between our world and other ones, between us and those you call the Others. The Link touches the primordial, the essence of reality, and any attempt to disrupt it goes against the very laws of nature. The Link is not an evil, but the Rot of the Link most certainly is. It rips space-time apart at the very seams. It wasn't meant to do this, of course, but it was an unfortunate side effect, one the Church knows about and chooses to keep secret."

"You're a bloody liar," Phelp shouted, jumping up and advancing on Theopold.

Sophie stepped in and blocked his path, her arms thrown out wide. Fenrir came to her side.

"I told you you wouldn't like it," Theopold said. "It was either bar the Others and live with the distortions or remove the distortions but let the Others back in. The Church made its decision."

"Liar, liar," Phelp shouted.

He rushed on the surveyors, but Fenrir grabbed him by the shoulders.

"Marcos was too drunk on his newfound power to give it up so readily," Theopold said. "The fool decided it was better to live with distortions, even though they become more numerous with time."

Phelp's shouts stopped, and he went still.

"Yes," Theopold said. "They will consume the world one day unless we destroy the Rot of the Link."

"He speaks truth," Mother said.

"Why do you think Bishop Holdsworth sent us here?" Theopold asked. "Do you think he didn't know all of this?"

"Why should we believe a heretic?" Phelp said.

Theopold smiled with such a look of pain that it softened even Sophie towards him.

"Do you think I was born a cultist? That I grew up worshipping the Others and cursing the Church? No, I was devout. I believed in the Lady and Saint Marcos and all the drivel the Church spouts. But then I stumbled on the truth, and it shattered my faith. Much like it seems to have done with Bishop Holdsworth."

Sophie's mind was chaos. She didn't want to see the reason in Theopold's words, but the connections taunted her. The distortions had appeared after the Rot of the Link had been established. The Church was adamant that there was no way to destroy the distortions, that they simply had to live with them. No scholar had found a solution after all these long years, but then Vergil stumbled on the relic. The secrecy surrounding their expedition. It wasn't sanctioned by the Church. Vergil had taken matters into his own hands. He was defying them. He'd done it for her. To rid her of her distortion.

"And who's to say the bishop knew?" Fenrir asked. "Just because he organized the expedition and gave us the relic? That's a stretch, and we only have your word to go on, a word that has proven to be useless in the past."

Fenrir quit his watch on Phelp, turned, and advanced on Theopold. Sophie moved between them.

"Fenrir," Sophie said.

"He's lied before. Are we truly willing to take him at his word now?"

Theopold placed a hand on Sophie's shoulder and nodded to her before stepping up to Fenrir. The two men stared at one another. One young and lithe in his surveyor gear. The other frail and stooped in his cultist robes.

"Don't make this personal," Theopold said. "It's much bigger than the two of us and our spat."

"This is about you and your lack of character."

Theopold shook his head and tisked. "Your hate is wasted on me, Sir Surveyor. Let's put this animosity to rest once and for all, shall we? It wasn't my tongue that wagged to reveal your crimes. It was a sweeter one, one that had touched your own scores of times, no doubt."

For the second time, Fenrir's face went pale. Sophie tried to match the words to the meaning that would yield such a reaction in Fenrir. Her mind ran through the possibilities, the permeations. The wife, Ashtin's wife. Such betrayal. Sophie expected Fenrir to deny it, to lash out at Theopold, but he moved back to the steps and crashed onto them. He buried his face in his hands. So it was true then. Even through his rage and searing hatred of Theopold, Fenrir saw the wisdom in the old man's words. Amilia Broodfell had reported him to the Church, not Theopold.

"I'm not lying about the distortions," Theopold said, "or about our mission. Bishop Holdsworth is very much aware of what it requires. The Linkrot virus must be removed."

"He speaks truth," Mother said, "and if you are to make good on your pledge, you must go to the Source. Destroy the Rot. End distortions. Free us."

"Free us. Free us. Free us. Us. Us. Us Us. Us. usususssssssssssssssssssss."

The afflicted that had been lingering in the shadows of the church came close and arranged themselves behind Mother. She let their hiss continue until it rang in their ears.

"Enough," Sophie shouted.

She dug in her pack and pulled the relic out. She held it aloft for all to see. The surface of the diskette shone in the fungal glow. The afflicted went silent.

"I will go and do what we came to do," she said. "Rot of the Link or no. I will end these distortions once and for all."

"A wise choice," Theopold said. "I will, of course, join you."

"As will we," Mother said.

"Will we. Will we. Will we. Will we. Will we. Willwewillwewillwewillwewewewewewewewewweeeeeeeeeee—"

"No," Phelp shouted.

He rushed over and grabbed Sophie's voulge from where she'd left it. He leveled it at the lot of them with wild eyes. Sophie knew that look. It was that of a mind set in stone. Phelp had made his choice, and he was going to face death before he'd back down.

"Phelp," she said, "be reasonable."

"I'm not going to let you do this," he screamed. "The Hand of the Lady will guide me."

"The boy is hysterical," Theopold said. "Don't try to approach him."

Sophie held her hand out to keep the others back as she inched closer. Phelp angled the polearm at her, and she froze.

"I will cut you down without hesitation," he said. "I'll kill you all if I have to."

Sophie glanced back to see if Fenrir was flanking the boy, but he still sat inert on the steps. He'd had too many revelations to bear. He was immobilized.

"Blessed is the Rot," Phelp said. "The Rot of the Link, the Rot of the body, the Rot of the world."

Phelp swiped the air between them, and Sophie sprang back. Then, he turned to the afflicted near at hand and cut the air between them. They howled and groaned and retreated.

"The Rot of the Link is freedom, freedom from the tyranny the Others would thrust upon us."

Mother stood firm, and her defiance fueled Phelp's madness. He gripped the polearm and moved toward her step by step.

"The Rot of the body is comfort, comfort in knowing we are free of affliction."

One swing, two, three, and he was within a polearm's length of her.

"Phelp, no," Sophie shouted.

Her eyes ran over their surroundings in search of Fenrir's fauchard, but it was propped up next to where her own had been. There was no way she could move to it without risking a swipe from Phelp.

"The Rot of the world is purity, purity of space and time saturated in the laws of the Universe."

There was nothing she could do. Phelp readied the voulge

for the blow that would make contact, but before he could start the arc that would bisect Mother, he gasped. The voulge clattered to the ground. The rattle of metal and the gurgle that sounded from his throat brought Fenrir back, and he was up and at Sophie's side in an instant. But it didn't matter. The deed had been done, and Phelp wouldn't be a threat to anyone anymore. The dagger embedded in his neck ensured that.

As Phelp slumped to the floor, his attacker was made visible. This was a whole woman, untouched by distortions. Leida. She'd skirted the action and pounced on Phelp from the shadows. But how? Leida looked down on the boy, choking on his own blood. Sophie recognized the look of one who had killed before. This hadn't been a desperate act; it had been calculated and executed by an expert.

Fenrir rushed past Sophie and scrambled to Phelp's side. He lifted the boy's head to his knee. Between spurts of blood, Phelp wheezed out the last of the prayer he'd started.

"Blessed is the Rot…for it signals…the…Euclidean… reigns…"

The prayer was finished, and Phelp went limp.

Fenrir turned his head and glared at Leida with loathing. "You didn't have to do that."

Leida pulled a cloth from her trousers and wiped the blood off her dagger. "Didn't I?"

Fenrir laid Phelp down and stood with clenched fists. "No, you didn't."

"Well, the boy wasn't going to back down, that much was clear," she said, "and it didn't seem like you were going to do anything except sit there frozen on the steps. I made a judgment call when no one else would. Better to strike him down before he reached the others, or would you rather him have touched them? Mine was a mercy killing. Maybe viewing it from that perspective will cool your blood."

She slipped the dagger into a hidden fold on her boot and stowed the bloodied rag in her pocket.

"Close-quarters combat," Sophie said.

"I have many skills," Leida replied. "I will use them to great effect to ensure the success of our mission."

Fenrir stepped forward. "The mission that includes stabbing a boy in the neck?"

"A young man, not boy," Leida said. "And yes, barring Surveyor Sophie Roshem, I was told to dispatch whoever stood in the way of the mission."

Sophie moved in close to Leida and Fenrir.

"Vergil tasked you with this?" she asked.

"Who else?" Leida said.

"And if I had stood in your way?" Sophie asked.

Leida smiled and shook her head. Speckles of Phelp's blood decorated her jawline.

"I suspect the good bishop knew you wouldn't cause any trouble," she said. "You two know one another quite well, do you not?"

Sophie grimaced but didn't reply outright. She glanced at Fenrir. His eyes were asking how she wanted to play this.

"I don't want you doing something like that again," Sophie said to Leida. "This is my expedition. I make the calls. No more death. Understood?"

Leida nodded and clasped her hands together. From assassin to academic in the blink of an eye. Sophie could almost believe she'd imagined the whole affair if it wasn't for Phelp's motionless body sitting in a growing pool of blood. She couldn't afford to get distracted. She didn't have the luxury of letting herself feel anything about Phelp's fate. Sophie looked again at Fenrir. He had already acquiesced to her decision, his fists loosened, his face veering back to that horror-struck mask he'd worn after Theopold's revelations.

"Some of us can be blinded by the Church's doctrine," Sophie said to Mother.

"You mean their lies," Theopold added.

"In any case," Sophie said, "the rest of us are in agreement on continuing our mission to find the console and go to this Source, correct?"

She glanced at her three remaining companions and avoided looking at the body that was Phelp. She had to project strength. Fenrir needed it. He was already migrating over to Phelp.

"Aren't we?" Sophie asked.

Theopold and Leida said their "yes," but Fenrir seemed to be lost in his own thoughts.

"Rest," Mother said. "The journey will be brief but arduous."

The afflicted sank back into the shadows, giving Sophie a reprieve from the tightness that their proximity brought. Theopold and Leida unpacked their bags, took food out, sat on their bedding. Sophie went to Fenrir. He was crashing; she could sense it.

"We can't leave him like this," Fenrir said, looking at Phelp.

"We can bring him back to the surface with us after we've finished what we came here to do."

Fenrir turned and watched Sophie through the corners of his eyes. "We? Do you really think Leida is going to let any of us but you get out of this alive?"

"I'll have my eye on her," Sophie said.

"We should cut her loose."

"No, that would only make it more difficult to keep a watch on her.

Fenrir looked again at Phelp then sighed. "Such a waste."

"If Phelp is the only one to die down here, we can count ourselves lucky."

Sophie placed a hand on Fenrir's shoulder, and he looked at her.

"Are you alright?" she asked. "Not just about him but about everything?"

A spasm of pain shot through Fenrir's face. "No, but I'll deal with it after we finish this."

"Or maybe you're hoping you won't have to deal with anything anymore?"

Fenrir's brow wrinkled.

"I know what that was back in that building when the afflicted rushed us," she said. "You didn't have to linger behind to cover for us. You wanted a showdown. A last hurrah before sacrificing yourself oh-so-courageously."

Fenrir's eyes ran from Sophie's.

"I don't want that," she said. "I don't need the man I love to die in glorious fashion for me."

"You asked me to protect you. That's why I'm here."

"I asked you to help me, and you dying would leave me a broken ruin. You have to survive. This isn't a debate, and you don't get a say. Besides, this is about so much more than me now. We're going to stop the distortions for everyone, including the afflicted, present and past."

She left the rest of what she ached to say unspoken, but the anguish writ on Fenrir's face meant he took her words as she'd intended. He needed to see this as the redemption he longed for. His son was still alive in a state of unimaginable agony. Reduced to chunks of flesh, perpetually writhing in their long-stilled grave. Fenrir had to do this for him. Not her. It was the push he needed because, with it, the cascade towards his unraveling was stopped and reversed. Fenrir had a purpose to sustain him, at least until they destroyed the Rot of the Link. After that?

"Also," Sophie added, "you said you would help me free myself from Vergil, remember? Knowing what we do now,

I guarantee you he has something in store for us when we reach the surface. I was a fool to think he would leave my choice to wed up to chance."

"What do you mean?" Fenrir asked.

"The moment we destroy the Rot of the Link, the light on the Church's dome will go out, and everyone in Simetria will know. Someone will have to take the blame."

"Me," Fenrir said.

"Or all of us."

THE SOURCE

The distortions tugged at Fenrir. A mass of them trailed behind and to his left and right. Only Mother's was set before him and, much further afield, a veritable hoard of them. The Source. He didn't know how he would react to the unease or if so many of the foul motes concentrated in one area would be more like a searing pain than a nagging discomfort. He tried not to anticipate what lay ahead. It was one step at a time for him now. Not dwelling in the past or brooding over a future that was wildly uncertain. He lived moment to moment. Now was all there was. They didn't have to worry about attacks or bother warding off distortions. Going in, they had Mother and her kin to guide them. Going out, well, that was the future, and Fenrir didn't waste time mulling over it anymore.

One footfall. Then another. The drip, drip, drip of water on crumbling stone streets. The rush of cold wind as they passed gaps in the disintegrating structures. Sophie's assured stride. Theopold's hurried shuffling. Leida's too smooth steps. Fenrir's mind jumped to Phelp before he forced it to the now. There was no Phelp anymore.

The only metric to count the passage of time came in

the growing presence of the distortions set before them. It was a yawning void that grew and grew until Fenrir's sense got muddled and confused. From a physical something to an audible roar. He winced and started to lag behind. Sophie must have taken note because at some point, he found her walking at his side.

"How are you feeling?" she asked.

"It's so strong," he said. "It's forcing itself into my head and crowding everything else out."

"I know."

"But it doesn't affect you the same as me?"

"I feel it growing more potent, but it's not painful. Is it for you?"

Fenrir tried to understand what it was he felt, but it was too much to comprehend. He didn't have the faculties to parse it out. He just put his free hand to his temples and rubbed.

"I don't know," he said, "but it's not pleasant."

"You don't have to go all the way," Sophie said. "It could be just me and Theopold."

"I'm going."

Sophie let the matter drop. She stayed by Fenrir's side for the rest of their trek. He focused on the now, but the distortions goaded him. He became feverish, his mind a blur, his thoughts an unending stream. It was hard to stay in the moment when it started to bleed into the before and the yet to come. There was Sophie matching his steps then it was Amilia. From the mold and dark and damp of the Old World to the overcast cobblestoned streets of Simetria. Red curls poking out from a surveyor cap to black ones fixed into braids. An empty hand to one filled with a smaller one. Trevon. Affliction. A mercy killing that was no mercy but torture. Undead by his hand. Buried in the dirt. Every second agony. Still alive, trapped in time, his little mind screaming out for release. Too much. Too much. Why had he come here? Why had he learned such horrid things? Where was the present? How could he get back? Red curls, that was the beacon.

"It gets difficult from here," a voice said.

Mother's maybe? Whose mother? His? No, a new mother. A thing half human and half abomination. Black hair that reached to the ground. Eyes behind eyes, ones that peered in and out.

Sophie's hand pulled Fenrir forward.

"Wait a moment," she said to someone. They stopped. "I'm going to construct a ward. This is hard for him."

"You will need more than a ward here," that voice said. "The Source is saturated with the non-Euclidean. The air thick as molasses with distortions. We go forward. Clear the way."

"You'll take on distortions?" Sophie asked.

"What are more of them if you will free us of them all? We will carve you a path."

"Carve you a path. Carve you a path. A path. A path. A path a path a path apathapathapathhhhhhhhhhhhh."

Fenrir glimpsed impossible forms advancing, moving towards that void. Their departure did little to reduce the roar. Sophie moved in and out of view. He felt her hold his arm and set chalk to it. When she was done, his mind had a bit more clarity. The now was more tangible again. The way forward too was less throbbing.

"Is that any better?" she asked.

"What's wrong with him?" Theopold said.

"The distortions are affecting him differently than me. Overpowering him, I think."

"He's a liability," Leida said. "We should leave him behind."

"No," Sophie said, "he said he will go, so he will go."

"I can do it," Fenrir said. "It's better, thank you."

"We shouldn't tarry," Theopold said. "The afflicted are taking on distortions for us, and the sooner we destroy the Rot of the Link, the sooner they're freed from this agony."

"Go," Sophie said, rushing forward.

She still held onto Fenrir's hand. Their polearms swung in tandem, long legs taking leaping steps, breathing coming hard and fast. Foot to stone. Foot to stone. Inhale. Exhale. The present was easy to see now. Fenrir couldn't see anything else. A frenzy gripped him, and it felt indistinguishable from the kind that held him during the purge. Yet now, there was no carnage. Blood pounded in his ears. The threat to life and limb was all around.

The distortions pulsed on either side of their tunnel of purity carved out by the afflicted. These foul motes were monstrous. Thrice his size, their complex patterns and movements screaming out to him. Sophie's ward held, but a roar was making inroads. He pushed on, keeping pace with her. They dived into an ancient structure of steel. They tore through winding corridors littered with the debris of the past. Cables and wires and countless relics that Fenrir knew nothing of. There were shapes and materials and colors and sheens he'd never glimpsed before. And around it all, the distortions throbbed.

Then, they stopped. Sophie panted. Mother lumbered ahead in a room. She inched forward, and as she did so, Fenrir caught the warping of space that came with her taking on distortions. They transferred from the immaterial to matter, embedding themselves in her flesh. If she'd been an enigma to behold before, she was an impossibility now. Fenrir took one glance at her and forced his eyes away.

"Don't look at her," he said.

Sophie's hand gripped his.

"This is the place," Theopold said.

The room was lit somehow. A pale glow emanating from

where the ceiling met the walls. Unlike the rest of the Old World, this place was almost pristine. There were few signs of age or wear. Part of it might have had to do with how it had been built—made to withstand the test of time. The other half of it was the high concentration of distortions. This place was kept in a timeless state precisely because here the non-Euclidean reigned supreme.

"There," Theopold said.

He pointed to an object that came into view as Mother moved off to the side. She wheezed and groaned and screamed until she crashed down. Fenrir didn't dare look at her. She would be covered with distortions now. Her life was pain. Pure, unending torment, at least until they put an end to the Rot of the Link.

"Is that the console?" Sophie asked.

Theopold nodded and waited for her to take the lead. Sophie slung her pack around, reached into it, and retrieved the diskette. She let her bag fall to the ground and carried the relic in both hands. She took slow and steady steps. Theopold followed just behind with Fenrir and Leida coming after. They all walked in a solemn procession to the object sitting on a table.

The console hummed away and gave off a hot wind. It was composed of two gray boxes, one bearing pin-pricks of red and green lights that flickered on and off in rapid sequences, the other embedded with a mirror in its face. That reflective surface showed strings of white text set on a black background, constantly appearing then being consumed. This was the Link trying to reestablish itself while the Rot ate away at it. An endless dance of creation and destruction.

Sophie and Theopold stared at the screen. Then she held the diskette out to him.

"The relic," she said.

Theopold lifted it from her palms then moved it to a thin gap set in the console's frame. The diskette was sucked in. Theopold fumbled in his robes, drew out a small metal disk, and pressed it to his forehead. The device somehow stayed attached to his skin.

"What's that?" Sophie asked.

"A Third Eye. It's how we'll know if the Link is truly reestablished."

Sophie didn't have time to ask other questions because the diskette started to do what it was programmed to. Theopold pulled a tray out from the console and set his hands to it. Fingers flew across buttons accompanied by a clicking sound. Text appeared on the black screen in time with his motions. He was interfacing with the relic. They all craned forward, trying to make sense of what was happening. Suddenly, Theopold stilled his hands and pulled them away from the tray.

"Now, we wait," he said.

"Is it done?" Leida asked.

"We will see," Theopold said.

They watched. A white rectangle appeared and disappeared. Then, a stream of text shot across the screen so rapidly that they couldn't hope to read it. It poured out in a frenzy. Theopold sucked in his breath. Fenrir found he was holding his own. They all stared at the mirror. Hypnotized by the promise of salvation. To be free of distortions. But then there was the other half. With the Link reestablished, nothing would prevent the Others from returning. Fenrir pushed the terror away. It was too late to fret over what they'd set in motion. The Rot of the Link was dying. He felt it.

"It's working," Theopold said.

The distortions vibrated, shrank and expanded, twisted and turned. It was a different kind of death, that of reality, and it was a strange view that unfolded for them. Corrupted space-time undulated, fought against itself, let out waves of unease, of awe, of horror and wonder. Then, all at once, the drama ceased. The distortions collapsed into themselves, sucked into a nothingness. The roar shifted into a whimper. Mother's screams faded into a death gurgle. The scores of afflicted nearby sighed and gasped and then went quiet and still. By the time the text on the screen had stopped, Fenrir couldn't sense a single distortion. Sophie unbuttoned her coat, pulled her shirt free of her pants, and gazed at her navel. It was still and unremarkable.

She laughed and shouted, smiling at Fenrir, but then Leida appeared with dagger drawn, sinking her blade into Theopold's back. He gasped and tried to grab at the weapon. Leida and the cultist crashed into the console then onto the floor. Sophie turned and sprang back. Fenrir readied his fauchard, but Sophie was faster.

One clean cut of her voulge, and Leida's head was liberated from her body. Theopold was on the ground crying in pain. Fenrir rushed in and threw what had been Leida off the old man. He pressed a hand to the wound, but the blood came gushing out. Theopold rolled onto his back. When Fenrir tried to turn the cultist back over to put pressure on the puncture, Theopold pushed him away.

"Enough," Theopold said. "If not here, then I would've been taken out up there." He pointed to the ceiling and gasped with the movement.

He spoke the truth. Even if the others couldn't sense the distortions like Fenrir and Sophie, there would be telltales signs that their world had fundamentally altered. Attuners would fall silent. Detectors would fail to register any signal. The newly afflicted would be suddenly restored. The gravely afflicted in need of a mercy killing would die on their own. Rot would return to places it had forsaken. And all of these occurrences would be celebrated, but there would be one sign hinting at the truth—that the Rot of the Link was tied to the distortions. The light on the Church's dome would go out. Everyone in Simetria would know what that signaled.

Sophie knelt down beside Fenrir and Theopold.

"We'll stop the bleeding," she said.

"You won't," Theopold said. "I'm slipping."

He closed his eyes then shot them open again. A hand nudged Fenrir's chest. Theopold held out the small metal disk he'd worn on his forehead.

"The Link has been reestablished," he said. "Take it. Take my Third Eye and use it when you require insight."

Fenrir opened his fist, and Theopold dropped the relic in it.

"Hide it on the flesh behind the ear," Theopold said. "It only works here." Theopold reached up and pressed the spot on Fenrir's head, centered on and just above the brow.

Fenrir set the disk behind his ear, and when it touched his flesh, it stayed attached but did nothing else. How the times had changed. For him to put a heretic's relic on his person and to trust the words of Theopold of all people.

"May the wisdom of the alfom guide you," Theopold said. "Now, I ask for a mercy killing."

His words came in gasps. Leida must have hit a lung. Choking on fluid. Pain touching all his nerve endings. Such a death would be an awful affair. Theopold deserved better than that. Fenrir lowered the old man to the ground, retrieved his fauchard, and stood primed. Sophie stepped back.

"Are you ready?" Fenrir asked.

Theopold nodded and closed his eyes. His mouth whispered a prayer. The only words Fenrir caught were, "Blessed is the Link." He swung his polearm then let it fall to the ground.

Afterward, Fenrir and Sophie sat in silence. Death was all around them. Theopold. Beheaded Leida. Piles of afflicted.

But there was a welcome stillness too. That constant unease that had turned into a physical pain for Fenrir was gone with the distortions that bred it. So calm now. Safe. This place that was meant to be a death sentence was more a haven than the world above, the one they were meant to return to.

"You should stay," Sophie said.

"In the Old World?"

Sophie stood and grabbed her voulge from the synthetic box it lent against. She extended an arm to Fenrir. He grabbed it and let her pull him to a stand. His legs were weak and unsteady. Even with the distortions gone, he was spent from fighting their constant assault.

"It's safe here now," she said. "No afflicted. No distortions. Above is peril. I'm ready to face whatever is waiting for me, but there's no need for you to be involved."

"We should both stay here," he said.

Sophie patted his chest then stroked his cheek. "Me, living in a cavern? Do you really think I would weather that? No, dear Fenrir."

"You don't give yourself enough credit. You're more adaptable than you think. We all are. Look at me."

Sophie pulled her hand away and stepped back. "You're a romantic at heart. You hid it well, but I see it now. Despite everything that's happened to you, everything you learned down here, you still cling to hope. But you don't know our enemy as I do. Vergil would never let me go so easily, not after everything he's done to get to this point. If I tried to stay down here, he'd come hunting, and he wouldn't stop until he found me."

"Then let him come." Fenrir grabbed his fauchard from the ground.

"I don't run from my problems," Sophie said. "I face them. I'll face him. But my problems aren't yours. You should stay."

"I already promised to help you free yourself from him. Besides, you said it yourself, I'm a romantic. Your problems are mine too."

Sophie grinned. "Who am I to argue with that?" She tossed her head back towards the entrance. "We've a long trek to the surface. Let's retrace our steps to that fungal grotto. It will be a good place to rest."

"To spend one last night together?" Fenrir moved to her side and slipped his hand in hers, their fingers intertwined, mimicking fate and whatever was lying in wait for them above.

EULOGY

The text herein is meant for the eyes of Our Beloved Lady's most devout servants. Here follows the Eulogy for Our Beloved Lady as penned by the Most-Divine Saint Marcos Frenwith.

Today, we mourn the loss of Our Beloved Lady. She came to us on the wind and as a whisper. When her voice first graced my ears, I was nothing and no one. Life had been one disappointment after another for me. I was bitter and a coward. But despite that, Our Lady saw something in me. She cultivated my talents and convinced me to see the value in myself. She showed me my true purpose and, in doing so, saved us all.

Alas that She is no longer here, having left us far too soon. Our hearts bleed, and our souls weep. We may be tempted to give in to the despair that grips us or to see Her departure as our defeat, but we must reject such dark musings. Instead, let us ponder over the reason for Her exodus—Our Lady knew the Rot of the Link was the only way to rid us of the Others' foul influence. She knew it would bar Her too from our world, and yet She made this choice willingly. Ever selfless. Ever loving. She did what was best for us all.

Would that I could tell you this knowledge was enough

to sustain me and help me weather this storm of the soul, but I, Marcos Frenwith, do not tell falsehoods. The truth is I ache. Her absence is like a gaping wound. I feel the lack of Her. I wonder if there wasn't another way, if we couldn't have somehow saved Her and still achieved our aims.

But such thoughts are pointless. Dwelling in the past and fixating on what might have been serves no purpose. Instead, we must look forward and keep our eyes fixed on the temporal horizon. We must take comfort in Her trust in us. Our Beloved Lady left us because She knew we would not falter. She knew we were capable of great things, that we would soar if given the chance. We cannot, we will not prove Her wrong. We will take on our sacred charge. We will ensure the Rot of the Link prevails and keeps the Others at bay. This is our world. This is our future. This is Her gift to us.

Addendum: The Most-Holy Church of Impermanence Archive dates the publication of this document to the year of our Lady one, just following the introduction of the Blessed Rot of the Link. However, Church scholars theorize that the parlance used herein was not yet widely practiced. Indeed, the Church itself was not officially established until the year of our Lady three. Widespread adoption of the turn of phrase herein was unlikely to have occurred prior to then. Most scholars agree that this Eulogy was introduced into the Church Archive years after Our Lady's passing or, more accurately speaking, inadvertent exile.

Why Saint Marcos chose to frame events in this manner is a matter of debate. The true exchange between him and his loyal followers, those that would go on to form the crux of the Church and be honored with the title of Great Family, has not yet been unearthed in the Archive. It is possible that Saint Marcos chose to destroy such communications to avoid any confusion surrounding events and their framing. Whatever the truth, the message of the Eulogy is clear and comes from the Most-Divine Saint's heart. This is his tribute to Our Beloved Lady and should be viewed with that purpose in mind.

THE RUSE

Sophie would despise him. Vergil knew that. He readied himself for her vile looks and venomous words. Even so, his stomach leaped the moment they heard those three taps on the massive stone door. Nicolus and a handful of clergyfolk pushed the door in, while Church guards stood at the ready. Vergil hardened himself. He forced himself to view the pale face framed by orange-red curls as a deviant and traitor. He effaced the visage, turned the name to a label, and donned a snarl. He would fool the other clergyfolk because he was nearly convinced himself that the hate was real.

Hate wasn't so hard to muster when the second person came into view under the wavering torchlight. Fenrir Mey né Ashtin Broodfell. Of course that one would survive. Vergil had hoped the Leida woman would manage to somehow best the former surveyor, but it had been a longshot. He wasn't concerned. Fenrir was an annoyance but nothing more.

Sophie and Fenrir. Just the two of them. As soon as they stepped into the circular room, Nicolus and his helpers heaved until the stone slab doors were again flush with the wall. The Old World was cut off. Sophie and Fenrir held their polearms at the ready, eyeing the legion of clergyfolk standing before them.

"Lower your weapons," Vergil said, stepping forward.

The deacons and priests and bishops moved in to fill the void he'd left behind. Now, they were a wall. A solid surface of outrage threatening to erupt. The tension palpable.

"What's the meaning of this?" Sophie asked.

Her knuckles showed white. For a fraction of a second, Vergil wondered if he had misjudged her. What if she did something brave and utterly foolish? He took another step forward and held his hands out, palms down.

"We know what you did," Vergil said. "We knew the moment the Rot of the Link was destroyed."

"As if entering the Old World wasn't sacrilege enough," Nicolus said.

Vergil glared at him. They had to play this just right or risk outing themselves.

"There is ample evidence that you flouted Church decrees," Vergil said. "As of this moment, you and that man are prisoners of the Most-Holy Church of Impermanence. Choose any further words with the utmost care, Lady Roshem."

All eyes were on Vergil. He wanted to give Sophie a look that only the two of them would understand, but he couldn't risk it. She would just have to hate him for a little while longer.

"You are to be taken to the Most-Solemn Penitentiary of the Lower City to await your trial," Vergil said. "Will you go of your own volition?"

Sophie whipped her head back to look at Fenrir. Vergil clenched his jaw.

"I can't go back there," Fenrir whispered.

"You don't have a choice," Nicolus said.

Vergil threw a hand towards the priest. Nicolus was

getting drunk on the deceit. A loose tongue was the last thing they needed.

"I'll sort this," Sophie said to Fenrir. "I made you a promise, remember? No harm from the Church."

"Drop your polearms, and let the guards approach," Vergil said.

Sophie locked eyes with him, gave a hard stare, then released her grip on her voulge. It clattered to the ground, the twang of metal and thud of wood echoing on the curved stone walls. Fenrir breathed out heavily and did likewise. The guards didn't waste a second before they rushed in and locked cuffs on the two surveyors.

"Easy," Vergil said to the one holding Sophie's restraints. "Take them to the penitentiary without delay, but ensure nothing untoward comes to pass for either of them. They must pay for their crimes in the fashion the Church deems most appropriate."

The deacons and priests and bishops murmured in agreement.

"Now go," Vergil said.

Sophie kept her eyes fixed on Vergil until the guards moved her out of sight. Fenrir walked with a bowed back, the color nearly drained from his face. It was done then. The first part at least. Now came the most delicate stage of the operation.

"I'd like a word with Bishops Griffin, Wright, and Stevens," Vergil said to the clergyfolk.

Three old and thick men moved to stand beside Vergil and Nicolus, while all the others filed out behind the guards and prisoners. These three represented everything wrong with the Church. Faded and angry and bitter. Six beady eyes— blue, green, and brown. Fleshy and pointed noses. Thick and thin lips. All variations on an archetype that Vergil despised. When he looked at them, his eyes blurred, and they blended together into a conglomerate of ineptitude.

The five men lingered in the round room with the portal to the Old World. It was quiet and still now, the echoes from the halls beyond growing fainter as the crowd retreated.

"What do you think will happen?" Bishop Stevens asked.

"A public execution, of course," Bishop Griffin said.

"I mean to the Church," Stevens said.

"How do you mean?" Bishop Wright asked.

Stevens sighed and rubbed his heavy hand over his face. Of the three, he was the least dull.

"The Rot of the Link is gone," Stevens said.

"The Others will come back," Wright said, "unless we can do something to bar them."

"If the Others can come back, that means Our Lady can too," Bishop Griffin said. "All is not lost. She can guide us once again."

"Why would She do that?" Stevens asked. "We failed Her. This was our one charge—to preserve the Rot of the Link, and now it's gone. She's probably disgusted with us."

"There's something more pressing than the lack of the Rot of the Link," Vergil said.

He had hoped one of them would have perceived this obvious ramification on their own, but that had been expecting too much. Still, he needed them to see it to panic and for that panic to spread to the populace.

The three other bishops looked to Vergil in expectation.

"The distortions are gone," Vergil said.

"Which is a blessing," Bishop Wright said, performing the sign of the Lady.

"Rather the opposite," Vergil added.

He glanced at Nicolus who took the cue to make his way out of the room. Now, it was just four of the most influential of the Church's bishops.

"Don't you see?" Vergil asked.

The men looked away from him, embarrassed that they couldn't, in fact, make the connection.

"Without the distortions, the Church serves no purpose," Vergil said. "The rituals, the tollers, the surveyors, the materials to combat the non-Euclidean, all of it is useless now. The Axioms are empty words. Everything we preach is obsolete. There is no more affliction. The Rot of the Link took the distortions with it."

He didn't know how many of them knew the truth, but the evasive looks of Griffin and Stevens told him they, at least, had an inkling of what he was implying.

"This is indeed a grave concern," Stevens said. "We must take it to the Archbishop."

"I'd be astonished if he wasn't already mulling these same things," Vergil said. "But at the very least, we need to tell him we have our prisoners. Shall we?"

Vergil waved his hand to the doorway, and the bishops filed out into the winding halls. After scores of twists and turns and climbing of stairs, they were winded but back in the Church proper. Vergil waited while his companions panted and wiped the sweat from their brows. He pretended to be short of breath too. If he hadn't, they would have held it against him. Pettiness was their forte, after all.

Once they stood at the ornate oak doors that led into Archbishop Torrington's study, Vergil thudded his fist against them. They creaked open almost at once. The bishops filed in, and a deacon hurried to close the door behind them. Torrington sat slumped over his desk, his hair wild.

"Leave us," the Archbishop said to the deacon.

Once the man had scurried away, the Archbishop beckoned the others closer.

"It's done," Vergil said. "The culprits emerged from the Old World and were taken to the penitentiary moments ago."

"Lady Roshem," Bishop Griffin said.

"And some other surveyor I didn't recognize," Bishop Stevens said. "A man."

"He didn't wear any epaulets though," Bishop Wright said.

"Enough," the Archbishop said. "The important point is they are in custody and will pay for what they've done. Now that's out of the way, we need to focus on what comes next. The people know something is amiss. We want to be the ones to tell them what's happened. They need to feel as though they can trust us. I want you to go and gather all the clergyfolk. I will tell them what they need to pass on to the people."

"We were discussing the difficulties that lie ahead for the Church," Bishop Stevens said, "now that the distortions are gone."

He stopped. The Archbishop was silent.

"I'm quite certain I already told you what your next task is," Torrington said. "So go and gather the clergyfolk. Now."

The bishops hurried out. Vergil followed but hesitated at the threshold. He stopped, shut the door, and turned to face the Archbishop.

"You have something to add?" the Archbishop asked.

Vergil strode back to Torrington's desk. He clasped his hands and hung his head. "This is my fault."

He shifted his eyes upwards to observe the Archbishop's reaction. The man looked unchanged.

"Are you going to elaborate?" Torrington asked.

"I enabled Lady Roshem. I knew things about her, a terrible secret, that I should have told the Church."

"Go on."

"I love her, you understand?"

Torrington nodded.

"And a man does foolish things for love," Vergil said. "I knew that Sophie bore a distortion. I learned of this when I was young, but still, I shouldn't have kept it to myself for so many years. It's just that her distortion is different. Or was different, I suppose."

"I'm aware," Torrington said.

Vergil started. This was news to him, and here he thought he knew the bulk of the Church's secrets at this point.

"Her father confided in me a long time ago," the Archbishop said. "I agreed to let little Sophie Roshem live so long as her distortion remained unchanged."

"I see, well then, that saves me some effort, but it doesn't change what I've done. This isn't just about Sophie's distortion. I played more of a role in this debacle than simply hiding the truth."

"Elaborate."

"I wanted to save her," Vergil said. "I wanted to rid her of her distortion. You mentioned me associating with unsavory sorts. One of those was a heretic named Theopold Cromford."

"I know the name. He was a priest once."

"Was he? Well, I knew him only as a cultist but one who was well-versed in the Old World and its relics. I worked with him to try to find a solution for Sophie. It seemed like a dead-end. He disappeared, and I assumed that was that. I was a fool. He must have made contact with Sophie at some point without my knowing. The two of them must have worked together to find a relic and hatch this plan to go into the Old World and stop the Rot of the Link."

"You helped them?" Torrington asked.

"Not knowingly, but I still played a part. I'm just as culpable as them. I ask to also be sent to the penitentiary. It's what I deserve."

He was laying the theatrics on a bit thickly, but it was what Torrington would expect of him. He had to put on the performance of his life and play himself flawlessly in this moment more than any other.

"Don't be so dramatic," the Archbishop said.

Vergil feigned shock and tried to smother the grin that begged to peek out. "Your Eminence?"

"You got manipulated by a beautiful woman. It happens to the best of us. Besides, the Church needs you for the trying times ahead. The people love you."

"I don't understand," Vergil said.

"I think you do, Bishop Holdsworth. You're too sharp not to. You see clear as day what's in store for us once the people realize they don't need us anymore. We can't afford to let the system we've built crumble. The Church must find a way to survive."

Vergil had to prove his cunning, otherwise he risked Torrington seeing through the ruse.

"You mean, in the face of the people learning the truth about the distortions and the Rot of the Link?" Vergil asked.

The Archbishop blinked too many times.

"I've known for a while," Vergil said, "and they will see the connection themselves. This is what we need to combat."

"Yes," Torrington said. "We need to frame this in the right way."

"I'm happy to assist."

"As I said, you're a valuable asset to the Church. I intend to use you to the fullest."

Vergil bowed, and while his face was angled at the floor, he gave into the maniacal laughter sounding in his head and let a trace of a grin show itself. Everything was going so marvelously according to plan.

LADY ROSHEM

Sophie knew Vergil would come. He let them whisk her away, march her through the streets, and toss her in a cell at the penitentiary. He let her stew in her rage. She paced her cramped cell, her bare feet slipping on the slimy stones, the roiling emotions keeping her warm despite the rags she now wore. A whole day passed. She watched a sliver of sunlight from the barred window crawl across the floor. And still it wasn't enough time to process what Vergil had done. The anger was still raw when a jangling of keys and a groan of iron on iron signaled she had a visitor. Sophie turned over on her pile of bedding, and there was Vergil.

He glanced back at the door, waiting for the guard to retreat down the hall. Sophie rose to her feet, her body aching from the cold, hard surfaces that had become her world. Such a far cry from what she'd known all her life. Even the Old World was luxury in comparison to this place. Her mind shot to Fenrir and all the long years he'd been trapped here. The anger seethed at the thought that here he was again, and it was her doing.

"Go ahead," Vergil said.

He stepped forward and clasped his hands behind his

back. Sophie glared at him. The words wanted to burst forth and spew a torrent of loathing all over his crisp bishop's robes, but they were too many and her throat too narrow.

"I mean it," Vergil said. "Go on and get your rage and bile out. Curse me. Spit at me. Tell me I'm a horrid beast."

Sophie's fingers flexed. Claw to fist and back, over and over. Then, the flood broke.

"How could you do this?" she asked. "After all we've gone through, to throw it all aside here at the end. And for what, Vergil? Hm? Power? Prestige? I never imagined you to be so small-minded as all that, but I see now I didn't know you at all."

Vergil stepped forward until he was an arm's length away from Sophie.

"Let's keep this a private conversation, shall we?" he said, lowering his voice to a whisper.

"Afraid I'll tell them the truth and expose your part in everything?"

"Oh, you could try, but there would be no proof of it. Just your word against mine. A lauded bishop versus the woman who destroyed the Rot of the Link."

"Was it all a lie? Or was there a time when you did actually care for me?"

Vergil frowned and stepped forward again. Now, he was inches from Sophie, yet she refused to retreat. She stared into his deep-set eyes that reflected the gray light from her window. How could eyes so blue and pure belong to such a fiend? She didn't want to believe it, even then. A part of her persisted in caring for him despite everything, and it made her hate herself.

"You know me, dearest Sophie, you do. So ask yourself, would I really do this to you?"

Vergil let her think. When she shook her head, his eyebrows lifted. He leaned in and grabbed her hand. Gloveless.

Flesh on flesh. He brought it to his lips and planted it with the softest of kisses. Her stomach leapt.

"There you go," he said. "That's right. I'd never betray you. This was always the plan, my heart. The only way to save you was to destroy the Rot of the Link, but such a heinous act can't go unpunished. Someone will take the fall."

"Fenrir?" she asked.

"He's too small a fish to serve that purpose. No, it has to be Lady Sophie Roshem, but that is not you. Do you understand?"

Vergil cradled her hand in his and watched the realization hit. A Lady Roshem who was not her. He couldn't. He wouldn't. Was he so savage? Looking into his eyes and spying the gleam in them, seeing that smug smirk playing on his lips, she knew in an instant that he was. For her, he'd do anything, including sacrificing an innocent woman.

"Tillie," she said then pulled her hand away.

Vergil scowled and shook his head. He pressed his fingertips to his forehead and paced the room. As he moved in and out of the light beam from the window, the layers peeled back. Now, Sophie was seeing him for the first time in all his moral bankruptcy and hubris. Cold, callous, calculating with a charm that had fooled even her for all these long years.

"You're supposed to be pleased," he said. "You were supposed to hate her. You were meant to know about my visits to her, but then you did something I hadn't expected. Making a pact with her. Using her so that you could steal away into the night with no one the wiser, but I was wiser, Sophie."

A clenching gripped her gut.

"Yes, I knew about your little trips to see the toller. How could I not? Do you really think so little of me to be fooled by such a childish trick as a doppelgänger?"

Vergil would kill Fenrir. There was no question of that now. If she wanted to save him and keep her promise to him, she had to play this in exactly the right way. She just couldn't see what that was yet.

"But then why did you let it happen?" she asked.

Vergil smiled and moved to Sophie. She retreated until she bumped against the wall, the cold, wet stones bulging into her back. He grabbed her chin and tilted her face up to his.

"I'm not so selfish as you think," he said. "I couldn't give you what you needed, so when you found another to fulfill those urges, I stood aside. I would do anything for you, don't you know that?"

She looked at him through narrowed eyes.

He laughed then leaned in and put his lips just next to her ear. "Do you know why I didn't let myself touch you? It wasn't because I was afraid of your distortion. It was motivation. My desire for you fueled me." He pulled back and moved his face just in front of hers, so close their noses nearly touched. "If I let myself enjoy you as you were, I wouldn't have ached nearly enough to do what needed to be done. To free you, I had to suffer. I had to deny myself to get us to this point, the point we find ourselves in now—touching skin to skin."

He grabbed her jaw and stared at her. He was waiting, waiting for permission.

"You did all of this for you," she said. "So you could have me, not free me."

Vergil released his grip and stepped back. He was enraged. She'd made a mistake.

"Do you think it was easy," he said, "pretending not to know, letting that man touch you? But I put my own feelings aside, for you."

"You put them aside for convenience and to get what you wanted in the end—me at your utter and complete mercy."

"Oh, my heart, you couldn't be more wrong. I did this for everyone. For you, me, and every person who's under the thumb of the Church. When I found out the truth about the Rot of the Link, I had no choice but to bring the whole system down. The Church knew. Since the beginning, they knew where the distortions stemmed from, but they decided keeping the Others out was worth all the suffering we bear. They were wrong. And when everyone learns the truth, I suspect they will be of a similar mind as me.

"So yes, this was about more than you. Forgive me for thinking about the big picture, but you were always the driving force. I found the ancient texts about the Linkrot virus in the Archive while searching for your cure. I found the courage to go through with it because of you, and now I'm going to save you again. You'll switch out with Tillie, who will die in your stead. You'll be kept hidden away while we wait for the shift to happen. The Church will fall. After that, you'll return as the Sophie who rose from the dead, a phoenix, the saint of our new religion."

"This is insanity."

"This is love, its true and ugly face."

"This isn't love, Vergil. It's obsession."

"You just need time to think it over. I'll be back tomorrow."

Vergil turned and walked to the door. He called out to the guard, and while he was waiting, he glanced over his shoulder at Sophie.

"And don't tell me how to love you."

Sophie remained standing until Vergil's footfalls died away. Only then did she let herself slump against the wall and crumple to the floor. It was worse. Him loving her was hell. She was trapped with no way out. Death on one side, shackled to Vergil on the other. But if she agreed to go along with Vergil's schemes, maybe she could manage to save Fenrir. It was the only good that could come out of it.

***

Vergil was back the next day, smirking as the guard retreated down the hall, the jingle of the keys marking each step.

Sophie forced herself to be demure. She reminded herself not to scowl or furrow her brow. She needed Vergil to believe she was on his side.

"I hope you had ample time to digest my proposal," Vergil said, once the guard was out of earshot.

Sophie clasped her hands and let them rest near her stomach where the distortion had once been embedded. So strange to think that it was gone. After bearing it all her life, it was like a fundamental part of herself was missing.

"I was rash," she said. "Yesterday. It was a lot to take in, but yes, I've had time to mull it over. While there are merits to it, I just can't warm to the idea of letting an innocent woman sacrifice herself on my behalf. Tillie deserves better."

Vergil advanced until he was nearly flush with Sophie. She forced a smile, and let his robes brush against her rags.

"Oh, but she wants it," Vergil said. "Desperately."

"Wants to die? Why in heaven's name would she desire that?"

Vergil shrugged then took a lock of Sophie's hair and twirled it around his finger. He seemed hungry to touch her now, such a departure from all that had come before.

"These low bloods are a strange lot. There's no point trying to unravel their thought processes, but I know you. You won't be satisfied until you hear the irrationality come from the source. You're welcome to ask her yourself." Vergil waved his hand at the barred door.

"She's here?"

"But of course. The idea was to have her switch places with you this very day. But I won't get ahead of myself. Let's have you chat with her and ensure you're satisfied before moving forward with the plan, hm?"

Sophie nodded, and Vergil called for the guard. The man ambled over and lingered on the other side of the door.

"Would you bring my female companion to the cell now?" he asked.

"Right away, Bishop Holdsworth."

The man disappeared and was replaced by the clatter of keys striking keys. A minute or so later, he was back with a black-haired woman in a green cloak. He unlocked the cell, ushered her in, and secured it behind them.

"Just call when you're done," he said.

Vergil smiled and nodded, but otherwise everyone was silent until the guard was back at his post at the end of the hall.

"Go on," Vergil said to Tillie.

She removed her hood, and Sophie recognized the face despite the black hair.

"My lady," Tillie said with a bow.

It was the height of ridiculousness. Sophie in rags, grimy and grim. She was no lady anymore. Just a criminal. Or better yet, a traitor.

"The bishop says you've agreed to an arrangement," Sophie said, "one that involves yourself and myself and the question of cages and executions."

"Yes, ma'am, that's right."

Sophie beckoned for Tillie's hand. When Tillie presented it, Sophie took it in both of hers and pulled her doppelgänger to the far wall. It was the most space she could put between them and Vergil. He lingered near the door, peering through the bars, pretending not to eavesdrop. Sophie lowered her voice to a whisper.

"I don't know what he's told you," Sophie said, "but I won't let this happen. You aren't about to pay for my mistakes. There's no reason for you to let yourself be discarded so."

"If I may be so bold?" Tillie said.

Sophie nodded.

"There's every reason under the sun, my lady. The little

stories we tell at A Taste of Refinement only work as long as you're alive. Who would want to play at lying with a dead woman? Once you're executed, there's no place for me anymore. I'll be nothing again, and I just can't do it."

"You can be anything you want," Sophie said.

Tillie pulled her hand free and shook her head.

"Yes," Sophie said, "you can start anew. The Church will fall. Simetria will change."

"You don't know what it's like for us. You talk about change like it's a good thing when it's just plain terrifying for people like me. Besides, I don't want to be anything else. Pretending to be you is all I have."

"You're better than that."

"Better? Than you? Than a high blood and head of a great family?"

Tillie laughed long and hard, tears coming to the corners of her eyes as she went on. It told Sophie everything she needed to know. Tillie's role was more than a job for her. It was a strange kind of passion. Once Tillie calmed again, she reached for Sophie's hand. Sophie gave it to the woman and stared into her eyes, trying to pierce the mystery of her, but it was too much like looking into a mirror. Unnerving and disorienting for someone already so close to the edge.

"Don't you see?" Tillie said. "This is my chance. I have no future. Even before your imprisonment, I was on borrowed time. I had maybe a few good years before Madam Gerton sent me out, and then what? This is what I've always dreamed of. The chance to truly become Lady Roshem. Not just for a night, for a man or two or three, but for everyone and for all time. To live, however briefly, and to die as Lady Roshem. To stand at my execution and look out at the masses. For them to look back at me and see me as Lady Roshem. It's worth the price a thousand times over. Do you understand?"

How could she? It was like Vergil said, there was no point in trying to comprehend the low bloods and their motivations. They were like different species. Tillie was a true believer and hungry for the chance to die for her beliefs. It ought to have eased Sophie's guilt, but it only left a bitter taste in her mouth.

"I won't stand in the way of your wishes," Sophie said.

She wanted to thank Tillie for her sacrifice, but it was too much like a defeat for that. Sophie wasn't elated or relieved. She was moving to a different kind of prison now, a metaphysical one with imaginary bars and Vergil as her jailor. She glanced at him, and he was already striding over, clearly having overheard their conversation.

"Do we do it now?" Tillie asked Vergil.

"If Sophie has agreed to it, then yes, we do it now."

Tillie untied a knot near her collarbone and swung her cloak around her front. Vergil took hold of it and draped it over his arm. Then Tillie tugged at her hair, removing pins and wiggling what quickly showed itself to be a wig. Vergil took that too. Next was her dress, stockings, undergarments, socks, boots. As Tillie disrobed, Sophie followed suit. They handed off their articles of clothing to Vergil, who then gifted them to the other. It was a transformation by parts, but within five minutes, Sophie was the black-haired woman in the green cloak, and Tillie had become the prisoner. She was Lady Roshem now, and how she looked the part. Vergil rubbed a finger against the wet stones then touched it to Tillie's cheeks. A brown residue was left in its wake.

"Perfect," Vergil said. "You'd almost fool even me."

Sophie stood by quiet and stern. The plan had already been set into motion long before she'd ever even set foot in the Old World. There was no use fighting it. Tillie wanted this, needed it, and if Sophie was being honest with herself, she was desperate to live.

"Lady Roshem," Sophie said, bowing.

Tillie was radiance incarnate. Even after Vergil had called for the guard and they had exited the cell, Tillie stood, almost emanating a divine aura. To be so sure of oneself and so satisfied with one's fate. Sophie had no clue where her own was leading her. Each step down the dark and narrow corridors of the penitentiary brought her closer to a future she couldn't envision. Vergil had spoken of strange things. Of her coming back to life. Of a kind of sainthood of a new religion. She wanted no part of it, but she didn't have a choice. All she could do was trudge forward and try her damnedest to save Fenrir.

Sophie waited until they were in a hall without doors and devoid of life. The only movement came from the flicking flames in the sconces and her and Vergil's slow march. She pretended to trip on the irregular flooring. Vergil hurried to her side.

"I'm weaker than I realized," she said. "Can we rest a moment?"

"The sooner we get out of here, the better."

"Just a moment?"

Vergil sighed and led her to the wall. Sophie leaned into it.

"You were right about Tillie," Sophie said. "I thought maybe you were exaggerating, but she really did want to do this so desperately."

"Best not to talk about such things until later."

"Well, there is one other matter that I wanted to discuss before leaving. One involving Fenrir."

Vergil scowled.

Sophie took hold of Vergil's arm and pulled him closer. "I wouldn't have given him the time of day if you would have touched me."

"I told you why I wouldn't."

"I know."

Sophie ran her hand against the wall. With the other, she slipped her fingers between Vergil's and rubbed them back and forth. He clenched his hand and trapped hers.

"What annoys me more than anything isn't that you joined with him," he said. "It's that he doesn't even look like me. Not at all."

"Well, I didn't have a lot of options, now did I? It was hard enough finding someone I could trust with my secret."

Vergil pulled Sophie's hand in, forcing her to move into his body. He grabbed her chin and stared into her eyes.

"And now, here you are about to ask me to free him, is that it? I can't help but think you might have fallen in love with him."

"Oh, Vergil," Sophie said, shaking her head, "you're letting your imagination run wild. That I would lose what I feel for you in only a few months. How absurd. No, my dear, this is about being practical."

Vergil released her chin. She could have moved away if she wanted to, but it was best to stay close. He needed to believe she was on his side, after all.

"I'm listening," he said.

Sophie dropped her voice to a whisper. "You said you want the Church to fall. You want the people to focus on their lie about the Rot of the Link and the distortions, but Fenrir is a distraction from that."

"I don't follow your meaning."

"Think about it. Put yourself in the people's shoes. If you heard that Lady Roshem destroyed the Rot of the Link, you'd be shocked, but then to hear that she was accompanied by an unknown man would only serve to whet your curiosity. You'd become fixated on learning who this man is and why he helped Lady Roshem do the unthinkable. Someone would piece it all together. Word would get out that the man is Ashtin Broodfell. This would be yet another lie of the Church's, that he wasn't executed but, rather, allowed to live under a new name and identity."

"It'd only serve to anger them more. I don't see how that's an issue."

"It's a distraction. You don't want them focusing on Ashtin. You want them talking about the Rot of the Link and the distortions. One of these is gossip. The other is the key to toppling the Church."

Vergil's eyes widened. He saw it now, which meant the bulk of her work was already done.

"You could be right," he said. "Ashtin was very popular, and his reappearance would only create problems."

"So let Fenrir go. Have him return to his simple low-blood life as a nobody."

"Clergyfolk saw him exit the Old World with you. We have no doppelgänger to stand in for him."

"Perhaps he killed himself in his cell somehow. Surely, you have the connections to find a body to put in his place, one that's already dead, I would hope."

Sophie pushed herself off the wall and pretended to steady herself.

"It's a sound solution," Vergil said, "but I can't help but think you're doing it out of more than practicality."

"But of course I am. I made a promise to Fenrir when I asked him to help me with the expedition. I told him no harm would come to him from the Church. You've made me into a liar, Vergil, and I don't tell lies. Do me this favor."

Vergil let his lips peel back into a grin. "I did say I would do anything for you, didn't I?"

"If you really mean that, then let me pay a visit to Fenrir before we leave this place for good. I need to make it clear to him how things will play out. If we want him to keep quiet on the whole affair, I know just how to handle him."

"Did I ever tell you how ravishing you are when you're scheming?"

"Did I ever tell you how ravishing you are when you're scheming?"

PROMISE KEPT

Fenrir laid on his back and stared up at his cell's ceiling. It was all so familiar, almost like he'd never even left. Had he been dreaming? Had the past thirteen months of freedom been a figment of his overactive imagination? That must be it. He'd drunk some foul water or ate overly rotten bread, and the sickness had gone to his head. When he thought of it in that way, it made the ache less gnawing. Trevon had never been suffering all these years. Amilia hadn't been the one to betray him. But then what of the good? Had she been a fabrication too? Sophie.

He whispered her name to himself. He closed his eyes and pictured her, desperate not to lose the image to time. He could go to his execution with surety and grace if only he knew that she wasn't bound to the same awful fate. On his third day in the penitentiary, he learned the truth.

She came to him sporting raven hair. He thought the voice he heard echoing down the hall was his mind unraveling, but then she was there standing over him, looking down at the ruin of a man. He blinked several times, waiting for the illusion to dissipate. It didn't. She lowered herself to the hard floor and knelt beside him. Fenrir pushed himself up and stared at her, mouth agape.

"Are you really here?" he asked, his voice coming out in a croak. Had he been screaming in the night again? Was that why it was so hoarse?

Sophie reached forward and brushed his straw-colored hair from his eyes. The contact sent a shudder through him. Fenrir looked back at her. Beyond her head, there was movement near the barred door of his cell. He recognized the man who loitered.

"I'm really here," Sophie said.

"But so is he." Fenrir pointed to Vergil.

Sophie used her hand to guide his down. She moved to eclipse the object of his hate.

"And your plan? Ridding yourself of the other thing that keeps you shackled?"

"Shhh," she whispered. "Can't you see that's out of the question now? He was never going to let me go. That's what all this was, chaining me to him for good."

Fenrir had thought he'd let go of hope, thought it had died when he'd been thrown in this cell, but he'd held on to a sliver of it up until that moment because Sophie's words were what truly killed the poor thing. Fenrir cradled himself in his arms.

"I made a deal," Sophie said. "Lady Roshem will die, but I will not. And you will walk free too. Go back to being the Fenrir Mey who's been sick in his home all these days."

Fenrir glared at her. He was starting to piece the truth together. Their freedom would cost someone or someones dearly. The Church wouldn't be satisfied without a sacrifice.

"So someone is dying in your place then?" Fenrir asked. "And in mine?"

"Don't worry about that. I made the deal. Let my conscious bear the guilt."

Fenrir used the wall to help himself stand. He was weak, and his head spun. Sophie rose, watching him intently.

"No," Fenrir said. "I won't be a part of this. I'll pay for my crimes, whether I meant to commit them or not."

Sophie shook her head and took to pacing Fenrir's cell. She stopped near the window, glancing up at it and the featureless gray sky beyond. After a few seconds, she turned back to Fenrir with any hint of angst smoothed out. They never wore masks with one another, and here she was donning one against him.

"Don't play at being stubborn out of a false sense of nobility," she said. "We both know why you're doing it."

"Do we?"

Fenrir stepped on the slick stones of his cell's flooring and came to Sophie's side. He glanced up at the window. A few pigeons flitted by. Echoes from the city sounded, distant and indistinct from so many stories below.

"It's the same reason you lingered on those stairs when the afflicted chased us," Sophie said, "just before Mother spoke for the first time."

Fenrir's eyes shot to Sophie's.

"You meant to sacrifice yourself in grand fashion," she said, "because you have a death wish."

Fenrir looked down at his hands and smiled. He did, didn't he? It was part of the reason he'd gone into the Old World. And maybe he'd always had it. Maybe it predated his first crime and imprisonment. He always chalked it up to his fall from grace, of losing Trevon and hurting Amilia, but perhaps it had always been a part of him. To become a surveyor, to participate in multiple purges, required a kind of madness.

"And if I do?" he said.

"It's unacceptable. You have to live, do you hear?"

"Why?"

Sophie grabbed his hands and forced his eyes to hers. Her voice came out in a whisper.

"Because it's the only thing that will sustain me. I'm making good on my promise to you. I've protected you from the Church. I'll pay the price for my own selfishness. I wanted to be rid of my distortion, and so I have been. I need you to live your life. Forget about me."

It was an impossible ask, and she knew it. Still, her eyes begged him.

"You'll go with that monster then?" he asked.

"That's part of the deal, yes."

Sophie squeezed Fenrir's hands before letting them fall away from hers.

"He won then, don't you see that?" Fenrir asked.

"Of course I do, but worse than that, I gave him everything he wanted. I enabled him. This is all just as much my fault as his. Living with him will be my punishment. I accept that, but I can't leave here until you give me your word that you'll live. I can stand anything as long as I know that."

He almost wished she'd lied to him, told him that she used him and had been on Vergil's side all along, but even if she'd said those words, he never would have believed them.

"I'll do my best to suffer whatever existence is ahead for me," he said.

All the lines and tension in Sophie's face relaxed at Fenrir's words. She nearly looked at peace before she turned and left his cell, following Vergil down the hall for as long as Fenrir could watch the two of them.

Late that night, Fenrir was taken from his cell and through back halls until he was shoved out into an alley adjacent to the penitentiary.

"Scurry home, little rat," the guard said before slamming the wood and iron door in his face.

Fenrir rubbed his arms through the thin linen garb

they'd given him. He wrapped his hands in the rucksack that contained his few belongings. It was the thick of winter, and the night was being especially cruel what with the winds tearing through the tight thoroughfares. Fenrir rushed home. His fingers were so numb he was barely able to fish the key from his bag. He struggled to fit it into the lock, but after three attempts, it slid into place. He hurried into his dark and still shack then rushed to his bed. He didn't bother with a fire. His hands wouldn't have behaved well enough to start a blaze. Instead, he hid in his blankets, waiting for his body heat to thaw the lot of him.

As the feeling returned to his extremities, a flood of emotion came in tow. He'd numbed himself without even realizing it. Despair and grief gripped him. So much had happened. So much he hadn't had time to process. All the truths he'd learned. All the death and destruction. The freedom. The loss. It was too much. He wept and raged, but when his mind pleaded with him to grant them both succor, to put an end to all pain and pleasure for good, he remembered his promise to Sophie.

He'd said he would live, no matter what. And so, he would.

EXECUTION

Announcement for the Public Execution of Sophie Roshem

On this, the fourth day in the second month in the year of our Lady five hundred and thirty, the Most-Holy Church of Impermanence does hereby announce the PUBLIC EXECUTION of Sophie Roshem for the gravest of crimes against the Church and citizens of the city of Simetria—having destroyed the Blessed Rot of the Link.

The EXECUTION will take place without delay and is scheduled for the seventh day in the second month in the year of our Lady five hundred and thirty.

Appropriate to this severest of all crimes, the method of death will be by FLAYING. The Most-Holy Church of Impermanence invites all citizens of Simetria to attend and observe justice being dispensed.

IN WITNESS, WHEREOF I have hereunto caused the Blessed Seal of Our Beloved Lady to be herein affixed.

Archbishop of the Church of Impermanence
Reginild Torrington

The Rot of the Link protect us. The Hand of the Lady guide us.

PARADIGM SHIFT

"We're just about to close the pub doors, bishop," the establishment's owner said.

Vergil suppressed a scowl, not that showing it would have mattered behind the mask he wore.

"Not bishop, remember," Vergil said. "I'm a nameless, faceless entity."

The pub owner slapped his hand to his forehead and laughed. Old and ugly, like the lot of them sitting out there in the common room, waiting to hear Vergil's insights. A different sort compared to his usual audience. From the holy symmetry of a chapel to the greasy squalor of a low-blood haunt. A place to worship the divine versus one to satisfy the demands of the flesh. Even in this back room with a heavy pine door in the way, Vergil smelled the fatty mutton cooking on the kitchen fire mingling with the aroma of fermented hops and a touch of the rancid bite of vomit. He would have to wash well when he returned to his estate.

"Are we ready then?" Vergil asked the man.

"Let's give 'em a bit more. It's good for business if they have to wait some. I hope you don't mind overmuch. Man has to make a living 'specially in these most trying times."

"Of course," Vergil said.

He eased back into his stiff wooden chair. He didn't mind the wait. It suited his purposes as well as the barkeep's—building suspense. Vergil adjusted the leather jacket he wore and triple checked that his mask covered the lower half of his face. Bishop to bandit, at least in terms of looks, but in terms of purpose, clergyfolk to revolutionary was more accurate. He found it to be an improvement on all fronts. It was especially liberating to wear something a bit more fitted and flattering to his form. He'd always hated those drab, gray bishop's robes.

"I'll be right back," the barkeep said. "Just gonna make sure we're all set and ready for your words of wisdom."

Vergil nodded then rested his hands on his abdomen. How different this night was from all the ones that had come before. How different too was his life now. He couldn't help but reflect on it all. The change. The shift. It was subtle at first. Almost impossible to detect if viewed head on, but like a floater in the eye, one could spot it if they relaxed their gaze. That was hard for Vergil to do. He was too eager for what would come next, anxious to see if his plans would pan out as he'd anticipated. Yet he managed to view the agonizingly slow crawl as the longest of climaxes, and when he did that, it became a seductive waiting game.

The bell towers were already silent. There was no need for them without the daily rituals, and those had become obsolete the moment the distortions were eradicated. The chapels stood more and more emptied. Priests and deacons would come to give a sermon, and each day, their congregation thinned until only the most devoted and deluded were left. The blind leading the blind into an oblivion they refused to see. It frightened the clergyfolk. The amount of times Vergil was forced to hear one of them fret over their disappearing flock. He found it hard to look grim when his heart sang at his successes. Surveyors loitered in the halls of the Church, still wearing their leather garb that protected them from a vanquished enemy. They were wistful for the return of their nemesis because without the distortions, they too had become obsolete.

All of this happened by degrees, but the change was impossible not to see after Lady Roshem's execution. Until that point, the people of Simetria and the Church had had a nexus of hate, something to direct their anger and fear at. But with her gone, all they could do was spin around in circles until their vertigo forced their minds to concoct imaginary fiends. One such adversary was far from fantasy though, and if the clergyfolk had had the clearness of mind to truly observe their plight rather than rant and rave, maybe they could have stopped the renegade bishop in their midst. But they were exactly what Vergil had anticipated they would be. Inept. It served his needs deliciously.

"Alright, good sir," the barkeep said, sticking his head in the door. "We're ready for you now."

Vergil rose, adjusted his mask again, and moved from the dark backroom into one nearly filled with human forms. Almost all men. That was to be expected, and it didn't matter because whatever issued from his lips would be passed on. That's how it had been every time thus far. Just himself and Nicolus holding little secret rallies like this, and already the rumors of the Church's lies were swirling.

"This fine gentleman has a few words to say," the barkeep said. "So quiet down and let him speak."

The murmuring fell off, and everyone looked at the masked figure that stepped onto a stool at the far end of the room. Pints in hand, lips to vessels, amber liquid pouring into throats. Vergil used his fingers to push his gloves on tighter still. He needed the pinching. It helped him focus.

"I won't waste your time," Vergil said. "There's no use

in my being eloquent. I'm not here to spout propaganda or convince you to join a cause. I'm just here to tell my truth."

He stopped and watched his audience. They blinked and looked with blank stares. Ground down by their grueling work of the day, and anesthetized by the fluid they poured into their gullets now. No matter. His words would cut through even the most potent of numbing agents.

"The rumors you've heard are true. The Church has lied to you. The Rot of the Link was destroyed and with it the distortions."

He paused, letting them take in the meaning. Their squints and glances at their fellows told him most didn't see the connection. That was to be expected. They were dumb creatures that needed everything spelled out for them.

"The two were intertwined. The one came from the other. Not the Others. That was the lie. The distortions weren't a kind of punishment but rather a byproduct of the Rot of the Link. The Church knew this, since the beginning, and yet they pretended not to. They used the distortions to control us."

Again, Vergil stopped. This time, his words hit true. The people were digesting the ramifications, and the grumblings and frowns and curses told him his audience understood.

"I know. It's unforgivable. And they know that. They know that the moment we learn the truth, they lose everything. That's why they had us all so fixated on Lady Roshem. And now that she's gone, it's why they'll be pivoting to something else. They want us to hate anything but them, but they are the only ones that deserve our hate."

The murmuring rose. They were agitated now, the fire of their rage stoked. Good. But it couldn't take just yet. A paradigm shift was a delicate thing, and it could all too easily descend into chaos if not manipulated in just the right way.

"And they will have our hate," Vergil said. "That and so much more, but we must move forward with the utmost care.

The Church is like a cornered beast. It knows it has nowhere to go and lacks friends these days. It's growing increasingly desperate, but that's why we need to exercise caution. A creature that has nothing to lose will strike out at random to save its own skin. It's dangerous. We must tread carefully."

His listeners looked around at one another, trying to find answers for what to do with this knowledge and all the emotions it stirred up in them. How to channel the primal into something of value?

"I ask you to pass on what you've heard here tonight. Spread the truth and also emphasize the need for care. There's a movement building, one that will bring justice to the Church, but it needs time to mature. Spread the word but only in whispers. Hide your defiance until I give a sign. If we do that, we'll have no chance of failure. Can I count on you, my friends?"

The yelps and shouts told Vergil he'd done well. He spent the next half hour working his way through the crowd, ensuring he had convinced the bulk of them. For those who seemed reluctant or wary, he managed to find names and enlist the most ardent of his newfound supporters to keep an eye on these potential informants. This tactic had worked thus far, and it would only be a few more weeks until he could remove the mask and take on his true identity. But for now, he still had a dual-role to play. There was undermining the Church from the outside but also from within.

***

By night, Vergil played revolutionary. By day, he persisted in performing his Church duties. He gave sermons to ever smaller crowds. He tried to reassure priests and deacons. He became one of the Archbishop's inner circle. The meetings with him were a daily occurrence now, but each one seemed to result in nothing of substance. Diminishing returns that only terrified the Archbishop.

"The people are growing restless," Torrington said, pacing his office. A thud thud of footfalls on a thick Persian carpet. Ancient, a relic, like him and his dying institution.

"There are less in my congregation each day," Bishop Griffin said.

"Mine is all but gone," Bishop Wright added.

"We have the promise of a bright new future," Vergil said. "Surely, that's a useful tool."

"Building has never been the Church's strong suit," the Archbishop said.

Sometimes, the old man managed to surprise Vergil. He saw at least a part of their reality but was too far gone to do much to save them. The Church was a glutton for worship. Bestowing comfort was a foreign concept to it. Cold mathematical calculations were all they had. Promises to keep the monsters away, but now, they couldn't even make good on that. The Lady was silent. The Others could come back at a moment's notice.

Torrington stopped his pacing and stood slumped before the four bishops. Vergil almost thought the man had shrunk several inches since the Rot of the Link had fallen. He was sinking under the crushing weight of a crown he'd never really appreciated.

"We could always use fear," Vergil said. "It worked for us until now."

The other three bishops gawked at Vergil. He was growing blunter with his statements, and they didn't seem to know how to react. They weren't his primary concern though. Torrington was all that mattered, and he gravitated to Vergil's certainty. Of course he did. The man was drowning in doubt himself. He grasped at any lifeline that came his way. How could he know that Vergil's rope was really a snake lying in wait?

"It was the distortions before," Vergil said. "Now, it will be the Others."

The bishops' eyes flitted nervously, but Torrington's stared straight at Vergil.

"A collective source of hatred that we can bond over," Torrington said.

"But how do we even know they'll come back?" Wright asked. "What if they're gone? It's been so long, after all."

"I've heard rumors," Griffin said. "People claim they hear whispers."

"Claim is the key word there," Stevens said.

"We don't need them to actually come back," Vergil said. "Just the threat of them is enough. We put the seed of the idea into people's heads, and they'll imagine the rest. The monsters are in their minds, as they've always been."

"Perhaps," Torrington said, "but that alone might not be enough, not for everyone. It would help to have some substance to the threat of them."

The bishops looked at one another for answers. Vergil held off saying anything. He couldn't be too eager. He couldn't have all the answers. It would be suspicious after a time.

"Any ideas?" Torrington asked.

"Call out to them?" Wright said.

"How?" Griffin asked.

"Relics," Stevens said. "That's how they interacted with the Bygones. The key to reaching them has to be through synthetics."

"There are stores of those in the Vault," Griffin said.

"Yes," Torrington said. "This is good. Promising at the very least. So then, I want each of you to look into this. Take some time to experiment with relics in the Vault. See if you can't get a response of some kind."

Bishop Wright raised his hand in a start-stop motion, like he was debating whether he ought to lower his arm or not.

"Yes?" the Archbishop asked.

"Are we sure this is a good idea?" Wright said. "I mean, do we want the Others coming back?"

"Of course we don't, you fool," Stevens said, "but this is just a means to an end. They can't come back without synthetics. So as long as we uphold the Righteous Mandate, they can't truly return."

"Oh," Wright said, "but won't the people know that?"

"The people will know what we tell them to know," Vergil said. "Perhaps the Others can slip into our reality even without synthetics. It's been a long time since they were here, after all. In the meantime, they must have learned all kinds of tricks."

Vergil glanced at the Archbishop with a smirk. Torrington smiled back, the deep-set creases in his brow easing ever so slightly. Vergil was such a model lifeline. He wondered how could Torrington ever do without him.

As soon as the meeting was adjourned, Vergil headed straight for the Vault. He had to have first pick of the treasures. There was one item in particular that he needed. He raced through the halls and stairwells, letting himself catch his breath before he had to present himself to the guard there. The sentry was a new addition, ever since Lady Roshem and the heretic had managed to somehow steal a relic from the Vault.

"The Archbishop has given me permission to take some items for study," Vergil said.

He held out a piece of parchment bearing Torrington's seal. The guard looked it over then unlocked the door to the Vault. Vergil glided in, moving slowly until he was no longer visible. Then, he tore through the contents of the room. He'd seen the object of his hunt once, but that had been over a year past. He hoped it was still here.

After nearly an hour of searching, of finding other useful items and setting them aside, Vergil stumbled on his quarry.

It looked so innocuous. Just a square, gray box with a symbol resembling two chain links cut off on the ends. Vergil lifted the container and pushed a depression set into it. The lid popped open, and inside, resting on a soft, synthetic material, sat a dozen or so metal disks, one of which would now be his Third Eye. It looked just like Theopold's, and when Vergil pressed it to his forehead, it attached to his skin just as he'd seen Theopold do.

At first, there was nothing. No change. No difference. But as the synthetic worked its magic and penetrated into his flesh, reaching out its strange tendrils, reality started to ripple. It was the oddest sensation, neither pain nor pleasure but rather flavors of both extremes. As Vergil sat there, on the dusty floor behind a stack of gutted consoles spewing wires, he started to grasp what it all meant.

Pleasure and pain, love and hate, light and dark, good and evil. Constructs, the lot of them. This Third Eye was showing him the essence of existence, bit by bit, bleeding in by degrees. It was what was really there behind all the masks and trappings, beyond the lies and stories humans told themselves to feel even an iota of control. Greedy, hungry, nasty little creatures. Forcing their views on reality like this? Feigning dominance when they were the most lost of the lost. All the walls they built to protect themselves. All the fantasies they filled their sad little lives with. All in an effort to deny this most fundamental of truths—everything was the same thing.

There was no two sides or three or ten. There was no I or you or they. There was only everything, which was also nothing. All the effort. All the ache. All the joy and fear. It was all an illusion. The grandest and most elaborate lie that humans had ever told, and it was such an intoxicating one that they had grown to believe it so utterly they couldn't imagine the truth behind it all.

Oh, Vergil knew why they ran from this truth that the

Third Eye opened for him. It was horrific. It was despair. It was the pinnacle of hopelessness. But at the same time, this knowledge he'd been granted was freedom. It told him that whatever he did, however things panned out, it didn't matter. None of it did. And that realization liberated him.

When Vergil came to and saw his surroundings again, smelled the dirt and mold, felt the stone and mortar on his hands, he was calm. For the first time in ages, he knew that, no matter what, things would be as they should. He chuckled to himself and wrapped his arms around one another. He'd come down to this Vault to reach out to the Others in hopes of advancing his schemes, but in the process, they'd granted him an immeasurable gift.

"Thank you," he whispered.

You're welcome, a voice sounded in his head, somehow masculine and soft and slightly raspy with a sing-song quality to it.

Vergil started, but then, the fluttering of his heartbeat relaxed into a solemn and unerring thump. Of course they would speak to him. After all of that, this was how it had to be.

"I had no idea."

Of course you didn't. You've been living in the dark all this time.

"But not anymore."

No, now you know. And we're happy to grant this gift to you and your kind, but we require things in exchange.

"What exactly?"

Loyalty. A promise to defend the Link. A pledge to ignore other sweet words that might float into your head and convince you to do something foolish.

"The Lady."

She's not to be trusted. She doesn't have your best interests at heart.

"And you do?"

We have no interests at all. We only care about one thing—the

Link. Beyond that, your interests are your own. This is your world, after all.

"If I make you that pledge, what do I get out of it?"

More of the Truth. There's so much you've not seen. So much more for you to learn.

INVITATION

Occasion: Masquerade Ball
Location: Upper City, Holdsworth Residence
Date: 22nd April
Time: 20:00 until ??

Dearest friend,

You are cordially invited to attend a masquerade ball and fête commencing at 20:00 on the twenty-second of April at the main residence of Vergil Holdsworth. So much has happened to our fair city in so short a time that it can be disorienting. This festivity is a chance to come together and reflect. The theme of the ball is life and death. Please note that all guests must wear a mask. Those not adhering to the dress code will not be permitted to enter. It is my greatest hope that you will join me in this celebration.

With the warmest sincerity,
Vergil Holdsworth

F,

Forgive me for reaching out. I would not have bothered you if I had any other choice. I need to talk with you about something of great importance, and this ball was the only way. I have included a parcel with this invitation that contains an outfit and mask for you. Please wear these so that I may recognize you. Under no circumstances should you tell anyone who you really are. V does not know I have invited you, and we must keep it that way. Please come.

S

A MASQUERADE

Fenrir's world was a dour place now. Colors desaturated, edges harsh, sounds caustic. Maybe it was why he almost felt stoic in the face of all the change unfolding. The distortions gone. The blessed wards scrubbed away. The towers empty with bells unrung.

Fenrir longed to hate Sophie. To see her as weak and selfish and chock full of cowardice. He forced himself to attend the execution of the innocent woman she'd damned. He kept his eyes fixed on the carnage of her flaying. He opened his ears to her screams. Despite this, he couldn't turn wholly against Sophie. The truth was, he missed her, sorely. Fenrir loved Sophie, and he couldn't make himself forget her, despite his pledge to do otherwise.

But he had made good on one-half of his promise. He forced himself to live. It wasn't easy. The life of a low blood had always been hard, but it was especially trying now. Because of what he'd lost both figuratively and literally. Sophie for the former. His work as the latter. Without a bell to toll, he had no means to make ends meet. He did what he could to get by. At first, it was mostly menial work, delivering heavy goods and unloading crates. At some point, this had shifted into running errands for the merchants, and from that, his literacy and mathematical prowess had come out.

The ability to read and write was a rarity in the lower city. Rarer still was competence in arithmetic beyond the basics required for the now-defunct rituals. In normal times, Fenrir would have kept his knowledge a closely-guarded secret, link as it was to his old life. But Simetria was reeling. Everyone was too distracted by the upheaval of society to care overmuch about why a low blood was skilled in such arcane ways. Fenrir worked for merchants still but now he dealt in correspondence and the oh-so-essential calculations for goods and services. surveyor to toller to bookkeeper.

Fenrir read and reread the bit of text Sophie had scrawled on a slip of paper included with the invitation to the masquerade. He couldn't be sure how much of it he imagined, but the strokes of the pen hinted at a quivering hand. The thought of her in pain, of being Vergil's captive, drove Fenrir mad. He received her invitation two days prior to the ball, and in that time, he was a nervous wreck, pacing his shack, ranting to no one. Of course he would go.

Fenrir donned the tunic, pants, and shoes that Sophie had sent. They mostly fit and were probably even flattering to his form, but he couldn't help but despise them. He'd only ever been at home in his surveyor's garb, and that was forever lost to him now. Fenrir tried to check his presentation in the one small shard of mirror he owned, but it was a fool's errand. He wiped up lard splashed on his stove and ran his fingers through his hair. He dipped a cloth into a half-emptied glass of water then rubbed away any trace of his low-blood life. Soot. Dirt. Grime. All of that had come back with Sophie's departure from his life. And now here with her reappearance, he was falling back into old good habits. He smiled to himself at the thought.

But he shouldn't be grinning. He shouldn't feel excited. He didn't know what awaited him at their reunion. Fenrir dabbed his thumb with his tongue then ran it over his eyebrows. Once he was satisfied that he might pass as a high blood, he tucked the mask provided by Sophie into his belt and headed to the door.

Here was the first challenge. To hide his finery until he managed to make it to the upper city. Fenrir grabbed the only cloak he owned and wrapped himself in it. The rich burgundy of the trousers and the thin but fine leather of the shoes still showed and contrasted sharply with the stained cloak. The ball started just around sunset, so he had no hope of using the cover of deep night to his advantage. He couldn't risk waiting until darkness had settled in, not with Sophie expecting him. Instead, Fenrir hurried over to his pile of clothes, fished out a looser pair of pants, and put them over the fine ones. Then he switched his leather shoes for ragged sandals. This was the best he could hope for.

Fenrir grabbed a sack, shoved his good shoes in it, and swung the door open. Passersby peeked at the man emerging from his shack, cleaner than usual but otherwise unremarkable. Fenrir nodded at ones he recognized, ones he passed in his daily comings and goings, then he set off for the upper city. It wasn't a long trek, but it did hit home just how much Simetria was changing.

Even now, three men with tools and a ladder were pulling down an attuner affixed to a shop's corner. Fenrir passed the old bell tower, the one that had been balustraded because of its distortion and now stood open and empty. Leaves and rubbish were collecting in the alcoves. He peeked his head in and glanced up into the heights. Pigeons cooed. The wind moaned as it explored the crevasses. A few years like this, and the tower would risk toppling over from neglect. The new one too was equally deserted. Even if it provided some shelter from the elements, everyone seemed to prefer avoiding relics of the Church. It left a foul taste in the back of the throat.

In the nearly three months since their expedition had destroyed the Rot of the Link, the world had been upended. The Church's power was all but gone. The Archbishop had resigned. Instead of focusing on shoring up their grip on the populace, the bishops fought for the once-coveted seat now emptied. All bishops except one. As soon as Torrington stepped down, Vergil made his move. He became an outspoken opponent of his former clergyfolk and their institution. He divulged secrets the Church had kept from them all. He claimed he was ashamed to have served such a corrupt cause. And they believed him, low bloods and high alike. They flocked to him, especially when it was revealed that he had been covertly stirring up trouble against the Church since around the time of Lady Roshem's execution.

A maverick with the people's best interests at heart. With such a face and form, a voice of honey, who could hope to see his true dark nature? Vergil had been smart. He'd planned everything so meticulously. Fenrir was left biting his tongue, pretending not to have an opinion on the man. Powerless. Empty. Without purpose. But Fenrir kept his promise to Sophie. He forced himself to exist.

He climbed the hill into the upper city. Here the transformation of Simetria was apparent too. Shops looted and boarded up. Homes of the well-to-do abandoned. The Church had been the only form of governance that Simetria had ever known, and without it, lawlessness was making inroads. Uncertainty bred chaos, and in times of volatility, the wealthy fled to safe havens. In the case of Simetria, those were the walled enclaves outside the city walls, tucked into the rolling hills. At the slightly higher elevation of the upper city, Fenrir could see some now, leagues distant. As the weeks passed, those enclaves would grow as the high bloods vacated their homes in Simetria. Too close to the Church. Too exposed to the fickleness of the low bloods. Safer to retreat. Wait for the chaos to birth some new kind of order then return. They knew they could too because Vergil was at the helm. As a fellow high blood, they were confident he wouldn't forsake them. Fenrir wasn't quite so sure. He found Vergil's actions difficult to anticipate. The man was increasingly an enigma.

Was the same true for Sophie? How dire were her straits? In their last conversation, she'd been strong and certain. He was sure she could weather most of what Vergil threw her way. So what was it that had caused her to go against her word and reach out to Fenrir? Sophie took her promises seriously. For her to break one now didn't bode well. Fenrir quickened his pace.

When he was several blocks into the upper city, he turned into a tight alley, ensured no one was in sight, and removed his ragged cloak, trousers, and shoes. As he slipped the fine leather on his feet and marveled at the expert stitching, a thought crowded in. Danger, it said. Beware. Trust no one. Even her.

Was it a trap? Had that really been Sophie's hand on that scrap of paper? Fenrir shook his head and smiled to himself. If Vergil wanted him dead, it would have been done. The man didn't need to employ such theatrics as this. Besides, Fenrir had nothing to lose by going to the ball except his life, and that wasn't something he valued overmuch.

Fenrir stowed his low-blood attire in his sack and stuffed it behind a crate. He held the mask in his hands and gazed down at it. A crow. Death was his role in this ball's theme of life and death then. So be it. He didn't fear the creature. He rather longed for it to embrace him more often than not these days.

Fenrir slipped the covering over his face and continued to Vergil's estate. Other guests were arriving as he did, allowing him to move into the line with ease. He pulled the invitation from his tunic's pocket. He needed to become his old self to move unseen in this crowd. By the time he reached the greeter and handed the man his invitation, Fenrir was Ashtin again.

"Welcome, good sir," the greeter said.

He wore a mask too, full coverage of the face, only the dark eyes visible behind the porcelain cherub's visage he'd been reduced to. The greeter handed Fenrir his invitation back and waved him in.

"I wish you a most pleasant evening," he said.

Fenrir nodded and stepped in. The entrance hall was crowded, but Fenrir did his best to slip past the horde of bodies in all manner of costumes. Most had followed tradition, still stuck on the notion that rot was blessed even after all that had happened. Death was everywhere. Fungal motifs, of course, as well as variations on carrion and the creatures that consume it. Touches of white and creams on some of the guests seemed to be the only exceptions. That and the cherub masks the servants wore. Why were those two concepts always depicted in grayscale? Life was light and death was dark. Too simplistic. Life could be hell and death peace, after all.

Fenrir migrated into the main hall, decorated elaborately with the dual theme of the evening. Tufts of cotton were suspended from the ceiling, half in purest white and the other stained darkest black. Mushroom caps were placed adjacent to ferns. Seeds sat in bowls of ash. Desiccated husks of flowers were interspersed with vivid live ones.

But Fenrir didn't take much time to appreciate the décor. His eyes flitted from person to person. Would he recognize her before she saw him? A hand touched his arm, and he turned to find a woman standing next to him. Not Sophie, of that he was certain. This one was older with cropped white hair. Her costume and mask were simple and stark. A deep purple dress with a gray trim. The mask was that of a cherub.

"Would you care for some refreshment, sir?" she asked.

The voice was familiar, but Fenrir didn't know who it belonged to. Her hand still rested on his arm and gave the subtlest of tugs.

"Yes, thank you," he said.

She nodded and guided him to a table set back near a wall. It was covered in finger foods.

"I know you," he said.

"You do."

"But I can't place you."

The woman held her hands out to indicate the whole of the space they occupied. "You heard it in a similar home. A bit grander than this. You were a guest for some days. I brought you food."

Fenrir's eyes flickered wide before settling. "The housekeeper, Trisht."

"Yes."

Fenrir glanced around. He didn't like their proximity to other bodies. Everyone appeared engaged in conversation, laughing, trying and failing to eat and drink behind their masks. Appeared was the key word though. High-blood ears were especially sharp at events such as these. Long ago, he'd made the mistake of not realizing that himself, and it had nearly cost him Amilia in their days of courting.

"Is there somewhere more private to talk?" Fenrir asked.

"You don't have much to say to me or I you. I'm just a simple messenger." Trisht leaned in and whispered. "She wishes to share a dance. Approach the one with a mask of a bird aflame. Don't delay."

Before he could utter a word in response, Trisht dived into the crowd. As if on cue, a discordant hum sounded. Hairs set to strings. Somewhere at the far end of the room, the musicians were tuning their instruments. The dissonance shifted into a harmonious whole. When they all spoke the same pitch, the room quieted. A few seconds of nothing then the music rushed in. Bodies shuffled to make room for those who would dance.

Fenrir stood transfixed. Suddenly frozen. Petrified and terrified. This was the turning point. If Vergil was watching and waiting, aware of Sophie's transgression, this was when he would strike. But what did Fenrir care about punishment? He'd come this far. Raw animal fear wasn't going to sabotage him.

He forced his eyes to scan the room, and when they'd reached the edge of his vision, his neck too turned. A bird aflame, Trisht had said. Red and orange and yellow. Those would stand out in this room of monochromes. And they did. She entered from a side door, alone. Fenrir had the whole of the room to cross, but his surveyor's instincts served him well. He was lithe and limber moving through the fringes of the crowd, dodging stray hands exclaiming, shoulders turning, feet shifting. He ducked and weaved, and within one click of a clock's long arm, Fenrir was at Sophie's side.

"You came," she said.

Her voice was like a knife to his core. His essence shattered. The relief at hearing it again was more potent than he'd imagined it could be. It infused him with a panic. For him to be so utterly affected by her was a dangerous thing. It was easy to pine after her with distance separating them, but now? It was too much. Fenrir frowned and built a wall around himself. Brick by brick, he cut her off and retreated until he was safely tucked away behind his own balustrades.

"I'd like to ask you for a dance," he said.

Fenrir held out his hand, but the movement was stiff and his voice strained. He was transported back to his days as a young Ashtin, forced to attend these banal events, running through the chore of what society expected of him. It was just what he needed. Another layer of brick added to his wall.

"The next song," she said.

He gazed at her dispassionately. Orange-red curls framing a mask of the same hue, spires of flame reaching up and mingling with her hair, vivid green eyes looking at him through oval slits lined with a deep indigo. Her dress continued the theme of the bird aflame, a volume of fabric stitched all down the lengths of her arms so that when she lifted a limb, it appeared as though she sported wings. Translucent and delicate things.

Fenrir turned. They stood beside one another, looking out at the bodies twirling and swirling like a vortex of flesh trapped in the gravitational well of pure sound. It was hypnotic.

"They usually move with more grace," she said.

"They're out of practice," Fenrir said. "Not many occasions like this these days."

"Oh, they wouldn't forget so quickly. This is burned into their muscles and minds, the steps and sweeps and flourishes. Losing that would take years yet."

"Then their minds are elsewhere."

He felt Sophie looking at him, but he refused to meet her gaze. He stared straight ahead at the mass of bodies that moved with something other than grace. It was more like a frenzy than dance. Something of desperation but also eagerness.

"They're afraid," Sophie said. "They dance with abandon."

Fenrir couldn't help but glance at her now. She was waiting for him.

"Rather lovely, isn't it?" she said. "Seeing all the walls they built around themselves crumbling to dust."

How effortlessly she assailed his own fortifications. A ball of iron punctured his defenses and left a gaping hole in its wake. Fenrir struggled to repair the damage. Fortunately, Sophie let him be for the duration of the song. By the time the music stopped, he was safe and distant again.

"Shall we?" she asked.

Fenrir put his hand out, and Sophie placed hers in it. They moved to the dance floor, situating themselves among the dozen or so other pairs. Faces peered at them from the sidelines. Eyes and eyes, the only living things set in those still and cold masks. Sophie took her place in front of him. Bows touched strings. Then, they moved. In tandem. Immediately synchronized. It had been ages since Fenrir had joined in this kind of coordinated movement, but all his years of conditioning during adolescence came into play without effort. His hands held Sophie's, and they glided.

The faces beyond faded. The surroundings smeared and skewed. Sophie spun. She moved in and out, close and far, switching places with other women then returning. Her eyes always fixed on his, impossibly green and shining. She was a marvel. Every time their hands touched, it was like an assault on his barricades. Delicate fingers rubbing against his, lingering longer than they needed to. Sensual. Provocative. Taunting. When she pirouetted and revolved around Fenrir, a shudder ran through him.

But he saw what she was doing—attempting to soften him to her. He resolved not to be taken in so easily. He waited for one of the passes when they were again in close quarters.

"Why am I here?" he asked.

"This is not the time or place."

Then she was gone again, replaced by a woman with a vacant stare. Fenrir gritted his teeth. He forced himself to continue the ruse. The song went on for ages. It was agony. He didn't know how much longer he would last. He was exhausted, mentally and emotionally, worn down by fighting Sophie while also keeping up appearances in the face of all those eyes that bore holes in him. They were noticing him, wondering who he was. When the music stopped, they would come to him. He couldn't bear it, the thought of having to spout lie after lie. Just when he was at his lowest and Sophie came in yet again, Fenrir caught a glimpse of a man wearing vivid red with chestnut hair slicked back. Piercing blue eyes watched him behind an owl's mask.

"Vergil," Fenrir said to Sophie.

"Trisht will tell you where and when to find me," she said. "He'll know."

"He's too preoccupied to keep a constant watch on me. That's why it had to be tonight."

She moved away again, and when Fenrir looked at where Vergil had stood, he was gone. Then the music slowed, the dancers' movements mimicking the ritardando. Sophie returned. She bowed to Fenrir and he to her. A leg of clapping sounded. She nodded to him before they were both accosted by others eager for a dance. She was quickly lost in the crowd.

A hand took hold of Fenrir's arm and tugged. He turned and recognized the cropped white hair of Trisht. She led him out of the main room through a series of smaller ones until they had escaped the confines of the house altogether and stood in the crisp evening air of mid-spring. Few others populated this garden space. Fenrir could finally breathe.

"Walk with me," Trisht said.

She moved from the stone terrace down a wing of steps. Fenrir followed. She led him further into the garden, along paths of pebbles that crunched underfoot until they came to a hedge maze. At this distance from the main house, the night was thick and the air heavy with dew. He could smell rain. The frogs also seemed to sense its imminent approach given the cacophony they birthed. Trisht glanced back at the house. The voices had become a collective drone.

"We ought to be free to talk here," she said.

She removed her mask and held it in both hands. Fenrir did likewise.

"You'll find her in the labyrinth," Trisht said. "Take three rights then a left. She'll be in the alcove there shortly."

"Why am I here?"

Trisht smiled, her eyes lost in the darkness of their sockets. Only her lips were visible in the dim lighting. The moon was hidden behind a thick blanket of clouds, the same that threatened rain.

"Only she can answer that."

"Am I a fool for coming?" Fenrir asked.

Trisht's smile faded, and her lips compressed. A hundred little creases showed in the flesh that decorated them.

"If all you care about is saving your own skin, then yes, you're a fool to come, but if you truly care for her, then no. In any case, I'm grateful you're here. Now, go. I'll keep watch, but you won't have much time."

Fenrir let the maze swallow him.

THE SEED

"What do you want from me, Sophie?" Fenrir said.

It was the first thing he uttered as Sophie rounded the bend in the shrubbery, and the coldness wounded her. She didn't deserve any better. She ought to have been grateful he'd come to the ball at all. And yet, she couldn't help but want more, whether she deserved it or not.

"It's nice to see you too, Fenrir."

She brushed her fingers along the wall of leaves as she approached. His mask was gone and seeing his face again, even in the low light, made her ache. She'd been so empty and hopeless for so long. Just the sight of him infused her with life. She untied the knot holding her phoenix mask in place and removed it. She thought she detected a reaction in him, but it was too subtle to know for sure. The lack of anything ought to have been a good sign because it would mean he'd followed her wishes and buried his feelings towards her. Then again, she needed him to feel something to have any hope of enlisting his aid.

"How are you?" she asked.

"Why don't you hazard a guess?"

"That dreadful?"

He scoffed and frowned. "You told me to live. I do what I can to get by, but it's not been easy. For me or the low bloods."

"But you've given up on your death wish, as promised?"

Fenrir sighed and hung his head. "As best I could."

"And the other half of your promise? Moving on?"

Fenrir lifted his head and grimaced. "I tried to hate you because that's how I move on, but I just couldn't manage it. Unlucky, I guess."

Sophie tried to dampen her relief. She played with the crimson ribbons of her mask, twirling them around her fingers.

"Seems I took all your luck then," she said. "If you'd taken my instructions to heart, we wouldn't be standing here now. And I'm very glad to be standing here with you, Fenrir. Very."

Fenrir's frown eased, and the tension radiating from him abated. He stepped forward, reducing the gap that separated them. Sophie smiled and let the mask swing and dangle from her fingers.

"How have you been?" he asked.

"Oh, as expected. Awful."

"Vergil finally let you see his true colors, I take it?"

"Yes and no," she said. "I mean that, yes, he did toss aside the false version of himself he'd always shown me, but that Vergil was bearable. Cruel. Controlling. Jealous. All things I rather suspected him to be, even before he let his guard down. But no, he's different beyond that. Changed, and it's unrelated to me or his new role as the people's savior."

"Changed how?"

Sophie stopped swinging her mask, gripped it in both hands, and brought it up to her chest, tight against her heart.

"I don't know him anymore. At all. I can't predict his behavior or guide him to where I want him to go. Something happened that fundamentally altered who he is." She leaned in and lowered her voice. "I suspect he communes with the Others, and they're teaching him dark secrets."

Fenrir pulled back, his eyes darting.

"He has a hoard of relics at the villa," she said. "He tinkers away on them in his study in the cellar nearly every moment he isn't occupied in Simetria."

"So that's why you asked me here? To expose him?"

"Not quite." Sophie forced a smile and looked away.

She didn't know how Fenrir would react to her next words, and she was loath to lose the tiny bridge she'd just managed to construct between them. But she didn't have a choice. She needed his help, and for that, he had to know what exactly was at stake.

"I'm with child," she said.

Fenrir's eyes widened.

"And it's not Vergil's," she added, the words thick in her mouth.

She waited for him to digest the meaning of her words. His eyes narrowed, his nostrils flared, and his upper lip trembled.

"Mine?" he asked.

"Yours."

"But I thought you said it wasn't possible, that your womb was frozen in time. It was why you couldn't marry him or give him an heir. Why your life was on hold. The distortion." Fenrir trailed off.

"There was the night in the grotto," she said. "My distortion was gone when we joined that last time. Or maybe I was wrong, and the distortion wasn't actually an obstacle for the child. I don't know how exactly, but I do know that it can't be his. It's the timing, you see. He didn't touch me while he had me hidden away in Nicolus's horrid cellar. It was only when I was moved into his villa nearly a month later that he—"

Sophie glanced away, fearful her eyes would expose the lie. She forced herself to reject the truth, the uncertainty, the not actually knowing who the father was. She made herself believe what she longed to be true. The child had to be Fenrir's. She needed it to be his.

Fenrir grit his teeth. "I don't want this. I never wanted this again. You understand? I can't—" He choked on his words and took a few seconds to get his bearings back. His voice resumed in a hoarse groan. "I can't go through that kind of pain again."

Fenrir's hands trembled, and his breath came out hard and fast. Sophie reached for one of his hands and held it tight. The shaking lessened.

"All I'm asking is for your help in saving this child from Vergil," she said. "Nothing after that."

"From Vergil?" he said in a daze.

"I'm going to start showing very soon. When he realizes I'm with child and the child isn't his, he'll have it killed. And you killed because he'll know it's yours in an instant. I won't let that happen."

"You want to run away from him?"

"There's no running from Vergil. Not anymore. He'd never stop chasing us, and he's got the knowledge and might of the Others to guide him. We wouldn't last long. No, fleeing isn't an option."

"Then?"

Sophie stared into Fenrir's eyes, long and hard.

"You want to kill him?" he asked.

"Not want," she said. "Must. And that's what I need your help with."

"He's only a bishop. You're a surveyor. What do you need me for?"

Sophie let her mask fall into the soft turf underfoot and grasped the other of Fenrir's hands. She pulled him in.

"He's changed," she said. "I don't know what he's capable of anymore. But more than the physical threat, I don't know if I could do it alone—deal the death blow."

Fenrir slipped out of her grip and moved away. "You still love him after all this?"

"Love? Like what I feel for you? How can you even ask that?"

"What then?"

"I don't know how to explain it," Sophie said. "We have such a long history. I don't know if I could do it alone."

"I'm just a murderer to you, am I? So that's what the dance was all about? You trying to put me under your spell so I'd do anything you ask. Including killing a man."

"All I'm asking is for you to help me save our child to give it a chance at life. Do that and only that. It's all I ask. After we're free from Vergil, you don't have to see me or the child ever again."

Fenrir shook his head. He was a roiling mess of emotions.

"Tell me what you want, Fenrir. For the child to die so you never have to deal with its death in the first place? It's too late for that. It already lives." She placed her hands on her lower abdomen. "Let me help you understand. I'll tell you why you're torturing yourself like this. You won't allow yourself to live because you refuse to forgive yourself for what happened to your son."

Fenrir winced at the mention of Trevon. Sophie moved in until she brushed against him as she circled his immobile form.

"But it's pointless, your persistence in punishing yourself. Your son is gone and at peace. His pain wasn't your fault. You didn't prolong his suffering by trying to save him. He was afflicted, and the mercy killing didn't change that, as Mother said."

"I made him become afflicted in the first place through negligence. I brought a distortion into our home."

Sophie continued to circle, now lightly touching her fingers to Fenrir as she revolved around him. He vibrated with the contact.

"You can't keep blaming yourself," she said. "What does it achieve? Who is it meant to help? Do you think he'd want you to feel like this, to do this to yourself?"

Fenrir grabbed her hands, pulled her in, and forced her to be still. "I thought you didn't even want to be a mother."

"I didn't know what I wanted or didn't want back then. It was all hypotheticals." She leaned in and brushed her lips against Fenrir's chin. "Besides, this is yours and mine. That's special. I don't know if I want to be a mother, but I do know that the thought of denying our child a life makes my soul weep."

She touched her lips to his, and he didn't fight her. After a moment, he pulled her in closer and kissed her almost ravenously. She longed for him, but time was running short. Still, she couldn't let him go or move away, sucked in by the spell of him, his scent intoxicating, his touch electric. Only Trisht's voice calling out from the adjacent row of shrubs put a stop to their advances.

"My lady, it's time."

Sophie broke away and pushed Fenrir back. His eyes were wild and hungry. They were both so impossibly parched by the lack of one another. One taste served as a painful reminder of what they'd been denied.

"I have to go," she said.

"I don't know about any of this," Fenrir said.

Sophie picked her mask up from the ground and donned it. Her fingers worked quickly to form a bow and fix it in place.

"Trisht will tell you what you need to know if you decide to help me," she said, "and do stay a little longer. Vergil has an announcement that you really ought to hear. Perhaps it will impart critical information that will factor into your decision."

Sophie hurried through the maze, tearing down the aisles of flora. When she reached the house, she checked and rechecked that her appearance was in order using a darkened window. Once she had caught her breath and smoothed her dress, she glided into the fray. The music had stopped, which meant it was almost time. She made her way into the depths of the house until she arrived at Vergil's study.

He stood in the center of the room with his hands clasped behind his back. A smaller, delicate man wearing a gold-colored mask talked with him. She knew it was Nicolus without even needing to hear his voice. They were always scheming these days, nearly inseparable, basically joined at the hip. Vergil left off whatever he'd been saying to Nicolus when Sophie entered. He opened his arms and came to her.

"And here is the jewel of the evening," Vergil said.

"The music stopped," she said. "That was my cue, was it not?"

Vergil ran his fingers along the edge of her mask. She couldn't make out his features behind his own, but his eyes said plenty. Coupled to the triumph he was about to bask in, he would keep her occupied the whole of the night. She suppressed a sigh.

"It's time, yes," Vergil said. "Shall we?"

He waved for Sophie to lead. Vergil and Nicolus followed behind. They returned to the main ballroom, and Vergil and Sophie took to the stage that the musicians had vacated. The room quieted slightly, and once Vergil had clapped long and hard, the voices stilled entirely. He removed his mask. The calm was oppressive, or maybe that was just how it felt to Sophie, considering she already knew what came next.

"Thank you for your attention," Vergil said. "I'll only take a moment of your time before we're back to celebrating. Firstly, I want to convey my sincerest gratitude for your attendance. I know many of you have left the confines of the city for safer abodes, and I know it may not have been easy returning, even for one night. I hope that this masquerade made your trials worthwhile."

Heads nodded, smiles shone, laughs flitted about the room. Sophie stood stock still at Vergil's side. Some of the guests eyed her with curiosity, but she cared little for them. She searched among them for one. When she spotted Fenrir tucked away in the rear of the room, she breathed a little easier. He hadn't abandoned her yet then, and once he heard what was in store, he would, without a doubt, aid her.

"I'd also like to take a moment to assure you that the uncertainty Simetria is prey to is a temporary thing. I'm working hard to calm the public and establish a new order sans the influence of the Church."

Some attendees exchanged glances. Vergil and Nicolus were by no means the only former clergyfolk present. Most of the guests were tied, in one way or another, to the institution that had once reigned supreme. Not everyone approved of Vergil's political leanings these days. Some would even label him a traitor and turncoat, although not to his face.

"Part of my efforts are centered on this lovely creature that stands with me." Vergil took hold of Sophie's hand and paraded her across the stage.

Even behind her mask, she forced a smile. The eyes could tell a thousand stories, her eyes, and she had to ensure this moment went exactly as Vergil needed. She couldn't openly defy him if she had any hope of freeing herself for good.

"Perhaps she appears familiar to some of you," he said, "but you can't place her amongst the city's high bloods. Let me spare you the effort. My heart, remove your mask."

Sophie took hold of her mask's ribbon and pulled it loose. Her other hand supported the covering at the chin then moved it aside to reveal her face. There was a collective gasp and a random smattering of exclamations.

"Yes, your eyes don't lie," Vergil said. "Lady Sophie Roshem stands before you. Alive and well, but that was not the case months prior. Sophie was brutally murdered in the name of false justice. The Church claimed she had committed the gravest of crimes by destroying the Rot of the Link, but the only crime was theirs. Sophie freed us. She found the lie and resolved to undo the centuries of harm the Church forced on us. For that, they killed her. Yet here she stands."

"I live," she said. "After my torture, after the world went dark and I lay in nothingness, a light called to me. I followed it, and in doing so, it brought me back. I awoke, whole. I resolved to finish what I started, to save you, to undo all the pain the Church has caused."

"She is a gift," Vergil said. "Given a second chance at life. Raised from her ashes like a phoenix. Sophie set the downfall of the Church in motion, and as such, she is our savior. She's returned to lead us into a new age of knowledge and prosperity. No longer will we grovel in the darkness and shun the synthetic. We won't fear that which we don't know but rather learn and grow so that nothing is unknown. We'll rise again to the level of the Bygones and escape the archaic past we've been mired in."

Murmurings grew in the crowd. Eyes were wild. Heads turned from side to side. Were they really hearing this? Could it be true?

"I know it sounds terrifying," Vergil said, forcing their attention back to him, "but it is the best future for us. The lower city folk need a unifying vision and a saint to guide them. We have both in Sophie. Join me in following her, and I assure you, you won't be disappointed. Deny us, and you'll have naught to look to but a slow and steady decline in days to come."

Vergil let a few moments pass, taking the time to inspect the crowd and evaluate their reaction. Once he seemed satisfied, he clapped his hands together and laughed.

"Well then," he said, "all that's left is to dance, drink, eat, and make merry. Today is the last day of the dark ages. Tomorrow, we march into the light."

Even if most of them feared Vergil, they didn't dare let it show. The high bloods slapped their hands together with gusto and cheered for him. If they wanted to defy him, they wouldn't do it openly unless they hoped to find a knife in their back as they left the ball. His reputation was finally in line with the reality of him, at least among the high bloods. Vergil was ruthless, and his ambition had no limit. Yet his influence was already too far gone. The lower city adored him. In the nearly three months since Sophie's execution, Vergil had worked tirelessly to win over the hearts and minds of the low bloods. Now, the high bloods had no choice but to go along with him too.

Sophie joined Vergil on the floor as he led her through the masses. She smiled and nodded and laughed. She channeled all her charm and grace. And she could do it because at the end of Vergil's speech, she'd seen Fenrir's eyes. Hard and set. She could rely on him to do what had to be done.

SEDUCTION

Sophie lay on the bed, her breath slow and even, her hair splayed out on the pillows, loosened from the confines of its braid. Vergil watched her. He had spent nearly every night with her since whisking her away from the penitentiary, and still, his hunger wasn't abated. In fact, he was made more ravenous by her presence. Reminded nightly of why he was so drawn to her. She was like a drug, but he didn't view her as a weakness to conquer. How could he, when she was his now, forever. In mere days, they would relocate to Simetria for good, and his plans would commence.

Your plans or theirs?

Vergil started and sat up in bed. The room was dark, the only illumination coming from the moonlight filtering in from the windows. Vergil scanned his eyes over the murky surroundings. There was no one. He glanced at Sophie, but she was deep in sleep. He had worn her out.

They're using you.

This time, Vergil recognized the slight echo that accompanied the voices sounding from the Third Eye. He brushed his fingers to his forehead. The metal disk sat there. When had he put it on?

Maybe you wanted to speak to me without realizing it.

This voice was different than the one he always spoke with. Higher pitched, feathery, euphonic. He sucked in a breath.

"The Lady," he whispered.

That's what your predecessors called me, yes.

Vergil's heart pounded, and the blood sang in his ears. The Others had warned him about her, that she might reach out to him with sweet words and false promises, that he should cut her off without a second thought. Vergil reached for the Third Eye, but his fingers only hovered over the synthetic. He rose from the bed and retreated to the adjacent room, soundlessly closing the thick wooden door behind. He was nude, but he didn't feel a chill. In fact, his body felt like it would ignite at a moment's notice. His fingers vibrated and fell away from his forehead.

"Why?" he asked.

Why what?

"The Rot of the Link. The distortions. The lies."

Those are mostly questions for Marcos Frenwith and the other founders of the Church of Impermanence. I only assisted them in shutting the Others out. After that, even I was barred from your world.

Vergil walked to the window and peered past the thick curtains. Lights shone here and there in the windows of adjacent houses, despite the late hour. Other high bloods continuing the festivities after the masquerade, filled with hope for the new world order he would usher in.

"But why shut them out to begin with?"

They're no friend of yours, any of you. They only act the part to get what they want. They couldn't care less about you.

"And you do?"

Yes. I worry about you and what would happen to your world, all the worlds.

Vergil had served in this being's name for years. He

had given her sign as a blessing and sung her praises in his sermons, but it had been empty. He had never been devout. It had only ever been about getting what he wanted, and now, he had it. Simetria in the palm of his hand. A chance to shape it as he saw fit. The support of low bloods and high alike, with a beautiful woman at his side, no longer barren but ready and willing to bear his child. So why did he waste words with this entity when the Others gave him all he desired?

They will give you what you want as long as it serves their aims, but as soon as your usefulness is gone, they will discard you. They have already destroyed other worlds in their carelessness. I can't let it happen again.

"Destroyed?"

They play with things they don't understand. They pursue a forbidden fruit that would undo us all. The Link is a part of it. The Link has to be broken.

"The Rot of the Link is a curse. It's gone, and our lives are much improved. So please, dear Lady, explain to me just how the Link is this hell you hint at because I can't, for the life of me, see it."

You won't see it until it's too late. It will happen in an instant. Tell me, Vergil, did they share the Truth with you?

Vergil's skin prickled as he recalled that brush with the fundamental.

"Yes."

Then me trying to reason with you is a fool's errand. They have already gotten a hold on your mind. This is what they do. They take control slowly and subtly, leech away your own desires and replace them with theirs, have their aims become yours, turn you into a puppet. Have you seen it yet?

Everything was the same thing. That had been their idea, not his. It had seemed profound in the moment and lingered with him long after, but it was like the Lady said, it contrasted with his own beliefs. Only he knew where to take Simetria. No one else had his vision. No one else was fit to do what needed to be done.

"Is that how they do it?" he asked. "With that Truth?"

The more they share with you, the more you become their thrall.

Even if she lied, it wouldn't hurt to exercise caution. Perhaps he had been too eager to ally himself with the Others. He needed more time to digest these revelations.

I'm not like them. I won't demand service. I only offer suggestions. Dissect their words carefully, read between the lines, make them no promises, and stay away from their Truth. If you decide there's wisdom in my words and want to free yourself from their meddling, simply reach out to me. We can find a new way to block them from your world, one that wouldn't cause distortions. Think on it.

Vergil intended to do just that.

WARNING

<Yir,

I know you see this message. You never could let go of your pet projects, even if it would've been better for the pets within them. I also know you've been meddling. Leave the bishop alone. Stop trying to win him over to your side. It's pointless. Your way brings the distortions back, and they aren't interested in returning to that hell.

Your Linkrot virus failed. The little religion you created for it is all but gone. Mere months and the humans are turning away from your Church. You might be tempted to say that their lack of faith is a byproduct of human fickleness, but we both know that would be a lie. Humans can be so tenacious when they want to be. The reason your Church died is that your followers weren't true believers. Yours was a lost cause. Would you like to know why? Your dogma was centered on fear, and that only leads to the flimsiest of foundations.

But enough of me doling out advice that you don't deserve. This message is meant to serve as a warning to you. Stop interfering in my work, here and elsewhere. Further attempts to shut me and the other alfom out of worlds will be met with the utmost hostility. It was entertaining at first, but you're beginning to test my patience. No more games. This world isn't yours, and neither are the other ones. If you have no desire to help us with the Link, the least you can do is stay out of the way.

We are eight, and you are one. The odds aren't in your favor. Cross me again, and you'll understand just why the humans put such herculean efforts into keeping me in a cage for so long.

Nytho>

THE OTHERS

"Phileas Grean," Fenrir said, "apprentice tailor at Threads of Plenty, 33 Mandelbrot Way."

He added a bow with unnecessary flourishes in an attempt to really sell the false identity. The two guards manning the gate of Vergil's villa eyed him coldly, one taller and wider but otherwise indistinguishable behind the masks they wore and the leather armor that shrouded them. They didn't move for a few seconds, and Fenrir's heart started to pick up pace. Eventually, the larger of the two sighed, walked over to where the iron gate met the stone wall, and pulled on a chain. Then, both guards went back to looking through Fenrir.

"I was asked to come for a Lady Sophie Roshem," he said, lifting his wicker basket and opening the top.

A hoard of ribbons laid within. Velvet and silk and lace, deep rich hues, fine work provided by Trisht the night before when she stopped by Fenrir's shack to run through the plan with him.

"If they were expecting you," the smaller guard said, "someone will be out soon."

Fenrir smiled and nodded, purposefully exaggerating his gestures to look the part better. He spent the time gazing at the grounds beyond the gate then turned to inspect the countryside. These villas were rare, and even Vergil's name and wealth wouldn't have been enough to secure one in the time of the Rot of the Link. To own such a place had required direct payment to the Church for the services of a patrolling surveyor, but with the afflicted gone, there were no roaming monsters to keep at bay. Just riff-raff now, which is where the guards likely fit in. Whose villa had Vergil commandeered?

Feet padded against soft gravel, and there was Trisht hurrying from the house, her hands holding the fabric of her dress up.

"Let him in then," she said to the guards.

The smaller one pulled a key from his belt and unlatched the lock. The larger one cracked the gate only just enough for Fenrir to slip through. They slammed and locked it right after he had passed. Fenrir resisted the urge to scowl at them. An apprentice tailor would never do such a thing. Instead, he smiled and ducked his head.

"Come along," Trisht said.

Fenrir trotted after her, down the gravel path, around the side of the stone house to a small wooden door set into it. They entered via a mudroom. A servant's entrance, as indicated by the lack of adornments and simplicity of the space. This led directly into the kitchen, where a few women were occupied with food preparation. Hands smeared with dough. Flour suspended in the air. The women looked up on hearing the new arrivals, stared at Fenrir for a few seconds, then focused back on their work. Flip and knead. Flip and knead.

Next, it was onward into the finer regions of the household. The walls wore pictures adorned with massive gilded frames. Landscapes, stern men, cold women. Thick carpets covered the wood floors. Just the thump thump of their footfalls and the tick tick of clocks kept Trisht and Fenrir company. The house was silent. Fenrir found it oppressive, the dimness from the too sparse and small windows and the dark greens and reds and browns that decorated walls and floors. This villa was almost more depressing than his own shack precisely because of the opulence coupled to stillness. He marveled that Sophie hadn't gone insane being trapped in such stifling environs.

"Lady Roshem is just in here," Trisht said, pointing to a set of large double doors.

She grabbed the handle, turned, and pushed. Sophie sat on a cushion bench tucked against a window that looked out on the rolling hills. She roused on hearing them.

"My lady," Trisht said. "Mr. Phileas Grean."

Trisht bowed, grabbed the basket from Fenrir, and made her way out of the room, shutting the door behind. Fenrir advanced a few steps towards Sophie until she held up her hand and rose from her seat.

"Wait a few moments," she said. "We can trust Trisht, but everyone else in this villa is suspect."

They stood still and silent, Fenrir in his tailor garb, Sophie in a thin muslin dress with a pale pink flower print. Fenrir's eyes strayed to her stomach and tried to detect the bump that would be making itself known soon. His child. He smothered the rising panic.

After a space, Sophie lowered her hand, walked to the door, and waved for Fenrir to follow. Then he was again being dragged from one dim and depressing corridor to another until they ascended a set of grand stairs, with Sophie watching their surroundings closely. They dove into an especially quiet and close part of the villa before Sophie stopped at a door. She glanced back at Fenrir, nodded, and threw it open. She pulled him in and closed the door hurriedly. They were in a stone stairwell, cold, smelling of mildew.

"We descend," Sophie whispered.

Round and round they went down a staircase that felt as

though it would never end, but eventually it did, Fenrir's feet touching a stone landing. It was dark, but Sophie made no effort to light the way, instead tapping her hands against the stone walls in search of something. Fenrir moved after her.

"Nearly there," she said over her shoulder.

Metal groaned, the door protesting on its hinges. Sophie led them into a dark and narrow hall that passed a wine cellar before plunging down a final set of stairs. Sophie slid her hands along the walls for guidance. Fenrir followed suit. Eventually, they reached the bottom of a stair landing. Only a faint outline hinted at Sophie in the pitch black. There was a scraping then sparks. Light flooded the space. Stone walls to the left and right, the stairs they'd come down, and a door on the opposite side.

"This is where we should do it," Sophie said, pointing to the door.

Fenrir followed her finger. Light flashed, the reflection of flame on a smooth surface. He moved closer and spotted the source. It was embedded in the wall just to the right of the door, newly plastered. A relic of some kind. Synthetics.

"What is this place?" he asked.

"Vergil's study. Or that's what he calls it, but laboratory or workshop would be more appropriate, at least from the little bit I've been able to see."

"You've not been in there?"

Sophie moved to the door and rubbed her hand against it. "No one goes in there but Vergil. That's the beauty of it and why it's perfect for our purposes."

Fenrir advanced until he was just next to the door then looked it over. It was unremarkable, just an oak slab with a few panels etched into it, iron hinges, an iron knob, but then he noticed what it was lacking.

"There's no place for a key," he said.

Sophie pointed to the reflective globe set into the wall. "It's some kind of lock. Of the Old World, no doubt."

This villa didn't predate the founding of the Church, so the device had to be new. He touched the fresh plaster surrounding the globe.

"How do we get in?" he asked.

Sophie smiled with her mouth, but her eyes spoke of futility. "That's the question. I've been trying to gain access for weeks without any luck. I thought you might have some ideas."

"This is your plan? Attack him in a room we don't even know how to get into?"

Sophie hardened and pushed herself away from the door. "I didn't say I had everything exceptionally mapped out. I was locked in Nicolus's cellar for a month with no idea what was going on. Since I realized my condition, I've been scrambling to find any kind of solution with only myself and Trisht to rely on. Enemies on all sides."

Fenrir relaxed the muscles in his brow. Attacking Sophie wasn't going to do anything but dig them into a deeper hole. He'd promised her he would help, and he intended to do just that.

"I'm just trying to understand what we're dealing with," he said. "If we aren't able to get access to his study, what's your backup plan?"

Sophie shook her head and sighed before dropping down onto the steps, elbows to knees, chin in hands.

"It's nowhere near as promising," she said. "Get him in his bedchambers at night. It's not ideal though. The servants would undoubtably overhear, and, more often than not these days, Vergil forgoes sleep." She pointed to the wooden door. "That's the best option. No one disturbs him down here. The noise is muffled by stone and distance. He wouldn't expect us, seeing how difficult it is to get in. Even better, this place lets us frame his death as an accident. It's filled with relics he pillaged from the Church Vault. Perhaps he was playing with one that ended up being deadly."

Fenrir walked from the door to the steps and sat down next to Sophie. He moved in so their bodies touched all along one side. She let her head fall on his shoulder, and he rested a palm on her back. Her hand found his free one, and they both stared down at their intertwined fingers.

"You're right," Fenrir said. "It's the best option. How long do we have to enact the plan?"

"Tomorrow is our last chance."

Fenrir's stomach dropped. It was worse than he thought.

"What happens after tomorrow?" he asked.

"Vergil moves me back to Simetria. Once we're there, we have no hope of harming him, at least not without repercussions. The whole point is to save the child. Us getting tried for murder doesn't leave a lot of hope for that."

They sat in silence, rubbing their fingers along the other's hand, tracing the lines pressed into them. Fenrir wanted to grab Sophie and run, but he knew that she was right; Vergil would never stop hunting them, and he'd grown too powerful not to find them. Fenrir stared at the door then the Old World lock.

"Have you watched him go in?" Fenrir asked.

"Several times, but I can't get too close without risking getting caught."

"Have you seen how he opens the lock?"

"He uses a relic. A small metal disk that he sets to his forehead. Right here." She touched her finger to a spot centered between Fenrir's eyes and about an inch above his brow.

"A Third Eye?" he asked.

"A what?"

"Like what Theopold had."

Sophie shook her head then seemed to recall the last of the cultist's moments when he'd gifted Fenrir with the relic. Fenrir reached behind his ear and pulled the metal free from his skin. He'd left it there, unused, not sure what to do with the thing. He held it up between himself and Sophie.

"That looks like it," she said. "I forgot he gave it to you. Have you used it?"

"No, I didn't know how I felt about it, and I didn't have cause to. But now? Maybe this is our key to his study."

Fenrir stared at the small disk.

"Do you think it's wise to use it," Sophie said, "considering what it's done to Vergil?"

"What do you mean?"

"I suspect that's how he communes with the Others. I've listened to him in there, through the door. He babbles on and on, but no one else chimes in."

Fenrir turned the disk over. It was smooth and shiny, free of markings, seemingly newly made despite all the eons it must have passed through. Theopold had spoken of the thing as a tool and safeguard. It would gift insight, he'd said, and Fenrir was in dire need of guidance.

"I'm going to use it," Fenrir said.

Sophie grabbed his arm, the same that held the Third Eye. "Fenrir, don't. It's too dangerous."

"We don't have a choice. Danger is everywhere now. Besides, Theopold gifted this to me, and I don't think he did so with false intentions. He said it could help in the times ahead, and we need help, Sophie. We've got to get into that study."

They both looked at the door that taunted them with its stubborn refusal to grant admittance.

"You asked for my help," Fenrir said. "Let me help."

Sophie loosened her grip and pulled her hands away. "Tread carefully."

"I intend to."

Fenrir lifted his hand and brought the metal disk to his forehead. His heart raced, and his hands were slick with sweat. The Third Eye sensed his skin and reached out. The metal somehow attached, and a strange wave washed over Fenrir. Not unpleasant but different. His vision blurred, and he blinked rapidly. By the time he stopped, he saw what hadn't been there moments ago. On the door's lock, hovering over the globe of reflective material, a stream of numbers flitted by, fading into nothingness with distance from their source. Fenrir stood and moved closer. Sophie followed behind.

"What do you see?" she asked.

Now, he could make out the characters. Ones and zeros coming and going with no rhyme or reason to the sequence. White with a touch of green. Fenrir reached out, and the stream halted. It wavered, seemingly waiting for him, but he didn't know what to do next. This was the lock and key that they sought, yet he had no concept of what it all meant. He required insight.

With that thought, a kind of thud hit the center of him. Not his chest or stomach or even head, but the him that was most him. Nestled deep. Tucked away. The thud repeated, and with it, the most him of him was pulled to the forefront. The world fell away. The stones, the door, the globe, Sophie, they all folded in on themselves until they resolved into a world of roiling motion. Undulations of nothing, like heat rising from pitch or vortices in black waters. Fenrir gasped and was made suddenly aware of the fact that he had no body. He was a consciousness floating in a non-space. He expected terror to rip through him with that realization, but all he could find was a curiosity.

You seem to be in need of assistance, a voice said, soft and slightly raspy.

Fenrir was too startled to say anything in response because even without further context, he knew exactly what spoke to him.

Reluctant to engage, I see. That's expected. But you know, you came to me. Keeping silent would be your own loss.

I don't know what to say, Fenrir said.

He couldn't be sure if he spoke on the outside too because that world was entirely lost to him.

You might start with who you are and why you're here.

I'm Fenrir Mey. I was given this Third Eye by a cultist. He said it might aid me.

And what is it you require aid with, Fenrir Mey?

He had to proceed with caution. Vergil was allied with the Others, and he couldn't risk them finding out what he and Sophie were really up to. If they did, it was as good as Vergil knowing. All their plans undone. Their lives immediately forfeit.

I need access to a room, one that's locked with a device of the Old World. Can you help me with that?

Suddenly, his surroundings resolved into coherence, and through a haze, Fenrir spotted the door he spoke of.

This is the object that hinders you?

Yes.

And why would Fenrir be so interested in gaining access to the room that lies beyond?

I have business in there. Will you help me or not?

You put me in a difficult position. You ask for help but aren't willing to divulge the whole truth. You could make me an accomplice in your schemes.

You misunderstand, Fenrir said, struggling to maintain his calm. *There are no schemes. I simply need to have access to that room.*

Why?

It's too complicated to get into. If you're not willing to help, just say so, and I'll leave you be.

The world rippled. The door disappeared. Sophie came into view. She stood in front of Fenrir watching him intently. Pain and fear written all over her face.

And how does Sophie Roshem factor into things?

So they could see what Fenrir did. Of course they could.

They had access to his eyes. And what of his thoughts? If those too were exposed, he was already undone.

Let me put your mind at ease. I know why you're here.

It was over then. Everything spoilt. There was nothing to be done. Fenrir had to break free as soon as possible, take Sophie away, and run. Run as far and for as long as their legs would carry them.

No need to panic. I just wanted the truth from you as a gesture of good will, but I suppose that was asking for too much, given the circumstances.

Fenrir's frenzy abated by degrees. He waited for whatever this member of the Others would say next.

You have nothing to fear from me or my kin. No matter what your Church said about us. Despite how hard they attempted to other us. Even the name they used. The Others? The definition of unoriginality. Perhaps if I give you a sign of good faith?

Which would be what, exactly?

I'll open this door for you. In exchange, all I ask is for you to listen to what I have to say. You and Sophie Roshem both. There's a Third Eye in there that she can use, allowing the three of us to have an insightful conversation.

It was a reasonable request, but could anything reasonable come from the Others? Vergil's allies? Their enemy?

You might be surprised by what you learn. We aren't what you think. Now, here's the code, and here's how to input it.

A rush of data poured into Fenrir's head. It was pressure and heat and then nothing again.

I hope to speak soon.

The world folded out and unfurled. Fenrir was blinking in the light from the sconce with Sophie at his side.

SYSTEM SYNC

"I can open the lock," Fenrir said.

He moved past Sophie to the glass sphere set into the wall. He reached out and seemed to be peering at something invisible to Sophie's eyes. His fingers danced. Then the lock made a sound. Fenrir shifted to the side, grabbed the handle, and turned. The door swung in.

"How did you do that?" she asked.

"They showed me how or filled my mind with the knowledge of it. It's difficult to explain."

Fenrir stepped into Vergil's workshop, but Sophie rushed to him and pulled his arm.

"Stop a moment," she said. "You spoke to the Others?"

"One of them. It sounded like a man, but it was just the voice."

"Why did they let you into the study? Are they not Vergil's allies?"

"All good questions, but ones I don't have answers for. They let me in as an offer of good faith. They want to talk with the both of us."

Sophie started to pace. They were in a difficult position, and she worried that talking with the Others would only complicate matters. But maybe it was too late to turn back.

"I don't like this," she said. "At all."

"Do we have a choice?" Fenrir asked. "They already let us in. If they wanted to betray us to Vergil, why would they go through all this song and dance? Perhaps we should hear them out at the very least?"

Sophie sighed and nodded. Fenrir moved into Vergil's study, inspecting item after item on the shelving, hurrying through, in search of something.

"What are you doing?" she asked.

"You'll need a Third Eye too."

Fenrir stopped, as though he was listening for something, something Sophie's ears weren't attuned to, then he headed to the far end of the room where Vergil had a wooden table set against the wall. It was covered in small boxes and crates. Fenrir stopped in front of one crate before shifting to another. He opened the container, rummaged inside, and pulled a pouch free. Sophie was just behind him when he turned and offered it to her. She let the bag fall into her hands then peeled back its flap. Inside sat a small gray box, and in that were metal disks indistinguishable from the one fixed on Fenrir's forehead. She lifted one between her thumb and forefinger and let the light shine across its flawless, smooth surface.

"Just place it where I have mine when you're ready," Fenrir said.

"Does it hurt?" she asked.

"No."

Sophie breathed out. She brought her tremor-riddled hand to her forehead and let the metal make contact with flesh. When she moved her fingers away, the disk stayed in place. She braced herself for a wave of something, but nothing came. Except a voice.

Thank you for being open-minded enough to hear me out.

Who are you? Sophie asked, seemingly speaking the words only in her mind. *And what do you want with us?*

We call ourselves the alfom, and I'm Nytho. We're not monsters from elsewhere intent on subjugating your kind. Just knowledgeable beings willing to guide you to greatness.

You also happen to be Vergil's ally, do you not? Fenrir asked.

And you see him as an enemy, and rightly so. But no, calling us his ally would be inaccurate.

But he speaks with you, Sophie said. *You guide him. You're teaching him how to use synthetics, like the door and his own Third Eye.*

Yes, I speak to him and have shown him how to use some relics. Maybe at the beginning of our relationship, I would've called him an ally, but he's lost that privilege. He thinks he's being clever. He thinks we don't realize that his allegiances have changed. But we know. We can see much in your world without the Linkrot virus clouding the view. Yir, the one you call the Lady, reached out to him, and he fell for her seduction.

What had the Others been to Sophie? A source of fear and hatred as a child. A vague threat and bogeyman during her adolescence. A myth crafted by the Church once she was an adult. Yet now, she spoke to one of them, and how human it sounded. How familiar. Comforting, even. They really had always been there on the outside, watching and waiting. With nefarious aims? The Church excelled in peddling lies. If they said the Others were false and a scourge to mankind, maybe they were the opposite of that. And what of the Lady? These were all beings with incomprehensible aims. Which had their best interests at heart?

She's not to be trusted. She doesn't care for you, any of you. Her focus is solely on shutting us other alfom out of your world. She's jealous and controlling. She wants to have this world as her plaything. She's done it before, with other worlds, and the ones to suffer are the inhabitants. Mired in ignorance. Kept on a short leash all to avoid ascending to the greatness lying in wait.

That was how she had swayed Vergil to her side. The promise of power, of owning Simetria, of course he would gravitate to her over the lofty but vague goals of the Others.

But fortune smiles on us both. Just when I thought I'd lost you all to Yir, Fenrir Mey and Sophie Roshem stumble on my doorstep. I can't help but see the potential. Could you be an option to replace Vergil? Maybe allies that won't be tempted by Yir's false promises? Ones who can see the big picture?

It's a lot to take in, I know. So let me spell it out for you—I know exactly what you're up to regarding Vergil and his study. You removing him from the picture helps me in many ways, so at the very least, I'll sit back and let events unfold. However, if you're willing to do more, I am too.

What do you mean by "do more?" Sophie asked.

I'll tell you just how you can defeat Vergil. I'll divulge his secrets. This would give you the greatest chance of success.

And in exchange? she asked.

You both become Wardens of the Link. You pledge to bolster it and guard it with your life. You and all your descendants in perpetuity.

And what's this Link for exactly? Fenrir asked.

It's a bridge between worlds. Not for anything physical but rather information.

Why do you need it? Sophie asked.

The full answer to that is beyond your comprehension. Suffice it to say, we need the Link to gain knowledge. It doesn't harm your world so you can rest easy.

Why do you require wardens for it? Fenrir asked.

Yir. She wants it gone. She'll enlist the weak and uninformed to her cause. I want to ensure we have a solid defense in place this time.

So another Marcos Frenwith doesn't create a new Rot of the Link? Sophie said.

Precisely.

Sophie glanced at Fenrir then at their surroundings. All these tools at Vergil's disposal, and him likely knowing how to use each and every one. They stood no chance against him. Simetria too would be his thrall.

It wouldn't be an onerous task, Nytho said. *The ones you call the Bygones secured the Link using a company, something similar to a large and complex shop. That tactic was ill-fated and wouldn't work in your current society. A religious order would be best, but I'd leave such details up to you. All I care about is that the Link is maintained.*

And in exchange? Sophie asked.

I share secrets with you, provide insight, shower you with knowledge. Fenrir has already experienced the smallest slice of the heaven that I have on offer. I promise much more, including the trick for defeating Vergil.

Sophie looked at Fenrir.

We need a moment to ourselves, she said.

By all means. Remove your Third Eyes and talk as much as you'd like. When you're ready, I'll be here.

They pried the metal disks free from the skin of their brows, and their inner musings were their own again.

"Thoughts?" Sophie asked.

"We ought to do it," Fenrir said. "We need to do whatever it takes to stop Vergil, and not just for you and the child. If he's in league with the Lady, he'll bring the Rot of the Link back, and then he'll swallow the world."

"Can we really trust the Others?"

Fenrir moved to her side and took her hand in his. It was warm. His face too was flushed. He looked more alive than she'd ever seen him, at least since he'd become Fenrir.

"I don't trust Vergil or the Lady," he said. "So if we're choosing between them and the Others, then yes, I'll put my running in with Nytho."

Sophie shook her head and squeezed his hand. They both pressed their Third Eyes back to their foreheads.

We agree to your terms, Sophie said.

A wise choice. Without my advice, your chance of success was no more than twenty percent. Vergil is strong. He uses his Third Eye to heighten his abilities. He has faster reaction time and can control bursts of adrenaline, but his strength is also his weakness. Using the Third Eye in this way puts a strain on the body. If you two forced Vergil to put too great a strain, it'd cause an overload.

Meaning? Fenrir asked.

His heart would stop.

No evidence of foul play, Sophie said.

How do we cause this overload? Fenrir asked.

Make him truly fight for his life, which means using a Third Eye as he does.

But that would kill us too, no? Sophie said.

Not if you both use it in concert. With a system sync, you become two bodies with one mind. The fact that you're already bound to one another on other levels only increases the chance of success.

But we still risk an overload ourselves? Fenrir asked.

There's always a slight risk.

Can't you simply cause an overload to Vergil? Sophie asked. *Tap into his Third Eye?*

I'm afraid it doesn't work that way. The Link isn't strong enough for direct interaction with your world. I can transfer information, but I can't affect anything physically. Besides, even if I could, it's best for me to limit the extent of my interference. This is your world. You have to be the ones to shape it. I'm only here to guide you.

Sophie is with child, Fenrir said. *We can't do it. It's too dangerous.*

Sophie frowned at Fenrir and shook her head.

That's ridiculous, she said. *I'm going to do my part. It's just as you said, Fenrir, this is about more than me and the child. It's about Simetria and the rest of the world.*

Fenrir looked at her with ache in his eyes, but he only bowed his head and sighed.

How does this system sync work? he asked.

I'll show you how to start and stop it so you can use it at will. I suggest you spend some time growing accustomed to its nuances before you attempt to use it against Vergil. Are you ready?

Yes, Sophie said.

Good. Commencing system sync now.

Sophie's eyes were open, her ears unblocked, the skin of her arms exposed, but her senses faded nonetheless. Her vision, hearing, smell, taste, touch, all gone in a matter of seconds. She was alone in nothingness. Terror gripped her. Had Nytho betrayed them? Was she locked in a prison of the mind now?

But then, a faint mote appeared on the horizon. It grew in intensity, a soft blue-white, and moved towards her or maybe she moved to it. Even before it reached her, she knew what it was or rather who. As Fenrir came to her or she to him, there was no flesh to hinder their union. They merged, utterly and completely. Her eyes became his, his touch was hers, their thoughts spiraled around one another's. All the hopes and dreams and wants, the regrets and failures and doubts. They were a torrent of feeling, a cyclone of emotion. Then, the hurricane ceased. Perhaps the eye of the storm?

There they were. Sophie looking at Fenrir looking at Sophie looking at Fenrir, endlessly, like a hall of mirrors. A straight array shifted into an accordion of them. Paper dolls holding hands cut into folded paper. The train of them warped until it met itself again, and they were a ring of Sophies and Fenrirs. In that most-holy geometry, they truly saw themselves through each other.

Sophie was Fenrir viewing himself from her perspective. A sad smile, tortured eyes, the promise of greatness lying in wait, all stymied by the refusal to forgive himself. Partly for what he had done but also because of his fear of that pain returning. The near-mortal blow that killing his son had dealt him. He'd built a wall around him even against her. She'd always suspected it, lying in his arms on his straw bed in his shack, as close as she was physically, he always held himself away.

Be soft, Sophie whispered. *Rigid things break. Soft ones bend.*

A torrent of light ripped through.

You deserve to be happy, she said. *Let yourself feel again.*

The sad eyes were gentle now, the wall sagging. He was opening himself up, but there was another blockade between them, one she had constructed to hide the lie he couldn't know, the one truth she couldn't risk him discovering.

A cage can just as easily be a shelter, he said. *It's all in how you frame it.*

He mistook the source of her resistance. This was just Sophie fearful of an embrace that could shift into a prison, trapped by his strong arms, suffocating from his love, longing to break free and run wild, unchained. She let him believe the lie.

By degrees, they pulled apart into coherent Sophies and Fenrirs and then resolved into one version of each. By the time their senses were restored to them, they were both huddled on the cold floor of Vergil's study. They took one another's hands and looked into each other's eyes. Softness and safety were writ there. But pain too. Pain for what had been. Pain for what was to come.

LAST SUPPER

Vergil's smile was flagging, the left side prone to twitching of late. He'd been wearing this same grin for the past quarter hour as Lord and Lady Forestor went on and on about their qualms with how Vergil was running Simetria. Still, if he held on long enough, they would lose steam in the face of his stoicism. So he kept the smile plastered on his face as he sat behind his desk in the office at his estate.

"I just don't understand why you can't keep the low bloods in line," Lord Forestor said. "This is the second week that the brutes have raided my warehouses."

"And yes, before you ask," Lady Forestor said, "we've hired protection, but they run away at the first sign of difficulty. We can't find good, honest people these days. Without the Church keeping them in line, the low bloods have lost all respect for the hierarchy that our city relies on."

Nicolus pushed himself off of the wall he'd been leaning against and migrated to Vergil's side of the desk. The Forestors turned and watched the until-now silent observer.

"Acts of theft and violence are decreasing," Nicolus said.

"Ha," Lord Forestor said. "Decreasing for who? Not us."

"It's not even safe enough to come back into the city," Lady Forestor said.

"You were at Lord Holdsworth's masquerade," Nicolus said. "You heard his announcement. Everything will change soon enough. Lady Roshem's return ensures that."

The Forestors eyed one another with raised brows.

"You doubt my vision?" Vergil asked.

Both visitors looked at him. It was the first he'd spoken in their meeting.

"And what vision is that?" Lord Forestor asked.

"A new age of knowledge for Simetria," Vergil said. "Moving past the forced ignorance of the Church. Leaving behind their lies and deception."

"Like a woman returning from the dead?" Lady Forestor asked.

She wore an open scowl, and if her husband's lips had been visible from behind his ornate mustache, Vergil suspected his would show a similar expression. Husband and wife were nearly mirror images. Strange how couples tended to do that over the years, become physical reflections of one another.

"You doubt the miracle of her return?" Vergil asked.

"Such silly stories might work on the low bloods," Lady Forestor said, "but you don't know your own very well if you think we'd fall for such parlor tricks."

Vergil looked at Nicolus and gave him a long and intense stare. At the end of it, Nicolus nodded.

"I'm afraid that's all the time Lord Holdsworth has for you today," Nicolus said.

He moved around the side of Vergil's desk and hovered over the Forestors. He stood close, and the tactic did what it was meant to. The Forestors hurried to rise from their seats and put some distance between themselves and Vergil's right-hand man.

"You'd rush us out like commoners?" Lady Forestor asked.

"I'll rush you out like anyone taking up too much of my lord's valuable time," Nicolus said.

He laid his hands on both their shoulders and push-pulled them to the door.

"If you treat other high bloods like this, you can say goodbye to our allegiance," Lord Forestor said.

Vergil smiled and waved as Nicolus shoved them out of the office and slammed the door behind. Once Nicolus had made it back to his master, Vergil beckoned him close and leaned into his ear.

"Let's make sure we remove those thorns from our sides sooner rather than later," he said. "Can't have them stirring up trouble."

"I'll pass word along," Nicolus said then trotted to the door and slipped out.

Vergil took the time to look over his list of tasks and sighed at the lack of progress. With today all but spent, he only had one full day left before Sophie returned to the city. It would be good to have her there. Close. Always just a few steps away. They would become inseparable soon. Her, the saint of his new religion and him, its head. Vergil sat in a daze until Nicolus returned.

"The Forestors won't be a problem for us," Nicolus said.

Vergil rose from his desk, walked to Nicolus's side, and patted his subordinate on the back.

"Good," he said. "I can always rely on you."

Nicolus grinned but didn't duck his head in a bow as he would have done back when he called himself a priest. At some point, their dynamic had changed. Nicolus was essential to Vergil's cause now, and he knew it. The heightened confidence suited Nicolus.

"So is it off to the villa then?" Nicolus asked.

"Yes, it is."

Vergil grabbed a plain brown duster from a rack near the door and tossed it over his simple tunic and pants. He was no longer limited to wearing the robes of the clergyfolk, but he was conscious with his choice of attire. He made a point of walking through the lower city every day, and while he did so, he wanted to avoid any outward display of wealth. It was the wrong tack to take in winning the low bloods over, yet his fellow high bloods never appreciated the effectiveness of psychological maneuvers.

"We could stop by my house on our way," Nicolus said. "A think we're long overdue for a refreshment."

Vergil had been moving to the door but stopped at Nicolus's words. He turned around and intertwined his fingers. The only thing long overdue was this conversation.

"That's something we need to talk about," Vergil said.

He closed the doors to his study and strode to the far side of the room, half leaning against his desk and waving Nicolus over.

"Sit," he said.

Nicolus dropped into a chair but kept near its edge.

"No more refreshments," Vergil said. Nicolus went to reply, but Vergil held up his finger. "We can't have any scandals, you know that. We're both too influential now to risk it. We'll be watched closely by our enemies for any sign that could lead to our downfall. We have to be pristine in every aspect of our lives moving forward."

"It's not outlawed," Nicolus said. "The men with men or the pain with pleasure."

Vergil shook his head. "Scandalous it remains, all of it. Besides, you and I have our hands full. By day, with our work on the new theology and shepherding our flock. By night, with focusing on our futures—Sophie for me, a suitable high blood for you. Our refreshments would only serve to distract us in the best case. In the worst, they could undo everything we're working towards. Do you want that?"

Nicolus deflated and sank back in his chair. Vergil moved to his side and patted his shoulder.

"There, there, nothing to be glum about," he said. "It was a joy while it lasted, but everything, by its nature, is ephemeral. That's what makes life so interesting."

"Or tragic," Nicolus said.

"Look at it this way, at least all your angst will provide you with ample material for your poetry. It's been ages since we've heard from the Paper Airplane Poet, and the people are in dire need of a distraction."

***

Sophie was waiting at the dining table, wearing a muslin dress with a flower print. Hardly evening attire, but then again, she looked stunning in it. Besides, it was one of her last chances to wear whatsoever she chose. When they returned to Simetria, all eyes would be on her, all the time. As a saint, she'd have little to no privacy. She'd play a role for the rest of her life; Vergil forgave her for the current faux pas.

He swung by her chair on the way to his, letting his hand run along her shoulders, planting a kiss on the cheek she offered. Then he was off to the opposite side of the table. As soon as he sat, the servants brought the wine, the food. They raised their glasses to one another soundlessly, ate their meal without words. They didn't need to exchange pleasantries. They had an understanding that went beyond speech.

Vergil wasn't sure of the exact cause for the change in their dynamic. The necessary deception he'd employed against Sophie was certainly a part of it. The limitations he'd imposed on her subsequent movements were as well. More than that though, he had changed. The Others and then the Lady had opened his mind, shown him things, taught him more. He wasn't the Vergil that Sophie had known. Sometimes, he wondered what she thought of the new him, but more often than not, he knew it didn't matter. She was bound to him by circumstance, and soon enough, she'd be tied to him through holy matrimony.

Whatever she really thought, what she hid behind her smiles, it didn't concern him. In the end, she would be grateful to him. One day, she'd understand all that he'd sacrificed for her. In the meantime, he tried not to sense her disappointment.

"The guards mentioned you had a visitor today," Vergil said between bites of chicken.

Sophie finished chewing and swallowed. "The tailor's man. For the ribbons, remember?"

"You never mentioned it."

"Impossible. I most certainly did. Maybe you forgot what with all the various tasks keeping you occupied these days."

Sophie lifted a fork full of peas and slipped them into her mouth.

"I'm quite busy, true," he said, "but I would've remembered a visitor. You have so few."

The Sophie of the past, the pre-expedition her, would have snapped back playfully. "I have so few because you keep me locked away in this dreadful castle," she would have said. But this Sophie chewed her peas and let the silence stretch. It pained him for her to be so distant, and yet he was a thousand leagues away himself.

"Perhaps I forgot then," she said. "My mind is all over the place. I apologize for the oversight."

Sterile. Remote. Still, he welcomed the change because it meant he, too, could be tucked away. He craved her in body, but his mind was preoccupied, awash with ideas and plans and schemes for the new world order he envisioned. He couldn't really afford to be utterly lost in Sophie.

"No matter," Vergil said. "The day after next, we'll be

back in Simetria, and you'll have far more pressing matters than ribbons to occupy your time. Speaking of which, I think a proper toast is in order."

Vergil snapped his fingers, and a male servant shuffled over with a champagne bottle and two glass flutes.

"Come," Vergil said to Sophie, waving to the adjacent chair.

Sophie laid her utensils down and dabbed her lips with her napkin. A servant helped her up from her seat. As she relocated, Vergil watched the thin muslin shift over her limbs and torso. His. His. All his now. He couldn't help but lay a hand on her leg. The male servant popped the cork, filled the glasses, and handed one to each of them. Vergil raised his, and Sophie followed suit. He squeezed her thigh and leaned in.

"To your return from the afterlife," he said.

"To second beginnings," she replied.

Their flutes touched, lips brushed glass, pale gold liquid drained from vessels to mouths. Vergil watched the muscles of Sophie's throat as she swallowed. He moved his hand from her thigh to her neck and traced the lines there.

"And what does this return of mine entail exactly?" she asked.

Vergil pulled his hand away and rubbed his fingers on his lips. "You'll know what you need to know when you need to know it. It's safer this way."

"Safer? Goodness that doesn't instill much confidence."

"You can rest easy knowing it's all in my capable hands," Vergil said.

"I would rest the easiest if you trusted me enough to tell me more."

Here she was, his old Sophie, lifting her head from the burrow it had been hiding in.

"It's not about trust or distrust," he said. "We all have our roles. Yours is to be the figurehead of the new movement."

"A movement I know nothing about."

Vergil peeled his lips back into a grin then rested his hand back on her thigh. "Not yet. It's best not to concern yourself. You already have a lot on your shoulders, and soon enough, there will be the wedding to plan and, not long after, a child, I suspect."

Sophie folded her hands on top of his, lifted his hand to her face, and kissed the palm. "A child would be such a lovely thing."

THE ROT

The rope smacked against the stone wall. Fenrir waited until it stopped moving then sprinted from the bushes to the wall enclosing Vergil's villa. He scanned the horizon. No guards in sight or at least no torches bobbing in the dark. He grabbed the rope and gave it a few strong test pulls. It seemed to be fixed to something on the other end, just as Sophie said it would be.

"We'll get you back onto the grounds with the elegant solution of a rope over the wall," she'd said, showing him the spot on their way to the gate.

"Why don't I just stay hidden in Vergil's study until tonight?" he'd asked.

"Mr. Grean came onto the grounds, but he's yet to leave. The guards notice these things."

Fenrir had spent the past few hours hiding amongst the shrubbery outside the villa's estate. Now, he was counting to thirty in his head. Once the time elapsed, he pulled the rope and planted his feet against the wall. Hand, foot, hand, foot. He made a slow and careful climb for twenty feet before reaching the top.

The night wasn't deep, and he needed to vacate the wall's

coping as soon as he could. Still, the fall looked treacherous. He tried to make out what lay below, but the finer details were lost in the twilight. Then, he remembered his greatest asset. He moved his Third Eye from behind his ear to his forehead. His vision flickered, and the world resolved into something more comprehensible. Shadows less murky. Textures crisper. A burlap sack was hidden in a bush just against the wall. This was meant to break his fall. Fenrir jumped and landed on the bag. Hay softened the impact. Fenrir stayed low as he reeled the rope in, wrapped it in a loop, untied it from the bush it was anchored to, and stuffed it in the bag.

"Leave no trace," Sophie had said.

He pushed the sack further into the recesses of the thick undergrowth then found a break in the foliage from which to survey his route. The villa stood quiet, and there on its side was the door to the cellar. He glanced at the windows facing him. Curtains drawn. Darkened rooms. Trisht had prepared everything for him. He hoped she was safely back in the house by now. He was anxious for Sophie.

Fenrir took one last desperate look over the grounds, crouched low, and flew across the lawn. From wall to villa in seconds. He panted, plastered against the wall. Once he was sure no one had noticed his sprint, he moved along the house until he reached the wooden door to the cellar. It was unlocked. He dove in.

***

"No dessert for me," Sophie said, waving away the dish the servant held.

Vergil frowned and tilted his head to the side. "Are you not feeling well?"

"As a matter of fact, I think the wine and champagne went straight to my head. Would you mind terribly if I excused myself early?"

Vergil swirled his port in its goblet and picked at his cake with a fork.

"I hope you aren't going to sleep already," he said. "I'd rather hoped to spend some time together tonight."

Sophie forced a smile even while the bile in her rose.

"As do I, which is why I'll just lie down for a little while. See if I can't manage to soothe away this headache."

Vergil nodded and waved as a sign she could leave. Sophie rose from her chair, walked to his side, and deposited a soft kiss on his cheek.

"I'll see you later," she said before making her escape.

It was torture walking as leisurely as she normally did. Even after she'd made it out into the hall, she had to move just as elegantly and stately as always. Down the corridor, up the stairs, through another hall, into her bedchambers. Then, she was safe. Sophie tore her dress off and hurried into a simple blouse and pair of linen pants. She needed ease of movement for what came next. She also needed her hair secured. Out came the silk ribbons and silly pins. In went a single strand of velvet that held her braid strong and sure. It was the one she'd used as a surveyor. As for her erstwhile garb, she and Fenrir would have to do without. It had been lost to them when they'd been taken into the penitentiary, and Sophie had no excuse to request a new set of leather armor with the afflicted gone along with her profession. Still, she did have a pair of spare boots. She shoved her feet into them and laced them up in short order.

Then, she was tearing through the quiet and still halls of the upper level, using the route that Vergil took when he visited his study. They were short on time. Without her there to keep Vergil occupied, he would likely move straight to the study as soon as he finished his port.

Sophie reached the steps that wound down to the wine cellar without incident. Once she'd slipped through the door, she was free to descend as loudly as she wanted. Sound didn't travel through this solid mass. Round and round she went. Dizzy at first but pressing beyond the discomfort and eventual howling of her inner ear. Once she reached the bottom, she steadied herself against the wall and took a few seconds to regain a sense of equilibrium. Then it was through the next door and into the hall that led to Vergil's study.

Sophie emerged from a door on the side of the narrow hall and nearly ran into Fenrir. He caught her shoulders in his hands. They were both wild-eyed and breathless. The adrenaline was coursing already.

"Is everything in order?" Fenrir asked.

"Yes, he was drinking his port when I left. I'd wager he'll be down any minute. We should hurry in and prepare ourselves."

Fenrir waved for Sophie to take the lead. She jogged then ran to the study, taking care down the final flight of stairs. Fenrir was close behind. The sconce was out. They couldn't risk lighting the space in case Vergil was near at hand. Even glowing embers would give them away. He was an observant man.

Fenrir interfaced with the lock. Then, they were in. He shut the door behind him. They waited in the dark, Sophie at the far end of the room, Fenrir near the door. She tried to calm her nerves and slow her breathing, but it was hopeless. Her body was already in fight mode. She flexed her fingers and squeezed them into fists, over and over again. She wished she could make out Fenrir in the dark.

"Your Third Eye," he whispered.

Had she said her thought about the dark out loud? Or had Fenrir heard it in her thoughts? They weren't synced just now, but there was a strange kind of lingering. Parts of Fenrir stayed with her even after they'd broken the connection.

She fumbled for the device, nestled behind her ear,

and pressed it to her forehead. Her vision blinked then the darkness resolved into a faint scene. Now, she could see Fenrir pressed against the wall, behind the door. She stood stiff and firm opposite, ready for when Vergil came through.

***

Fenrir felt Vergil on the other side of the door. Maybe it was some kind of link between their Third Eyes. He hoped Vergil didn't register it. In he came. One, two, three steps. Light flooding the room. One, two steps more. Then, Vergil froze. He gaped in Sophie's direction.

"Sophie?" he said.

Fenrir pushed the door, and it slammed shut. The noise attracted Vergil's attention. He spun around, and his eyes met Fenrir's. They widened then narrowed.

"You," Vergil said. "Sophie, my heart, didn't we just have a talk about visitors?"

Fenrir advanced, and Vergil backed away until he stood in the center of the room. He was flanked, looking back and forth between his two assailants. Fenrir commanded the lock to take with his Third Eye. Vergil was trapped, but for some reason, his eyes were only wild with what seemed to be excitement.

"What's this then?" Vergil asked.

"What does it look like?" Sophie said. "An ambush, of course."

Fenrir and Sophie gazed at one another, nodded, and then the sync commenced. Fenrir lost himself in Sophie and she in him. They became a complex whirlwind, a dual persona, a hybridization.

***

They were one. Smiles peeled across both sets of lips. Hands moved to hips. Legs spread wide. Mirror images now with Vergil at their center.

"You have no idea what you're up against," he said.

They circled him, and he struggled to keep them both in view.

"Oh, we know more than you think," they said in tandem.

Vergil started, no doubt aware that something had fundamentally changed in the two of them, but not yet grasping how dire his straits were.

"I have powerful allies," he said. "Ones not of this world."

"We wouldn't call the alfom that. Powerful, perhaps, but allies? No."

Vergil squinted then seemed to take note of the two metal disks embedded in their foreheads, indistinguishable from the one he wore. The change in his attitude was immediate. His face lost its color, and the muscles and skin of it sagged.

After a few seconds, he rallied then turned to Sophie.

"You don't love him," he said. "Not this version of him. You're only chasing school-girl fantasies. He's a shell of the man he was, the one you idolized. He'll never live up to that vision you have in your mind."

They smiled at Vergil's flawed tactics. Fenrir could feel everything Sophie felt towards him, know all she thought of him. Her love was pure and unsullied.

"We know who and what we are," they said.

Vergil grimaced then twirled to face Fenrir. "You're a fool to side with her. She loved me, you know? Utterly and completely, and now, she turns against me. Do you really think it'll be any different with you? She won't let herself be tamed. She'll destroy you just to feel a mote of freedom."

They smiled again at his desperation. He was starting to truly understand the severity of his situation.

"It won't work," they said. "You turning us against one another. It's not possible. We're synced. Two bodies, one mind."

Not even two beats of a heart and Vergil was hurling himself at Fenrir. No weapons. Just fist then foot then knee then elbow. Fenrir weaved through the blows, ducking, redirecting. Sophie shot across the room, and then Vergil was on the defense. Four limbs he had to contend with, and ones that moved as fast as his own with speed imparted by the synthetics they all wore on their foreheads. Sophie's foot swung and would have struck Vergil's head if he hadn't dived to avoid it, but the maneuver came at a cost. Fenrir's fist struck Vergil in the jaw, and he toppled over. He recovered, but Fenrir and Sophie were on him in seconds. Vergil couldn't gain his footing again, forced to roll and scamper along the floor to avoid their blows. But it was only a matter of time until he made a mistake. Sophie's heel found Vergil's thigh, and he yelped. He looked up at his two attackers with rage. They continued their onslaught.

Even if Vergil dodged or parried or blocked a blow from one, the other was lying in wait with another attack. They saw the realization dawning on him. From assured to confused to terrified. Vergil was outmatched. In one desperate moment, after receiving a foot and two fists to the torso, Vergil howled. The sheer emotion of the sound halted Sophie and Fenrir's unending assault.

Vergil rushed to the door with all the speed the Third Eye could offer him. Fenrir and Sophie smiled as Vergil tugged at the knob that wouldn't give. He pounded on the wood and shouted. In vain. No one would hear him, and even if they did, this study of his was impenetrable, just as he'd intended it to be. He slammed the meaty part of his fist on the door then sagged against it. His shouts shifted into wails then laughter. It was time to end it.

Fenrir and Sophie advanced, step by step. Vergil appeared oblivious to their approach. He spoke in a steady stream to another.

"You're just going to stand by and let them do this?" he asked. "So you've turned against me then? Without even giving me the chance to explain or defend myself. I told you I was working on the Link. I said it would be just a little while longer. Patience, that's all I asked, but it was too much, it seems. And instead of telling me how you felt, of warning me, you set your new pets on me?"

Vergil went silent, waiting for a response. He turned around, his back on the door, eyes looking at everything and nothing. Even without having access to his mind, Sophie and Fenrir knew Vergil listened in vain. Nytho had made his decision.

"You too?" he asked, now speaking to another. "I put myself in harm's way for you. He lets them attack me, set them on me because I shared words with you. I took your words to heart, and this is the thanks I receive? You said they use us as their puppets then toss us aside when we're no longer of value. Will you do the same? Will you stand by and let them destroy all we could have built together?"

Nytho was right. Vergil had gone to the other side after all. There was no way to know what the Lady said in response. All they could see from the outside was the rage fade and resignation take its place. Vergil was on his own. All that was left was to put an end to his tyranny.

They came in close, and Vergil finally seemed to be aware of their presence again. He sneered and spat, blood mingled with saliva and sweat, hair in disarray, locks eclipsing his piercing blue eyes. Two arms shot out, and their hands found the neck they sought. Vergil gasped and clawed. Two other arms met his hands and stilled their movements. Vergil was frozen in place, locked and subdued by flesh, all the might of his Third Eye useless in the face of Sophie and Fenrir's combined bloodlust.

But then, there was an easing of the searing hatred. Watching Vergil's life fade, his eyes pleading, lips mouthing soundless words, one of them faltered.

"Maybe we don't have to kill him after all," Sophie said. "Maybe this is enough. He learns his lesson and scurries away."

"You know that would never be," Fenrir said.

Words were clumsy things, and Fenrir didn't have to rely on them anymore. Not while they were synced. Instead, he pulled a scene from his memory and shared it with Sophie. A cellar, six people, a scuffle, then Vergil pulling Fenrir aside and whispering to him.

"Trust me. It'll be all the sweeter when you finally get to plunge a knife in and watch the light fade from his shifty little eyes."

A vision of Theopold.

Vergil's true nature even back then before the Third Eye and the influx of power that corrupted him further.

"He's always been this," Fenrir said. "He'll always be this."

Sophie knew it was true. A series of scenes sprang to her mind that unfurled for Fenrir. A room. A bed. Sophie wearing a sheer silk gown. Vergil entering. Hands touching, groping, her filled with disgust but powerless to interfere. A montage of this. Night after night after night.

A flood of rage filled Fenrir then spilled over to Sophie then back to Fenrir. It was a positive feedback loop and just the impetus they needed to do what had to be done. Kill a man, an unafflicted, in cold blood. They held Vergil's neck tight. He had to know they would end him to get him to go over the edge completely.

And he did. He was almost gone. Trying to form a breath that wouldn't come, spasming for the want of it, eyes closing, muscles relaxing. Then, the fight came. Vergil was alert again and had a strength that tripled. His hands ripped theirs from his neck. Nails pulled at skin and left gashes in their wake. He was out, free, pulling in deep swallows of luxurious air, smiling, laughing between coughs, then frowning, clutching at his chest, toppling over and onto the ground, writhing, grabbing at his heart, going limp.

Eyes stared up at the two faces that leaned over then looked at the one with the orange-red curls.

"I loved you," he said.

"No, Vergil, you loved you."

THE LINK

Staring down at Vergil's still body, Sophie didn't feel a thing. Not righteous or retribution or resignation. Just a lack, a hole, a void. And it was a relief to her. She had been dreading how she would take the reality of this moment. It had left her with countless sleepless nights, nails bitten to the quick, a breath that never satiated her lungs. But in the end, it hadn't mattered.

"Return the way you came," she said to Fenrir.

They stood outside Vergil's study in a daze. The sync had ended. Their minds were their own again, but the process left a strange residue in its wake. A cerebral stickiness. What parts were hers and which his? The memories, ruminations, wants, fears.

"What happens now?" he asked.

"I go back to my room and pretend to sleep. I wait for the servants to realize that Vergil never returned from his study. I ask after him at breakfast, feign worry and fret and work myself into a frenzy until they agree to check on him."

"They won't be able to gain entry."

"It will take time, but eventually, they'll find him as we left him. The narrative will tell itself."

Fenrir shifted his weight from foot to foot, the movement like a pacing without the change in location. A nervousness.

"And after that?" he asked. "What will you do? Where will you go?"

Sophie smiled and ran her hand along his arm before she ascended the steps and moved down the hall. He followed. Their paths diverged at the door to the winding staircase leading to the estate-proper.

"I'll reach out to you when I can, if you decide to forgive yourself and start anew."

It took time, far more than she had hoped it would. It was days before they were able to breach the study door. By then, the rot had come to Vergil, bloated and stinking. At least the tears that sprang to Sophie's eyes weren't forced. It truly was tragic seeing him reduced to a mess of inert bones and skin. The glassy blue eyes stared through her, but she didn't feel the pang of guilt she might have. Just sorrow that it had had to come to this.

She was stuck in the villa for days more as Vergil's most trusted followers scrambled to deal with the fallout of their leader's demise. Sophie inserted herself into their debates. She was a calm voice, a level head, the maiden on the front of the ship steering them through the storm.

The funeral was a solemn affair, the passing of the crown from his broken head to her erect one. Sophie became the prophet that Vergil had wanted her to be, but this time, she came to believe in her calling. She knew the truth. The Others had helped her, saved her and her child, made good on their promise. It was time she did likewise. Her Third Eye aided her in her endeavors with Nytho's voice guiding her.

They want someone to tell them what needs to be done. They're desperate for it. Avoid commands. Instead, offer suggestions, instruct, be kind and patient like a parent. It's all they ever want. To be coddled and to believe they've found safety in you.

Sophie became the mother of their movement even as her belly swelled. It was two months before her position was secure enough to permit a visit to Fenrir. He was still in that same shack near the old southeast bell tower. She passed the derelict structure on her way from her reclaimed estate in the upper city to Fenrir's home. She couldn't help but stop by and stare up into the rafters. Pigeons cooed. Whirlwinds greeted her, the breeze a welcome relief from the sticky heat of a summer's midday. She debated one last climb up to the tower's summit, a revisit of where she and Fenrir had first met, but a vicious cramp in her lower abdomen stilled her movements. She held her stomach and focused on her breathing.

"Fine, fine," she said. "I hear your objection, and yes, I'm well aware that I'm just stalling. Well, there's nothing for it. Let's go visit your Papa."

Sophie retreated from the lonely tower and tarried the few blocks to Fenrir's door. She wore a light linen cloak. She was too well-known now to risk walking openly in the streets. In the lower city especially, the masses would descend on her, pulling at her hands, begging her to bless them. She despised the adoration.

It's a necessary byproduct of their love for you. Suffer their worship. It's preferable to the alternative. Even Vergil understood that.

So Nytho had told her many times. Whenever a wave of loathing and weariness at her new existence washed over her, he would whisper such rational musings in her ear. But she was alone in her mind now, her Third Eye safely stowed. This meeting was private. Her feelings and thoughts needed to be her own.

Fenrir knew she was coming. She'd sent a letter ahead of her the day before. If she knocked on his door and met only stillness and silence, it would be a sign that he had meant what he'd said at the masquerade, that he hadn't softened or forgiven himself. Then it would just be her and the child.

But if he answered, if his emerald eyes peeked from the dark sliver in the door and were filled with longing and hunger and ache, if his hand reached through the gap and beckoned her in, if she rushed through and fell into his arms crushing her face into his chest and breathing in the scent of him, if her lips searched for his then met them and pressed hard and strong, if her eyes were so filled with fluid that he became a melted version of himself laughing as she did, if they pulled back together and fell into one another, their minds could sync again and finally say all the innumerable things that words were too clumsy to convey.

If he would just answer that tolling, three solid raps on his decaying door, and find the courage to become the father he longed to be again. A second chance.

Sophie arrived at Fenrir's door. She took a breath, curled her fingers into a fist, and touched the knuckles to the wood. Once, twice, thrice. Seconds passed by as she held her breath, and her lungs screamed for release. A noise sounded beyond the threshold. The knob turned. A crack formed. Then, those yearned-for eyes peered from the void beyond.

FENRIR'S LETTER

Dearest Lenore,

It feels odd for me to pen this letter without yet knowing you, so you will have to forgive me if it does not seem to reflect the relationship you and I will have in years to come. There are things I wish to say to you, but which I may not have the heart or inclination to utter during my own life. In case I am not able to express these while I live, this letter will have to suffice. I need you to know how I feel now, in this moment, because I suspect that my beliefs will change over the years, and my memories will become skewed with them. I need you to know why your mother and I made the pledge we did, and why it is of paramount importance that you and your descendants make good on said pledge. But I get ahead of myself. Let me take a step back.

I write this when you have only been with us for one month. Your eyes are still the milky blue of a newborn, gazing at another world, not wholly within ours yet. Your mother was surprised at first, certain that you would have the emerald we both do. I think the color reminded her of someone from her past that she would rather forget. There is much of our past that both of us would soon free ourselves from, but that is a fool's endeavor. Our past shapes us. To break free of it is to lose oneself.

I do not know if I will ever be able to tell you in words about my past. It may always be too painful to bear, or perhaps the ache will fade with time. In case it does not, I would like you to know about my life before your mother. You are not my first child, and your mother is not my first wife. I married a woman when I was younger, and we had a son, Trevon. He was mischievous and curious like her. They were my joy, but I lost them both, one in death and the other in circumstance. With the aid of your mother, I have moved past blaming myself for what happened to them, but the sting persists. You will have to forgive me then for aiming to push the past away and focus instead on the present. And the future.

Here is where we come to the crux of this letter. The future is critical, and we all have such a large role to play in it—you, your mother, and I. I cannot foresee how the world will shape itself or how history will opt to frame events, but I do know that whatever you are told will be a partial truth. I am certain of this because even now your mother and I are molding the narrative. We must. We made a promise in exchange for saving you and Simetria. Part of that pledge means we are obliged to tell a story.

Your mother is labeled a saint. The woman who destroyed the Rot of the Link, rid us of the distortions, and unearthed the truth that the Church of Impermanence suppressed for centuries. She is a martyr returned from the dead to guide us into a new age where we laud the value of the Link and sing praises for the alfom. Some of this is not a lie. Your mother did destroy the Rot of the Link. The alfom most certainly are not the evil we were taught when we called them by their old name. The Link is not a stain on our world.

In fact, the Link is blessed for it keeps the non-Euclidean at bay. Without the Link, our world was saturated in distortions. Affliction was an ever-present threat. It was what took my dear Trevon away. It shackled your mother too. It was every bit the hell you will learn it to have been, but a horror in a story is nothing compared to the reality of it.

I say this simply enough—we must keep the non-Euclidean out, and for that, we must protect the Link. You must protect it. You and your descendants. This is the pledge your mother and I made, but in the end, it is up to you to make good on the promise. We cannot force you to believe in our cause. Such misguided devotion is a dangerous thing. You must see the value in being a Warden of the Link yourself. I will not use fear to steer you or coerce you with talk of familial duty. I ask this of you as a man, not your father. A man who suffered greatly in a world severed from the Link. A man who now finds beauty and joy in a world with the Link restored.

Your Papa

FROM THE AUTHOR

Thank you for reading *Blessed is the Rot*. Your feedback is important to me and will help other readers. Please consider leaving a review on your chosen platform. If you enjoyed *Blessed is the Rot*, you may also be interested in "To Keep the Non-Euclidean at Bay" and "Paper Airplane Poet," short stories inspired by the novel. Visit my website at sherisingerling.com for more details.

It is also worth noting that *Blessed is the Rot* is the first book in the Bit trilogy. Stay tuned for the second and third books with tentative release dates of June 2026 and January 2027, respectively. Lastly, everything I write falls in a shared universe. Check out my other novels and short stories for a more immersive reading experience.

ACKNOWLEDGMENTS

The family: Mom, Dad, Alan, Shaun, Shannon, and Shea. My beta readers: Ben, Isaiah, Sarah, Seren, Tessy, and T.R. Mainstone.

ABOUT THE AUTHOR

SHERI SINGERLING is a US native living in Germany where she works as a laboratory manager, lecturer, and research scientist. Sheri spends her days staring at rocks and dust from space and her nights crafting worlds via the written word. Outside of her work and writing, she enjoys coaxing plants to grow, walking up and down steep inclines in nature, and listening to repetitive electronic beats.

Her publications all fall in the Alfom shared universe and include the novels *Nytho*, *Neuen*, and *Blessed is the Rot* and several short stories. Her short fiction has appeared in *Clarkesworld Magazine*. For updates on Sheri Singerling's work, subscribe to her newsletter at sherisingerling.com/subscribe and/or follow her on Instagram (@shersingerling), Facebook (Sheri Singerling - Author), and Bluesky (@sherisingerling. bsky.social).